PRAISE FOR
A POTION TO DIE FOR

"What Heather Blake always achieves so skillfully, both in this debut series and in her Wishcraft Mystery series, is the creation of a complete mythology for her paranormal world.... The relationships between characters are developed realistically, and the romantic elements are never forced, making this an intriguing novel with a satisfying mix of mystery and the paranormal."

—Kings River Life Magazine

"Heather Blake's books are always favorites of mine, filled with magic, mystery, and romance, so ... twists and turns, secrets and lies abound, but all of the loose ends fall into place when the surprising revelation of the killer is made." —Melissa's Mochas, Mysteries & Meows

"Blake does it again with the debut of another great paranormal mystery series. As witch Carly tries to prove herself innocent of murder, a shocking turn of events makes readers tear through the pages to find out the real story. This reviewer can't wait for more fun from this talented author." —*RT Book Reviews*

"Heather Blake once again thrills readers.... Carly Bell Hartwell is a great heroine.... The ending was a surprise, though reading a good book from Heather Blake never is. She is one of the best paranormal cozy writers around, and you'll not want to miss the beginning of this new adventure." —Debbie's Book Bag

continued ...

Other Mysteries by Heather Blake

The Magic Potion Mystery Series
Book 1: *A Potion to Die For*
Book 2: *One Potion in the Grave*

The Wishcraft Mystery Series
Book 1: *It Takes a Witch*
Book 2: *A Witch Before Dying*
Book 3: *The Good, the Bad, and the Witchy*
Book 4: *The Goodbye Witch*

One Potion in the Grave

 A Magic Potion Mystery

HEATHER BLAKE

AN OBSIDIAN MYSTERY

OBSIDIAN
Published by the Penguin Group
Penguin Group (USA) LLC, 375 Hudson Street,
New York, New York 10014

USA | Canada | UK | Ireland | Australia | New Zealand | India | South Africa | China
penguin.com
A Penguin Random House Company

First published by Obsidian, an imprint of New American Library,
a division of Penguin Group (USA) LLC

First Printing, October 2014

ISBN 978-0-451-41631-5

Printed in the United States of America
10 9 8 7 6 5 4 3 2 1

For my family, who fill my life with love and laughter.

ACKNOWLEDGMENTS

"Piglet noticed that even though he had a Very Small Heart, it could hold a rather large amount of Gratitude."

—A. A. Milne

I'm a huge fan of *Winnie-the-Pooh* and the simple—yet wise—life lessons the silly old bear and his friends impart to readers. Like Piglet, my very small heart holds much gratitude for all the help and wisdom I received while writing this book.

I can't thank my editor, Sandy Harding, enough for her patience, support, and guidance. She's been an invaluable resource who has not only made Carly a stronger character but has helped me become a better writer as well. A huge thank-you, too, to everyone at Obsidian/New American Library who has helped bring Carly's story to bookshelves, from the cover artist and copy editor to publicists and the marketing department and everyone in between.

Many thanks to my agent, Jessica Faust, who's always the first one to cheer on my crazy ideas.

To my readers, who embrace those crazy ideas ... I say it a lot, because it's true: I can't do what I do without you. Thank you for buying my books, visiting with me on social media, telling friends about my stories, and for being the reason I keep writing. Along with gratitude, my heart is filled with happiness because of you. Happy reading.

∞ Chapter One ∞

M y nerves rocketed to high alert the moment the woman glided into my shop, her eyes masked by a large pair of black designer sunglasses, a gauzy scarf draped theatrically over sleek blond hair and then loosely wound around her neck.

She looked very Jackie O, and in Hitching Post, Alabama, the official wedding capital of the South, people like Jackie O stood out like peacocks among sparrows.

Despite our wedding flair, we were casual folks.

Her peacockiness didn't explain the jumpy nerves. That happened only when danger was near. My *witchy senses*—labeled so by my best friend, Ainsley, when we were teenagers—were at work.

The customer didn't look all that dangerous, but I'd been fooled by people before. Lesson learned. However, I also had to keep in mind that the danger I felt might not be coming directly from her—it could just be associated with her. My witchy senses weren't finely honed, so

I couldn't tell which it was. All I knew was that this woman meant trouble to me.

Poly, one of my two cats, lumbered over to greet the customer and assess whether the elegant newcomer had any hidden treats lurking beneath the flowing designer caftan that swished dramatically around her thin body. Poly was forever starving to death, as his twenty-five pound frame could attest. Roly, my other (much lighter) cat, stayed curled up on the counter, basking in a puddle of sunshine, preferring naps to treats. The siblings' breed was of unknown origin, but I suspected a mix of calico, white-and-gray ragdoll, and lethargy. Both were long-haired fluff balls of orange, gray, and white, their diluted coloring more pastel than bold. Besides their weight, another way to tell them apart was that Poly had more orange while Roly was mostly gray. They often came to work with me here at the Little Shop of Potions, and I adored each and every one of their lazy bones.

I wondered what this customer knew of my shop, a place that on first look appeared to be a blend of an herbalist and a bath and body boutique. On a daily basis, tourists wandered inside drawn in by the colors, curiosity, the allure of the window vignette, and the store's tagline written on the window: *Mind, Body, Heart, and Soul.*

Early-morning light streamed through the display window, glinting off the treasures I'd collected over the years. The weights and measures, the apothecary scale, the mortar and pestle my grandma Adelaide used in this very store. The sunbeams also bounced off the wall of colorful potion bottles, splashing prismatic arcs across the shop.

I inhaled the various earthy smells from the fresh and

dried herbs I used in my potion-making and absorbed the vibrant colors, the simple charm, and the magic in the air.

That was the most important part. The magic.

Most tourists didn't know that I hailed from an unusual combination of hoodoo and voodoo practitioners, and was a healer who used my inherited magic to treat what ailed. From sore throats to broken hearts, I could cure most anything—thanks to a dose of magical lily dewdrops (Leilara tears) and the recipe book of potions left behind by my great-great-grandmother, Leila Bell.

The customer bent to scratch Poly's head, and he flopped onto his back to playfully paw her hand. The big flirt. He lacked basic moral principles and would do just about anything for the possibility of a treat.

Another surge of warning tingles crept up my spine and spread to my limbs. Instinctively, I latched onto the engraved silver locket that dangled from a long chain around my neck. The orb was a protective charm given to me when I was just a baby, not to defend me from others but from *myself*. Being an empath, someone who can experience another's physical and emotional feelings, was something else I'd inherited from Leila. The locket engraved with two entwined lilies wasn't foolproof, but in most cases it blocked other people's emotions so I wasn't bombarded with everyone else's feelings. It was also something of a security blanket—offering me solace and comfort when I was troubled.

Like now.

"Feel free to browse around, and let me know if you need any help," I offered, though really I just wished she'd walk out the door. I didn't know what had kindled my witchy senses, but those warnings were rarely wrong.

If she stuck around, I had to prepare for the proverbial anvil to drop on my head.

The woman lowered her sunglasses a fraction and peered at me over the dark rim. "Will do."

A flash of recognition sparked within me but didn't flame. I had the feeling I knew her somehow, yet I couldn't place her for the life of me. She certainly wasn't local.

"Nice shop you have here," she said, her slow cadence that of a cultured Southern belle, one who'd been raised up prim and proper.

Still alert, I said proudly, "It'll do." I just hoped she hadn't heard about the murder that had taken place in the back room a couple of months ago. There were some things tourists needn't know. Fortunately, that case had been solved, the culprit brought to justice, my reputation restored, and life went on.

Slowly the woman stood, leaving Poly splayed out on the floor (treatless), his chubby belly the only proof needed that he was well fed. He wasn't that good an actor to be able to cover the pudge.

Her designer strappy gold high heels clacked on the wooden floor as she wandered over to a display of bath oils and surreptitiously glanced over her shoulder.

Although I usually only read people's energy to create a perfect potion, I didn't like waiting for that anvil—I'd had my fill of trouble with that murder and all, thank you kindly—and thought it best to be proactive. I let go of my locket and let down my guard to feel what she was feeling.

I sensed no menace toward me at all, so the danger swirling around was most likely due to the same reason her anxiety level was through the roof. Her stress coursed through my veins, increasing my blood pressure as surely as it did hers.

Taking hold of my locket again, I let out a breath. If she were interested, I had some calming cures and sleeping potions that might soothe her a bit. Temporary fixes to an obviously bigger issue but helpful nonetheless.

As she continued to wander the store, browsing, touching, perusing, and generally acting suspicious, I eyed the big fancy bag on her arm and wondered if she was a shoplifter. Over the years I'd learned that they came in all shapes, sizes, and pedigrees.

When she picked up a handmade soap, I walked over to keep a closer eye on her and said, "The lilac is nice."

Sniffing a bar of honeysuckle soap, wrapped in a muslin bag and tagged with a custom label, she said, "I prefer the honeysuckle myself. It brings back sweet memories."

Clear polish coated her short professionally manicured fingernails. She wore only one ring—an enormous pink star sapphire on her right hand—so apparently she wasn't in town to get hitched this weekend. Most likely she was a wedding guest. Probably the big Calhoun affair. The town was buzzing from the excitement of those nuptials. Especially my mama. She was in a full-blown tizzy because the wedding was being held at her chapel, Without a Hitch.

Mama in a tizzy was quite the dizzying experience—one I'd get to witness firsthand as she'd roped me into helping her get the chapel ready this afternoon for the big to-do. My arm hadn't needed much twisting. It was, after all, the Calhouns, and I'd have to be dead not to want an up-close peek at the family.

Headed by patriarch Warren (a U.S. senator who had

just launched a bid for the White House) and his wife, Louisa, the rich and powerful (and somewhat corrupt) Calhoun family was Southern royalty. They were firmly rooted in politics and had recently branched into the entertainment industry via son Landry, who was a rising country music star. News of Landry's speedy engagement to recent college graduate and former pageant queen Gabriella "Gabi" Greenleigh had sent shockwaves through the whole country, hitting the front pages of every tabloid in the checkout stand. "Little Orphan Gabi," as she had been called in the press, was the only child of one of the wealthiest couples in the state, both of whom had died in a tragic plane crash several years ago. Gabi's father, an oil executive, had been one of Warren's biggest supporters, and her mother had been best friends with Louisa. After their deaths, Louisa vowed to care for the girl, and took her under her wing. During this past year Landry and Gabi had fallen in love. The picture-perfect couple, America's newest—and wildly popular—sweethearts, were due to be married right here in Hitching Post in two days' time, this Saturday.

"Can't go wrong with either." I handed the woman a small wooden basket so she could shop. Might as well make some money off this strange encounter.

Turning to face me straight on, she said, "Carly Bell Hartwell, do you remember that one time you dared me to sneak into your aunt Marjie's yard, knock on her door, and run? Only I got all tangled up in her honeysuckle vines and she caught me? My rear still aches sometimes from the switching she gave me. Despite that incident I continue to love the scent of honeysuckle so don't be pushing your lilac wares on me."

In a split second the woman's voice shifted from high class to a local twang. I stared in shock at her and finally said, "Hush your mouth! Katie Sue Perrywinkle? Is that truly you under all that fanciness?"

Katie Sue whipped off her sunglasses, and familiar blue eyes danced with mischief. Throwing her arms wide, she rushed at me, wrapping me in a tight hug.

We spun in a circle, our squeals scaring Poly out of his stupor. His belly hung low to the ground as he dashed behind the counter.

"Just look at you!" I said. "How long's it been?"

Without missing a beat, she answered, "Ten years."

"Tell me everything." I pulled two stools over to a worktable. "Did you get to college like you wanted? Are you a full-fledged doctor now?"

Laughing, she glanced at her diamond-faced watch and said, "I only have but a minute."

"Talk fast, then." So, Katie Sue was back. I'll be damned.

I drank in the sight of her, trying to note the many changes. Her hair had gone from brown to blond, her skin from deeply tanned to pale cream, and her whole countenance from hillbilly to high society. "I'm so shocked you're here." I stumbled for words. "You're . . . unrecognizable. The hair, the clothes, the accent."

"Everything," she said firmly. "It took years, too, with thousands paid to a finishing school, voice coaches, a stylist . . . The list goes on. Oh, and my name's Kathryn Perry now. I had it legally changed right after I left town." Her voice dropped to a melancholy whisper. "I didn't want them to find me."

Them.

Her family.

My stomach twisted at the old memories. Katie Sue had what my mama would call an "unfortunate" childhood. Her daddy had died in prison after being sent there for killin' a man in a bar fight. Her mama liked the hooch a little too much, and hadn't been above raising her hand—or any other object in the vicinity—to keep her three daughters, Lyla, Katie Sue, and Jamie Lynn, in line. And when she remarried? *Shoo-ee.* Her new husband had an even bigger problem with addiction and a hair-trigger temper. And after one particularly bad fight with each other, the state stepped in and awarded custody of the girls to Katie Sue's granddaddy, a hardworking man who lived simply and loved those girls fiercely. It was a move that had probably saved the lives of all three sisters, but eventually tore the siblings apart.

Last I heard, Katie Sue's mama, Dinah Perrywinkle Cobb, and her husband, Cletus Cobb, had been released from the local pen, having served two years each for cooking up drugs in their trailer near the river. They'd been free going on five months now and had so far managed to stay out of trouble.

With wide eyes, Katie Sue glanced around the shop. "I can't tell you how much I've missed this place. It was more my home than that old ramshackle trailer."

As a young girl Katie Sue had spent hours and hours here, learning about herbal medicine at the knee of Grandma Adelaide, same as I did. Katie Sue would talk on and on about how one day she was going to become a doctor and use the knowledge Grammy had taught her to help others.

Grammy had always encouraged her lofty goals, though truthfully, I'd never thought Katie Sue would leave. Hitching Post had a way of holding on to its own. "Did you get your MD?" I asked, hoping her dreams had come true. With no lack of determination or stubbornness, I imagined she wouldn't have given up on her goal without a knock-down, drag-out fight.

"It surely wasn't easy, Carly, and I'm still in my residency down in Birmingham, but I did it."

She spoke softly, the pride in her voice coming across loud and clear, though I wasn't the least bit surprised to hear it. Even though hers hadn't been an easy upbringing, she'd always retained a sense of pride. Almost too much sometimes, not always wanting to accept help when offered. Fiercely independent, she was always determined to get things done—her way. I figured it to be a defense mechanism, an ability to have some semblance of control in an out-of-control environment.

I squeezed her hand. "Good on you."

Taking another peek at her watch, she said, "I have to get going. I have an appointment. Can we meet up later to continue catching up? I want to hear what you've been up to. Anyone special in your life?"

"It's complicated," I said.

She lifted both eyebrows. "*That* sounds like a story. Let's get coffee later, okay?"

"Are you back in town to see Jamie Lynn?" I asked, referring to Katie Sue's baby sister. She'd been just ten years old when Katie Sue left. "I heard she's bad sick."

Pain flitted across her eyes and she paled.

"You didn't know?" I asked, cursing the foot I just stuck in my big mouth.

She shook her head.

I should have realized as much. It never ceased to

amaze me how money could tear a family apart. Lyla, the eldest Perrywinkle sister, had married straight out of high school and never looked back, leaving Katie Sue and Jamie Lynn to mind their granddaddy when his heart began to fail. Mostly the task fell on a teenaged Katie Sue since Jamie Lynn was so young, and she never once complained about it, though it sopped up what was left of her already pathetic childhood. After the man died, the whole town was shocked to learn that the old coot had been buying stocks and stashing away money all his years. In his will he left all his worldly goods solely to his full-time caretaker—his granddaughter Katie Sue, who at that time had just turned twenty. She inherited almost two million dollars.

No one was more stunned than Katie Sue's own kin, who crawled from the woodwork without a lick of shame, their palms out. When met with a firm refusal— Katie Sue proclaimed the only other person who deserved a share of the inheritance was Jamie Lynn—her mama and stepdaddy made horrible threats, but it was Lyla who dealt the most painful blow. She filed for custody of Jamie Lynn. The court agreed that the older, married, and more settled sister deserved custody. Katie Sue tried to fight the matter in court again and again, but lost every time.

Eventually, she gave up trying. A heartbroken Katie Sue set up a trust fund for Jamie Lynn to access when she turned twenty-one, and did the only other thing she could think of. She took her share of the money and ran, leaving town and never looking back.

No one in town blamed her. Not even a little.

Katie Sue's voice cracked as she said, "What's wrong with her?"

"No one knows. It's a bit of a mystery illness from what I hear."

"Why hasn't she come to see you? At least for a diagnosis?"

By tapping into Jamie Lynn's energy, I should be able to pinpoint what was wrong. But that didn't necessarily mean I could fix it. There were some limitations to my magic. "My guess is Lyla. She keeps a tight rein on Jamie Lynn," I answered. Katie Sue's older sister didn't care for me much, knowing how close Katie Sue and I had once been, but she tolerated me just fine when I bought herbs from her massive gardens. Business was business, after all. Plus, she didn't care much for anyone so I didn't take her bad attitude too personal.

"But Jamie Lynn's almost twenty-one and able to make her own choices."

I bit my nail. "It's not so easy to break some ties. Especially when it comes to family."

"Don't I know it." Anger tightened the corners of her mouth. "I'll try to sneak in a visit with Jamie Lynn while I'm here. Do you think you can get her a message without Lyla catching wind of it?"

"What kind of question is that, Katie Sue? Of course I can."

"Kathryn," she corrected with a smile.

"That'll take some getting used to."

"Try, Carly. I worked too hard to make Katie Sue disappear for her to be popping up now." She sighed. "It doesn't help that this town brings back a whole host of bad memories I'd rather forget. Fortunately, my stay is only until Saturday; then I can return to Shady Hollow and go back to forgetting this place even exists."

I raised an eyebrow at the mention of Shady Hollow. A suburb of Birmingham, it was the wealthiest city in the state. Things sure had changed for her—her determination had paid off big time.

Reaching into her bag, she moved aside a small manila envelope that had a coffee stain on the edge and pulled out a notepad and scribbled a quick letter. She folded the note in half, then in half again. Absently, she stared at it for a second before saying, "When I first left, I set up a PO Box and wrote letters to Jamie Lynn every week for years. They all came back unopened." Giving her head a shake, she handed the note to me. "I asked her to meet me tonight at six thirty in my hotel room, so the sooner you can get that to her the better."

"Where are you staying?"

She smiled, and I realized she'd had her teeth corrected, too. They were now perfectly straight, perfectly white, and perfectly perfect. Which described all of her, not just her teeth. It was a little unsettling.

"At the Crazy Loon. I'm fairly sure your aunt Hazel recognized me but couldn't put a name to my face."

All three of my aunts, Marjie, Eulalie, and Hazel Fowl (my mama's sisters), collectively known as the Odd Ducks, owned aptly named inns in town. All four Fowl sisters were matrimonial cynics and weren't too keen on ever gettin' married, which was kind of ironic, considering where they lived. My daddy, a hopeless romantic, was still counting on my mama to come around, but so far she hadn't changed her mind. She was as happy as the day was long to stay engaged forever.

"I'm surprised you got a room," I said. "Everything's booked up."

"Friends in high places," Katie Sue said in a strange tone.

I took the note. "Well, don't you worry none. I'll see Jamie Lynn gets this." I only hoped that she hadn't been so brainwashed by Lyla that she refused to see Katie Sue.

"Thank you, Carly. You and your family are the only things that make this town the least bit bearable for me."

"Quit it now. You know we're always here for you."

She gave me another hug, we set a time to meet for coffee at my house, and she headed for the door.

"Wait! Katie—Kathryn?"

She turned. "Hmm?"

"If not for Jamie Lynn, why *did* you come back to town?" Now that I knew who she was, I couldn't help but wonder—and worry—about the dangerous energy she carried.

Something dark flashed in her eyes, and a wry smile creased her lips. "I'll tell you all about it later, Carly, but for now I'll say this." She put on her sunglasses and pulled open the door. "As a doctor I may have taken an oath to do no harm, but as a country girl who's done had it up to here with that family and their lies, I'm fixin' to give the Calhouns a taste of their own bitter medicine."

❧ Chapter Two ❧

"What do you know about the Calhoun family?" I asked my best friend, Ainsley Debbs, later that afternoon as she ran a feather duster over the potion bottles. She worked here a couple of days a week, partly as a favor to me and partly to escape her kids, who were known around town as the Clingons. She also held a part-time job at the local ob-gyn's office as a registered nurse.

Ainsley had already dispatched Francie Debbs, her mother-in-law, to deliver the note Katie Sue had written to Jamie Lynn Perrywinkle. Since Francie and Lyla were in the same gardening group it wasn't the least bit suspicious for Francie to pay a call on the sisters (and slip the note to Jamie Lynn). Francie was more than happy to help, especially when Ainsley promised her a box of wine and a hangover potion in return for the favor.

She knew exactly how to motivate her mama-in-law.

"You still worrying about Katie Sue?" Ainsley asked.

"I can't help it." My skin tingled just thinking about it. The danger surrounding Katie Sue was very real. I had a bad feeling. A mighty bad feeling. No one crossed the Calhoun family without retribution. Everyone in Alabama knew that.

"Did you call Dylan about it?"

Dylan Jackson. As a sergeant with the Darling County sheriff's office, he needed to be notified that there was danger in the air, and as my twice-former fiancé, he knew to take my witchy warnings seriously. "Not yet."

"You should."

"I know."

A smile quirked the corner of her lips. "What're you waiting for?"

I narrowed my eyes at her, and she laughed.

She knew why. Dylan and I were, as I told Katie Sue, complicated. We were in a strange place, the two of us. Friendly—really friendly—but not quite dating. I wasn't sure I wanted to go down that road with him again. My brain said *no* (real quietlike), but my heart was yelling *oh hell yes* (and that sucker was loud).

"Third time's the charm," Ainsley said, stepping over Poly.

"Isn't doing the same thing over and over again and expecting a different result considered the definition of insanity?"

She blinked at me. "Says who?"

I shrugged. "Probably some wise person who'd been burned by a relationship one too many times."

Like I had. Almost literally in my case.

"Sometimes, sugar," she drawled, "it's fun when things get a little hot, if you know what I mean."

I tipped my head. Right about now, a little heat sounded good. Really good. It had been downright glacial in my bedroom for a good long while. "Fine," I said, reaching for the phone. "I'll call. But only out of concern for Katie Sue."

Ainsley laughed again, not buying my excuse for a moment. She knew me too well.

We'd been best friends just shy of forever. Her mama claimed I was a bad influence on her baby girl, but Ainsley and I both knew she masterminded most of our crazy schemes. She'd stuck by me through thick and thin, including my two broken engagements to Dylan Jackson, my arrest (it was a misunderstanding, I swear), and of course when I was suspected of murder. I loved her like a sister and wasn't sure what I'd do without her.

Many years back she fell hard for a man who didn't seem to know she existed, so she hatched one of her famous plans to catch his attention. Carter Debbs didn't know what hit him—literally—when Ainsley ran him over with her car.

It hadn't been an accident.

After that Ainsley became a somewhat reformed wild child, the change coming about because she decided she needed to clean up her act to be the wife of a preacher man. They'd been married almost eight years now and had three kids. Twin four-year-old boys, Toby and Tuck, and three-year-old hellion Olive (who I thought should have been named "Karma" because she was so much like her mama).

Dylan didn't answer either of his phones, at his house or his office, so I left a message at both, asking him to call me back. Part of Hitching Post's quaintness was that it was cell-phone free—there wasn't coverage within town limits—so getting hold of someone right away was quite the challenge.

"So what do you know about the Calhouns?" I asked Ainsley again, revisiting my original question.

Wrinkling up her nose, her violet eyes sparkled. A lovely yellow sundress accentuated her generous curves. "I know about as much as you do," she said with a shrug. Her light brown hair had been recently cut into a choppy layered bob that swung as she worked. The hairdo exemplified everything about Ainsley. Refined but a touch untamed. "They're like the peaches in my backyard. Pretty on the outside, rotten to the core on the inside."

"Wait a sec." I studied her. "You didn't use those peaches in the cobbler you brought in yesterday, did you?"

Mischief twinkled in her eyes. "Why? You been feeling puny?"

This was why she was a *somewhat* reformed wild child. Every once in a while the crazy popped right out of her, like a jack-in-the-box.

Shaking my head, I nudged Roly off my mouse pad and fired up my desktop computer. She yawned and stretched and gave me a suspicious look while twitching her long whiskers. To reassure her all was well, I ran a hand down her fluffy spine, and she curled into a ball once again.

I wasn't sure what I could discover about the Calhouns online that I didn't already know, but I aimed to find out.

"One thing I've been wondering on," Ainsley said, pointing the feather duster at me, "is why Landry and Gabi's wedding was moved here to Hitching Post. It was supposed to be at a fancy estate down near Mobile, wasn't it?"

Everyone round here had taken to calling the soon-to-be newlyweds by their given names. The whole Calhoun family, in fact. Warren, Louisa, Cassandra, and Landry. As though we all knew them personally. Thick as thieves. Tighter than ticks. The Calhoun family better watch out, or they might have to set a few more—like a few hundred—plates at the family's Thanksgiving meal. The town had adopted the lot of them—whether they knew it or not.

"And wasn't it supposed to be a thousand guests?"

"The Calhouns told my mama that the bride and groom wanted something smaller, quainter, and that Gabi fell in love with the look of Mama's chapel. The guest list was cut to a measly three hundred."

"Ain't no way your mama's chapel will fit more than two hundred," Ainsley said. "And that's only if they're as skinny as fence pickets."

My mama would have found a way to squeeze them all in, but she didn't have to. "The ceremony's being held outside, around the gazebo."

"In this heat? Are they crazy?"

"Very possibly. Because it's a sunset wedding and with the rental of outdoor air conditioners, it probably won't be the heat that gets to the guests; it'll be the mosquitoes."

"Blessed be." Ainsley laughed and shook her head. "Well, if anyone can pull it off, it's your mama."

It was true. There was no stopping Veronica "Rona" Fowl when she had her mind set on something.

Ainsley's nose wrinkled again. "Why do you think Katie Sue's dander is up with the Calhouns?"

"I honestly don't know." It was hard to even speculate. I didn't really know Katie Sue anymore, and what I knew of the Calhouns made me worry about her well-being.

"What she said about giving them a taste of their own bitter medicine makes me think they did her wrong in some way," Ainsley said.

Poly hopped onto the counter and waved his tail under my nose. I rubbed his ears and scooted him out of the way of the computer screen. "Could be they did."

"But how does she even know them? She's Katie Sue Perrywinkle from itty bitty Hitching Post, Alabama, and they're"—her forehead scrunched as she searched for the right word—"famous."

"Well, she's not Katie Sue anymore, remember. She's Kathryn Perry, MD, and she has loads of money. Maybe she's a political supporter."

"Even still." Ainsley dragged the feather duster across a shelf. "Do you think the bitter medicine she talked about is literal? That it's actually a hex? Maybe she's been to see Delia."

Delia Bell Barrows. My cousin and former nemesis. We'd managed to stick a bandage on our broken relationship, but underneath old wounds ran deep. Because we practiced very different types of magic, I couldn't fully trust her. And wasn't sure I ever could. But that being said, we'd recently reunited and were trying to get to know each other as friends rather than rivals.

Though we both called ourselves witches, the term wasn't quite accurate but was used for lack of a better one.

People around these parts didn't care a whit what we were labeled as long as our magic worked when they needed it.

Our family tree had been split down its middle by mine and Delia's births. One side opting to use white magic for good (my side). The other choosing to practice black magic (her side).

Fundamentally our beliefs were night and day. Healer versus hexer. Good versus evil.

Delia sold hexes at her shop Till Hex Do Us Part, located across the Ring, the town center, and it was just the place for Katie Sue to scare up a bottle of revenge or a pox on the Calhoun family. "Maybe so, though the old Katie Sue would never touch a hex in a million years. She was all about healing."

"But you said she changed."

I couldn't argue that. Maybe her transformation ran deeper than hair color and speech patterns. I called up my favorite search engine and typed in the Calhoun name. Loads of information filled the screen.

"Find anything interesting?" Ainsley asked after a minute.

"Not really." Warren and Louisa had been college sweethearts, though rumors swirled of Warren's various affairs throughout the years. Seemed to me Louisa turned a blind eye to his dalliances, whereas if he were my husband, I'd be poking his eyes out with my handy-dandy pitchfork, my favorite weapon of choice.

The couple had two children. At age twenty-nine, Landry, the groom-to-be, was the youngest child and a classic ne'er-do-well. Three years ago, during one of Warren's reelection campaigns, several gossip magazines reported that Landry had been caught cheating during his final year of law school and that Warren bought him out of trouble. The family denied everything, but Landry never graduated and Warren's poll numbers tanked until not long after when tragedy struck the family. That's when Landry's older sister, Cassandra, had been hit by a car while crossing the street near her daddy's Washington, D.C. office, where she worked as an aide. She survived, but a broken back left her paralyzed from the waist down. The doctors were hopeful at first that she'd walk again, but it wasn't to be, and she was still bound to a wheelchair. Heartbreak for the family, but the sympathy vote bumped Warren's numbers through the roof.

I was about to click off the search engine, when a location caught my eye.

Shady Hollow.

It was where Katie Sue mentioned she lived—but it seemed the town was also home to the Calhoun family. On a whim, I typed in her new name along with "Calhoun" and was surprised to see her pictured at several Calhoun fund-raisers over the past couple of years, often framed in the same shot as Warren himself.

"Looks like Katie Sue *is* one of Warren's campaign donors." I showed Ainsley the photos.

"Or she's one of his mistresses," she said, her eyebrows raised and wiggling. "It wouldn't surprise me none with Warren's reputation."

It was a theory I couldn't dismiss even though I wanted to. Warren was known for chasing after young, beautiful, accomplished women.

"And if she recently found out he has himself another woman on the side . . . *Shoo-ee*. She might have gotten a hex from Delia to make his willie fall off or something."

I couldn't help but laugh. "I didn't need that image in my head."

But the more I thought about Katie Sue and Warren being together and her strange warning about bitter medicine, the more worried I became. *Mercy.* How'd I get mixed up in this mess? "I'm calling Delia. If she'd sold Katie Sue a revenge potion, a warning to the Calhouns might be in order."

"I don't know," Ainsley said. "I think it's high time Warren's willie shriveled up. If I were his wife, I'd be buying that hex myself. Cheat on me, will he? I don't think so."

I studied my friend. "Carter knows about the vigilante side of you, right?"

"Of course."

Shaking my head, I grabbed up the phone and punched in the numbers I now had memorized. Delia answered on the second ring, and as soon as she realized it was me, she said, "I was just about to call you."

"What's wrong?" I asked. The tone of her voice immediately set me to worrying.

A dog barked in the background—Boo, Delia's little black puppy. "You're not going to believe the—"

I glanced up as the bell jingled on the door, and a woman came inside. Ainsley shot me an incredulous look, her eyebrows practically in her hairline.

"I have to call you back, Delia," I said in a whisper.

"But Carly—"

"I'll call you right back." I hung up in a hurry.

The customer was Gabi Greenleigh, Landry Calhoun's intended. Oh, she tried to hide behind a big straw hat and sunglasses, but there was no concealing a beauty like hers. Tall and lithe with sleek auburn hair spilling down her back, I could see why she'd been crowned Miss Alabama two years ago.

"Hi there," I said. "Come on in, take a look around, let me know if you need any help."

"Thank you," she said softly as she approached the counter. Nervously, she bit her lip. "I do actually need some help. I hear you make potions." Her brow wrinkled; then she smiled, and it lit the whole room. "Your mama sent me over. She's ah . . . something."

It was a statement I heard often. "That she is."

"She said your potions are magical. Is that true?"

"Guaranteed to fix just about anything," I said. "You have something that needs fixin'?"

Glancing over her shoulder, she turned back to me and said, "Kind of."

Ainsley, never one to willingly be left out of a juicy bit of gossip, leaned on the counter. "Wedding day jitters? You need a calming potion? Carly can whip one right up. You'll be positively Zen in no time at all."

Gabi sighed and slipped off the sunglasses. "Poor excuse for a disguise, I suppose. You know who I am?"

"Your wedding's kind of a big deal round these parts," Ainsley said, putting it mildly.

Gabi stared at the counter for a second, then looked me dead in the eye. What I saw in her gaze near to broke my heart. The sadness was all-consuming.

Gabi rubbed Roly's head and took a moment before saying, "I need one of your magic potions."

"What kind?" I asked. "For the wedding jitters?"

"It's not jitters, I have," she said.

Ainsley patted her arm, consoling. "What is it you have, sugar?"

From the way Gabi was acting, I expected an answer along the lines of an STD or somesuch. Tears filled her big green eyes and pooled along dark lashes.

"What I have," she said, "is a man who doesn't love me. I need a love potion. The sooner, the better."

Chapter Three

A insley *tsk*ed sympathetically. "What do you mean he doesn't love you? Of course he loves you, sugar. He's marrying you Saturday in front of God and everyone, ain't he?"

Gabi sniffled and mumbled, "He doesn't love me. But that's okay. For now I love him enough for the both of us."

Ainsley tipped her head. "Is he gay?"

I shot her a look.

"Well, I mean, look at her!" Ainsley said.

I rolled my eyes.

Gabi snuffled—she even did that prettily. "I—I don't think so."

"Is there another woman?" Ainsley asked, *tsk*ing again. She turned to me. "Remember that time Widow Harkins started sweet-talking Carter? Asking him over to help her with this, fix that, stay for some fresh-made cinnamon rolls? And him being a pastor and all couldn't rightly say no, could he? Lordy be. She was lucky I didn't

pull her hair out by their bleached roots." She harrumphed. "And I still can't abide looking at cinnamon
rolls to this day."

"You did pull her hair out by the roots," I pointed out.
"Left her with a bald patch the size of a MoonPie."

"Oh, that's right. I did." Ainsley winked. "*Accidentally*, of course."

Gabi's eyes went wide.

I said to her, "Widow Harkins took to wearing wigs
and suddenly started going to church in Huntsville."

Ainsley said, "You just don't go stealing another girl's
man without consequences. Know what I'm sayin'?"

Gabi laughed nervously and nodded. "Why are women
so sneaky? It just ain't right."

"Well," I said, "sometimes wanting something so badly
makes you forget right from wrong. Especially when it
comes to matters of the heart."

"Kind of like knowing it's wrong to slip Landry a love
potion, but I'm going to do it anyway?"

I smiled. "Kind of. But there is a hitch with my potions
that you should know about." I hated to tell her about the
Backbone Effect, one of the supernatural rules that gov-
erned my potions. It prevented someone from being
duped by a potion by taking their free will into consider-
ation. Whoever the potion was intended for had to
want—consciously or unconsciously—the potion's result.
It was especially important for love potions.

Twin vertical lines creased the smooth plane between
her eyebrows as I explained, but then disappeared by the
time I finished saying my piece.

"That won't be an issue," Gabi said. "He wants to love
me . . . he just doesn't."

"Is there another woman?" Ainsley asked again. "You never did answer."

Gabi blinked as though never truly considering the notion. "I don't think so."

Ainsley slid me a *what-the-hell-is-going-on-here* look. "Then why is he marrying you if he doesn't love you?" she said, sounding truly puzzled by the notion.

Tears puddled again. "He's only marrying me because his daddy is forcing him to. Some sort of political ploy, an agreement they made years ago."

Dang. That was low, even for Warren Calhoun.

"You're okay with that?" I propped a hip against the counter. "With marrying a man who doesn't love you? Seems like you're borrowing trouble, and I don't think that's the 'something borrowed' meant for your wedding day."

"I know I should have more pride, but he's just . . ." Her voice trailed off, and her eyes once again filled with a sadness so deep it nearly broke my heart. "He's everything I want."

"Is he?" I asked softly. "Truly?"

Gabi looked between us, and I knew instantly the moment she realized she'd said too much. A cloud crossed her eyes—a flash of panic—before she slipped on a mask of indifference.

"You didn't hear any of that from me," she said. "I should go."

The door swung open and Caleb Montgomery came into the shop carrying a cardboard tray filled with coffee cups and a take-out bag from Dèjá Brew. "Carly Hartwell, just for you I snatched the last fudge brownie straight off the plate of some national news reporter from

who-knows-where who then called me a two-bit hillbilly."
He snorted and set the bag on the counter. "I'm worth at
least four bits. I mean, come on."

Divorce attorney Caleb Montgomery was one of the
town's peacocks and was probably the least hillbilly of
anyone in Darling County, with his fancy clothes and
haircut, which cost a lot more than four bits. We'd been
friends since second grade.

Gabi quickly set her hat on her head. "Look at the
time. I best get going."

"What about your potion?" I asked. "It'll only take a
second. . . ."

Emotion tumbled across her beautiful features. "I
should go. Thank you for your time and for listening to
me go on and on." She dashed out the door.

Caleb lifted the tab on his coffee cup and an eyebrow
at the same time. "Something I said?"

"Just your usual way with women." Ainsley dug into
the bag and pulled out a chocolate cookie.

Caleb smiled at her jab, taking it in stride. He was
used to it. "At least I don't have to bribe my mother-in-
law with hooch to watch my kids."

Ainsley bit into the cookie. "Not yet, leastways. Your
time will come."

A look of pure terror crossed his face—I wasn't sure
which comment hit him like a two-by-four. The fact that
he might some day have a mother-in-law . . . or kids. He
was a confirmed bachelor and liked it that way just fine.
I, however, was determined to set him up. I had someone
in mind, too, but getting them together was easier said
than done considering they couldn't abide being in the
same room.

"Was that . . ." He gestured toward the door.

Crumbs littered the floor as Ainsley nodded and spoke around the cookie she was chewing. "Poor girl." Poly happily pounced on the crumbs, lapping them up with a swift pink tongue. "If I were her I'd run and never look back."

Caleb looked between us. "I give them six months. If that." He had an uncanny knack for predicting how long a marriage would last. I'd never had the nerve to ask him if he thought Dylan and I could make it to happily-ever-after. There were some things this witch didn't need to know.

"Only because she left without a love potion," Ainsley said.

Poly stared up at her, hoping for more crumbs. He was out of luck.

"She was looking for a love potion?" Caleb set his coffee on the counter and leaned forward. "Spill."

Ainsley and I filled him in on the strange visit—and on Katie Sue's return as well.

His eyes widened. "I can't believe Katie Sue is planning on going up against the Calhouns. It's akin to playing with fire."

"Maybe Katie Sue's the one holding the matches," I said, thinking about her possibly being a woman scorned. My skin tingled again. Trouble was in the air, and it swirled around Katie Sue like a mini tornado.

"Or she's the one who's going to end up in ashes," he said, then added a dramatic *"Duhn-duhn-duhhhhn."*

"Stop that," I said, swatting him.

But he was on a roll and couldn't be deterred. "Seems I've heard Warren Calhoun has a reputation for getting rid of people who cause him trouble. Isn't that so, Ainsley?"

Her eyes alight, she nodded eagerly, a willing accomplice to his theatrics. "I heard that, too."

Caleb said, "Didn't he poison a rival who was inching too close in the polls?"

"That was a rumor," I said. "That guy died of a heart attack."

"Oh, I don't know." He tapped his coffee lid. "How about his campaign manager who vanished and still hasn't been found?"

"He was found. In Switzerland with a lot of the Calhouns' money." I wrapped up my brownie and stuck it back in the bag. My stomach churned.

"Oh right. I forgot." He winked. "Well, I'm sure I've read in the tabloids that his former mistress went missing."

"Mistresses," Ainsley cut in. "Plural."

There was a playfulness in their eyes that told me they were teasing. But this all felt too real to me. "*Alleged* mistresses," I said, feeling a lump growing in my throat.

"All I'm saying," Caleb leaned in, "is that Katie Sue best be careful . . . or else."

I could easily picture the "or else." I had a good imagination.

Ainsley, however, apparently decided to act it out.

She staggered around making choking noises. Slamming shut her eyes, she stuck out her tongue, and collapsed into a spasmodic bundle, her yellow dress billowing about until she finally settled in for her eternal rest.

Her little death scene was loud and dramatic. Much like she was.

Caleb laughed as the ever-hopeful Poly tiptoed forward to sniff Ainsley's outstretched fingers.

My stomach twisting, I said, "Don't even joke about it."

Caleb said to Ainsley, "She's gone and lost her sense of humor after finding the dead guy in the back of her shop."

I glared at him. "I didn't lose my sense of—"

The front door whipped open, and an ice-blond typhoon blew inside, her black cape flying out behind her.

Only one person could get away with wearing a black cape in the ninety-five degree weather of an Alabama August.

My cousin Delia Bell Barrows took one look at Ainsley lying on the floor, stepped over her prone body, and stormed to the counter. "I can't believe you hung up on me!"

"Well," Caleb drawled, his gray eyes narrowing on my cousin, "look what the devil done dragged in."

Delia speared him with a death stare.

He winked at her.

No, it wasn't going to be easy setting these two up, but I was game for the challenge.

Delia ignored him but grabbed on to the locket dangling around her neck—an identical charm to mine—as if to block his energy. She leveled her icy gaze on me. "It best have been a matter of life and death, Carly Bell Hartwell."

"Look," I said innocently. "Ainsley's dead."

Ainsley's body jerked twice in deathly emphasis.

"Nah, she's not dead." Caleb straightened. "She's just doing a fair imitation of Francie Debbs after keeping the Clingons for a bit."

"Bite me," Ainsley said, sitting up. "Your time to have a family will come, Caleb Montgomery."

He scooted around her on the way to the door. "Not if I can help it any. Keep me filled in about the—" Drawing his finger across his throat, he winked at Delia again, and slipped out into the sunshine.

As we watched him go, I caught the reflections of mine and Delia's faces in the glass door panel. We looked a lot alike, Delia and me, yet were easy to tell apart. Aside from our bitten-to-the-quick fingernails, my blond hair was darker than her platinum, my eyes brown to her frosty blue. Plus I had dozens of light freckles dotting my face, and she had a beautiful clear creamy complexion.

Six months ago, if someone had told me Delia and I wouldn't only be speaking but would be friends, I'd have laughed at the absurd notion. We'd been sworn enemies since the day we were born.

Enemies, because this shop and its secrets had been destined to me upon my birth—the legacy was passed down to the eldest child in the family, and thanks to being born two months prematurely, I was older than Delia by six whole minutes. Outraged, my aunt Neige, Delia's mama, had argued that gestationally Delia was the older of us, but my Grammy Adelaide turned a deaf ear.

Furious, Neige had rebelled by opening Till Hex Do Us Part, a shop that sold hexes, and started embracing her dark heritage wholeheartedly. Though she had no access to the Leilara, the enchanted lily drops, her black magic was still strong and her shop prospered. But she'd do anything to attain the Leilara—and the power that came with them.

Delia and I had grown up as rivals.

But then Aunt Neige had followed her heart to New Orleans, Delia had taken over the hex shop, and just a few months ago had taken a leap of faith to bridge the chasm between us when she learned I was in danger. Since then we'd slowly been getting to know each other.

But—and it was a big but—there was still a tiddly bit of worry on my part about the Leilara secret. And if Delia's friendship was only a ploy to get her hands on the legacy that should have rightly been hers.

"*Argh,*" Delia said. "How can you be friends with him? He's impossible."

Under her cape, she wore a pair of black skinny jeans, a black tunic top, and black sandals. Even her dog Boo was black, but I noticed she hadn't brought him with her. He usually sat in a wicker basket that hung from her arm, ala Toto from *The Wizard of Oz*.

On me, the black would have made me look like I'd done lost my mind, but on Delia it just made her look more mysterious.

"Impossible not to love," I said, laying the groundwork for my matchmaking. I reached in the bag for the fudge brownie—my appetite was back now that we weren't talking about death anymore.

"Gag me." Delia scratched Roly's head, who twisted her head for easier access to her chin.

Okay, so I had my work cut out for me. I broke the brownie in half and handed a piece over to my cousin.

"What was with the neck thing?" she asked. "Did someone really die?"

Ainsley dusted herself off. "Possibly a murder in the making."

"There's no murder in the making," I said. But even

as the words left my mouth, a tingle slid down my spine. I wished Dylan would call me back as I gave up for good on the brownie. What a waste of perfectly good chocolate.

"Is that why you hung up on me?" Delia asked, narrowing her eyes. "Like I said, I could forgive you if it was a matter of life and death."

Ainsley picked up the feather duster and went back to work on the potion bottles. "Nah, it was because Gabi Greenleigh came in."

Something dark flashed in Delia's eyes.

"What?" I said.

"What, what?" she countered.

"What was that look?"

She lifted a shoulder. "She's why I wanted to talk to you. I had a dream about you, and she was in it. Or maybe I had a dream about her, and you were in it. Either way . . ."

Delia's dreams were often premonitory and akin to my witchy senses—they were to be taken very seriously. Another warning tingle slid down my spine. "What was the dream about?"

There was caution in her clear blue irises. "You two were together at your mama's chapel . . ."

"And?" Ainsley prompted.

Delia shifted uncomfortably. "Carly was trying to calm her down, but she was screaming to wake the dead."

"Why?" I asked.

Delia said, "It could have had something to do with her being covered in blood."

✎ Chapter Four ✎

A couple of hours later, I left the shop in Ainsley's capable hands. She couldn't diagnose ailments as I could, but she could sell premade potions better than anyone I knew, and she'd call me at my mama's chapel if any help was needed.

I set Roly and Poly in the basket of Bessie Blue, my turquoise bike, and took a look around the Ring. Tourists roamed the stone walkway, window shopping at the shops that lined the cozy circle. An idyllic park was set in the middle of the Ring, with picnic benches, pathways, and a gazebo that was often used for weddings.

Hitching Post was consistently named one of America's most beautiful small towns, and it was easy to see why. In the distance, verdant Appalachian foothills overlooked the Darling River, and the town's landscaping committee went above and beyond with its colorful flowerbeds and hanging flowerpots. Everything was neat and clean, picturesque and quaint.

The discordant image of a blood-covered Gabi Greenleigh didn't mesh with the peaceful setting, and I hoped that Delia's dream had been just that ... a dream, or rather, a nightmare. Not a premonition. But I couldn't shake the tingles of my own internal warning system and feared that all hell was about to break loose in this charming little town.

What I wondered was if I could prevent it from happening ... or if the trouble had already been set in motion.

I was pondering that as I pedaled toward home to drop off the cats before heading to my mama's chapel. As I passed Dèjá Brew, I did a double take when I spotted my curmudgeonly aunt Marjie, one of the Odd Ducks, and her new boyfriend, Johnny Braxton, sitting at an outside bistro table.

Along with a host of other businesses around town, Johnny owned the Little Wedding Chapel of Love and was my mama's biggest competitor. Their rivalry knew no limits, and neither was opposed to fighting dirty. My mama had recently one-upped him in a big way, and he was undoubtedly looking for retribution.

Johnny knew my mama's Achilles heel was her family, and I didn't think it was any kind of fluke that he'd started dating Marjie not long after Mama bested him. An added incentive for wooing Marjie was that he wanted to buy her inn, and would do just about anything to get it from her, including trying to slip her one of my love potions. Fortunately, I'd thwarted that plan.

Marjie knew all this.

So *why* she had agreed to date him was still a bit of a mystery. However, my aunt was no one's fool, so I wasn't too worried about her getting hurt. She had her own motives, and though I didn't know what they were, I was curious about the game they were playing with each other.

I rolled up to their table to say hello.

If Bluto from *Popeye* had a grandfather, he would look like Johnny Braxton. Barrel chest, white hair, trimmed white beard, permanent scowl, and a hint of villainy. He was one of the richest and most successful businessmen in Hitching Post, but his sour personality had kept him a bachelor all his life.

Johnny eyed the cats with disdain (they returned the look), and said with a measure of judgment, "Quittin' early today. Some might question your work ethic, Miss Carly."

"I'm off to help my mama at her chapel," I said, sugar sweet. "There's some kind of big wedding there this weekend."

The vein in his forehead pulsed. He'd just about busted a gut when he found out the Calhouns had chosen Mama's chapel over his, a fact my mama had managed to mention each and every time she'd run into him. My mama wasn't above a little gloating.

Marjie lifted an eyebrow, and I swear her eyes were twinkling. *Twinkling.* Then she said to me, "You'd best get on with yourself then."

I noticed that she'd actually tried to tame her brown Brillo-pad brown hair into some semblance of a style, and that there was a smear of blush on her cheeks.

I lifted my own eyebrow. My aunt was taking this dating game very seriously indeed if she altered her normally nonexistent grooming habits.

Johnny's cheeks reddened. Just the sight of me tended

to have that effect on him, but I also knew he had heart troubles.

I couldn't help but prod him. "You're looking a little flushed, Mr. Braxton. Are you feeling okay? How's the ol' ticker?"

Steam practically billowed from his ears. "I'm fine."

"Right as rain," Marjie said, shoving his buttery scone closer to him.

His jaw set as he eyed the pastry. "I was just about to ask your lovely aunt to go on a nature hike this afternoon."

I nearly choked. First, the only thing growing in nature my aunt liked were weeds, and *hiking*? The word wasn't in her vocabulary.

"The wildflowers along the river are mighty pretty right now. But not nearly as pretty as she is," he said through clenched teeth, patting her hand. "Ain't she a beauty?"

I gazed at my aunt. I wasn't sure she'd been called beautiful a day in her life, but when you looked beyond the bad attitude, the scowl, and the unfortunate hair, her skin was perfection, and her eyes were big, brown, and absolutely enchanting. She *was* beautiful. "Yes, she is. Really lovely."

Surprise flared in her eyes before her jaw clenched, making her lips pucker like she'd been sucking on a sour candy. "A hike sounds wonderful. Just perfect. I've been aimin' to get back on the Lover's Leap trail for a while now. It's been years. I think today's the day. We can pack a picnic and make an occasion of it."

Johnny blanched. "Splendid." His lips pressed into a tight smile.

ONE POTION IN THE GRAVE 39

"It's a bit hot for a hike," I said. With these high temps it would be easy to get heat stroke.

"Nonsense, Carly," my aunt replied. "It's merely a little warm."

Johnny tugged at his collar. "Perhaps we should wait until evening, when temperatures are a bit more tolerable for a long walk. And we'll be sure to pack extra water."

Marjie shrugged. "If you think you need it . . ."

His brows furrowed, making him look even more cantankerous.

"Maybe while we're there, we should jump off the leap," she suggested. "Us being loverly and all."

Lover's Leap was a spot high atop one of the bluffs overlooking Darling River. It was accessed via a three-mile looped trail that started—and ended—smack dab between Mama's and Johnny's chapels. The "leap" was a thirty-foot drop into a deep section of the river that was particularly popular with teenaged couples who had a bit of a daredevil side. It was a risky jump—because one false move and the leaper could miss the water and land on a rocky section of riverbank. There had been more than a few deaths there over the years.

His chest rumbled as he attempted to laugh. "I think my days of leaping are long done, Marjoram."

"For shame," she mumbled.

He narrowed his eyes on her, but she paid no mind.

I was suddenly reminded of the movie *War of the Roses*, and wondered if that was what was going on with them. They were out to kill each other.

Johnny didn't stand a chance.

"You two have fun. I'll see you later." If they survived.

I smiled and waved and headed into the neighborhoods that branched out from the Ring and soon turned onto my street, which had only five houses—three on one side, two on the other. Old quintessential Southern homes, with big porches dripping in ferns, gabled roofs, dormers, and prerequisite fences, some wooden, some wrought iron.

Roly and Poly cautiously eyed a swooping cardinal as though afraid of an air raid (they were scaredy-cats) and tolerated the bumpy ride on the brick road fairly well. They were used to it. Old live oaks lined the street on both sides, creating a continuous canopy that made it look like the road wound through a leafy tunnel, and flowerpots filled with colorful annuals hung from lampposts. More cars than usual dotted my charming lane, most likely due to the Calhoun wedding and its numerous guests. But all was not scenic here, oh no. There were two blights on this lovely little stretch: My aunt Marjie's inn . . . and my house. My place was under heavy renovations, and Marjie's place . . . well, it was a lot like she was: contrary.

Her inn, the Old Buzzard, sat at the end of the street closest to the Ring, and looked like squatters lived there, with its peeling paint, weed-infested yard, and rotting clapboards. A No Vacancy sign swung on a leaning post. The inn hadn't seen a guest for as long as Marjie owned it, which was how she wanted it. She owned the place only as a result of a bizarre pact with the other Odd Ducks: What one did, they all did. So when the other sisters wanted their own inns . . . Marjie had to get one, too.

The thing about the Old Buzzard was that it was a diamond in the rough—something a businessman like

Johnny recognized. A little TLC would turn the inn into a gold mine.

Right next door to Marjie's, Aunt Hazel's Crazy Loon was the epitome of Southern charm yet was as eccentric as she was. Across the road, my aunt Eulalie owned the Silly Goose, which was absolutely lovely with its touches of whimsy.

I eyed the Crazy Loon and my thoughts turned to Katie Sue and why she was in town. I'd waited all afternoon to no avail for Dylan Jackson to return my calls, and as soon as I turned my attention to my house at the end of the lane, I knew why he hadn't gotten back to me.

I'd been looking for him in all the wrong places.

The butt end of his beat-up pickup truck stuck out of my driveway.

As I passed my neighbor Mr. Dunwoody's house—his place was sandwiched between my house and Aunt Eulalie's—I wished he weren't out of town this weekend. His portentous weekly relationship forecasts were the marital barometer around here. He might know if Gabi and Landry's nuptials would go off without a hitch . . . or if they were doomed. But unfortunately, the retired math professor was visiting his brother in Mobile this week. I rolled up to the mailbox and took out the small stack of mail and set it my basket. He'd put me in charge of watering his plants and collecting his mail while he was gone. The mail I could handle just fine, but his plants were already starting to droop. I was a menace in the garden.

I pedaled on with Delia's dream nagging my subconscious. Living in a wedding town, I'd pretty much seen it all. Breakups, makeups, runaway brides, grooms having flings with maids of honor, bridezillas ... you name it. But I'd never seen a blood-covered bride-to-be. And *mercy*, I didn't want to ever see one.

Trying to push aside the thoughts of Delia's disturbing dream for now, I admired my newly built front porch. It was so much prettier than the one that had been here before—the one that had come crashing down after an out-of-control truck rammed into it months ago. My tires bumped over the curb and onto the sidewalk, and I parked my bike next to my garage. As I plucked the cats from the basket I heard hammering coming from within the house and smiled. Dylan had adopted the role of handyman, and was helping me repair my fixer-upper. He was hoping to be paid in kisses. Instead, I paid him in suppers.

As I climbed the back steps, I knew I shouldn't accept his help but I really needed it. Plus he looked mighty fine wielding a hammer, very easy on the eyes.

And, okay, I liked having him around.

There. I said it.

I knew people thought we'd get back together no questions asked, but there were a couple of big things keeping us apart, the biggest being his mama, Patricia Davis Jackson, who couldn't abide the sight of me. Then there was the dark cloud of two broken engagements hanging over our heads.

Not too long ago Dylan had suggested that I wasn't so different from my mama's side of the family—that I was just as opposed to marriage as they were.

A big part of me scoffed at the notion. After all, I'd been ready and willing to walk down the aisle twice with him, but the first attempt was ruined by his mama, and the second by his doubts.

Or at least that's what I told myself.

And until he'd suggested I hadn't fallen too far from the Fowl family tree did the thought even occur to me that he might be right.

So now, a small part of me wondered. Did I take after my cynical mama and aunties? Because I certainly hadn't taken after my daddy, who believed his happily-ever-after was just a trip down the aisle away. He'd been waiting thirty-some years for my mama to marry him—and vowed to keep on waiting.

I didn't know. And I didn't like that I didn't know.

As the hammering continued, I pulled open the back door leading into the kitchen and set the cats down. Poly immediately hopped onto the counter and stood next to the treat canister, and Roly slinked off to find Dylan. She had a crush on him.

I knew the feeling.

"Hello!" I shouted as soon as there was a break in the hammering.

"Up here," he hollered back.

I climbed the scarred wooden stairs to the second floor, noticing every little pockmark in the stairwell plaster. I'd been renovating the house bit by bit ever since I bought it from my mama and aunties for a dollar a few years ago. They'd inherited it from Grammy Fowl and were more than happy to keep it in the family and not let some outsider in on "their" road. Mr. Dunwoody was fortunate to have inherited his house from his parents, or else his place would have been snapped up by the Odd Ducks long ago.

Personally, I think my mama and my aunts got the better of our real-estate transaction, money wise, but I loved living in the house my mama had grown up in. It just had a lot of problems that needed fixin', which seemed to cost a lot more money than any of us anticipated.

I noticed a floor fan aimed into the bathroom as I hit the landing. When Grammy Fowl put in central air-conditioning, for some reason a vent was never added to the upstairs wash room. It was one of the many projects on the to-do list, seeing as how it could heat up mighty quick between those four walls, even with the window wide open. Roly sat in the doorway, her tail swishing.

Dylan stepped out of the bathroom shirtless, his light brown hair damp and curled into soft waves, his chest slick with sweat, a hammer in hand.

Lordy. Be.

"Hey," I said dumbly, latching on to my locket as I tried desperately to keep my gaze on his face and my hands off his body. Talk about heating up mighty quick. I suddenly recalled what Ainsley had said this morning about heat and felt a flush creep up my neck.

"Hey." He frowned at his watch. "You're home early."

"I need to help my mama at her chapel," I mumbled.

He swiped a hand through his hair, raising brown spikes, then reached for his T-shirt that was draped over the doorknob. "That's right. Here I was thinking I'd surprise you by getting this framing done today, and you're the one surprising me."

Oh, I was surprised all right.

Slipping on his shirt, he said, "I should have known."

I said, "Known what?"

"You're forever surprising the hell out of me, Care Bear."

Usually the nickname bugged the hell out of me, but right now I didn't mind so much. "Someone's got to keep you on your toes."

"That's Roly's job, isn't it, girl?" he said as he scooped her up and cuddled her next to his chest.

Her purrs carried easily.

"Well," I said, trying to ignore my melting heart, "I'm about to really surprise you. I've been calling around for you all morning about some news I have, but I didn't realize you were here."

His green eyes sparkled. "You finally decide you can't live without me and want to elope?"

Yes. "No."

"That *is* surprising. I thought for sure you'd finally come to your senses."

I cocked a hip. "Why do you have to tease me like that?"

He set Roly on the floor and took a step closer to me. His voice dropped. "Who said I'm teasing, Care Bear?"

Before I did something stupid, like agree to run off with him, I said in a rush, "Katie Sue Perrywinkle is back in town, and she's mixed up with the Calhouns in a bad way."

Whistling low, he said, "You've had yourself quite the day."

"That's not even the half of it."

"Oh?"

"Delia had a dream about Gabi Greenleigh. She was covered in blood. I was there."

His eyebrow inched up. "Maybe you should start from the beginning."

I motioned for him to follow me to the kitchen, where I found Poly still staring mournfully at the treat canister. Solely for his persistence, I gave him a treat and one to Roly, too.

The kitchen itself was still in the midst of a remodel, but the floors had been refinished—gorgeous hearts of pine that now gleamed. I bustled about, making two grilled cheese and tomato sandwiches as I explained my visit with Katie Sue, how my witchy senses had kicked up, and told him all about Delia's dream. I set his sandwich along with some chips on a paper plate and handed it to him.

I cut my sandwich in half. "I'd like to prevent whatever is about to happen."

"The blood Delia saw . . . Was it Gabi's? Had she been injured?"

"Delia didn't know. Pretty much all she saw was Gabi covered in blood, screaming, and me trying to console her."

"Doesn't give me much to go on. Where'd the dream take place?"

Why I made lunch for myself, I had no idea. I couldn't eat while talking about this. I surely didn't learn my lesson from the brownie this morning. "Delia said my mama's chapel." I set my sandwich on his plate. "Can you assign someone to watch over Gabi?"

"I don't have that kind of manpower."

The Darling County Sheriff's office was tiny, the building itself three whole rooms with a basement lockup. Besides the sheriff and Dylan, there were only four other deputies and an office administrator on staff.

"We've got to do something," I said.

"There's a mess of U.S. Marshals in town along with

private security for this wedding. Someone is probably already assigned to Gabi. I'll get a message out about an anonymous threat. That'll bump up security around her."

"Thanks," I said but couldn't help feeling it wouldn't help.

"Do you think the danger you feel around Katie Sue is tied to Delia's dream?"

I folded the top of the chip bag and used a clothespin to keep the bag shut. "I wish I knew. Could be. But it could be that Katie Sue is out to get the Calhouns for some reason. Or that they're out to get her."

There were days I wished my witchy senses came with a little more information. Like a two hundred and twelve–page manual.

"It isn't likely anything will happen to the Calhouns, if you're worried that Katie Sue's going to act out. No one's going to get within ten feet of that family unless they want them there." He held up the plate. "This is good. Thanks."

"You're welcome. Thanks for fixing up my bathroom. But you're not going to distract me with your manners and all. What if Katie Sue's the one in danger from the Calhouns? Who's going to protect her?"

He sighed. "You're not going to let this go."

It wasn't a question.

"I have a soft spot for Katie Sue." I set the frying pan in the sink and listened to it sizzle as I ran water over the hot cast iron.

He dumped his paper plate in the trash can and walked over to me. Nudging up my chin, he said, "I understand soft spots, I do. But she's not Katie Sue anymore, is she? She's Kathryn now, and you don't really know who she is."

"I know. But do you really think people can change their core, their heart, so easily? I want to believe she's the same ol' Katie Sue under all that . . . fanciness."

"People change," he said. "Sometimes not for the better."

I nibbled a fingernail as I thought about that. I didn't want to believe it, but I knew it to be true.

"I'll see what I can find out about Katie Sue's business in town," he said, then leaned down and kissed me loudly on the lips.

A quick kiss. A tease. I wouldn't have minded a bit if he'd lingered—and I had the feeling he knew it.

I was getting entirely too comfortable with him around. I grabbed hold of his T-shirt and was about to go in for another kiss when someone started pounding on the front door.

"Carly! Carlina Bell Hartwell!"

"Hazel," I said to Dylan as I went to open the door.

"Lousy timing," he grumbled.

She was peering in the leaded panes, her hands cupped on each side of her face, her nose pressed to the glass. Most knew her as the strangest Odd Duck, but that wasn't saying too much.

Her flaming red hair burst about her head like some sort of fiery halo as she charged into the living room, her hand on her heart, her color high. She gasped as though trying to catch her breath, but I thought it was only a ploy to show off her generous cleavage to Dylan.

Hazel was a bit of an exhibitionist.

Her outfit of choice today was a short leather mini-skirt and pink halter top, of which her bosoms were practically hanging out.

Before I could even ask her what was wrong, Eulalie

(the sanest Odd Duck), came racing inside, hot on the heels of her sister. "You said you'd wait for me to come see Carly," she snapped at Hazel. She flung her hands in the air and adopted an *I'm-wounded-to-the-soul* tone. "I should have known you'd go behind my back."

Eulalie had a flair for the dramatic.

The fact that she looked like Meryl Streep's twin didn't help the matter. She fancied herself an unfulfilled actress. The world was her stage.

Including my living room.

Hazel gained her breath and waved Eulalie away. "I never promised such a thing. You're delusional. Heat stroke or something."

"Well, I never!" Eulalie countered, peeling off her wrist-length white gloves one finger at a time.

"Why are you here to see me?" I chimed in, hoping they'd get to the point sooner rather than later.

"We want men," Eulalie said, fanning her face with the gloves.

I stared at her. "What?"

"We want you to find us men," she said. "Use your matchmaking talents on us like you did on Marjie. It's not fair she has a man and we have no one at all to look after us. I had to change my own lightbulb this morning. Can you imagine?" She batted her eyelashes at Dylan.

"You should have called me, Miss Eulalie," he said.

I rolled my eyes. It was just the opening she was looking for.

"I'll do that next time. You're a sweet boy. Carly never should have left you at the altar the way she did. Twice."

"I agree." He nodded sagely. "And then she went and burned down the place the second time."

I kicked his shin. "Don't make me throw you out."

"You wouldn't know what to do without me," he said, smirking.

I said to my aunt, "The fire was *accidental*."

Hazel readjusted her breasts as she said, "Let it be known that *I* have a man. Leave me out of this."

"You have a *child*," Eulalie countered.

"John Richard is twenty-seven," Hazel corrected. "Of legal age, last time I checked."

"You're not still seeing him, are you?" I groaned. Attorney John Richard Baldwin had tumbled into my life—quite literally—a few months ago, and I couldn't seem to extricate him. He'd been fired from a law firm in Birmingham and had moved to Hitching Post, where he was apparently getting quite cozy with my aunt. I had believed their flirtation with each other was just . . . flirtation. The thought of them actually getting *together* was too much for me to stomach.

Eulalie kept waving her gloves in front of her face as a fan. "The poor boy doesn't even know he's dating her. Just keeps coming over at her beck and call. Fix this, tend that, all the while her boobies are heaving out of her tops. You should be ashamed. Ashamed!"

"Calm yourself down, Reverend Green," Hazel said snidely.

"Men?" I asked loudly, hoping to stop a catfight before it started. I'd broken up more of their brawls than I cared to admit. "I can certainly set you up."

"I already said I don't need a man," Hazel protested.

"Then why'd you come sprinting over here, first chance you got?" Eulalie demanded to know.

"I didn't come to see *Carly*," she said as though that made a lick of sense. "I came to see *Dylan*."

Dylan straightened in alarm, as though she'd suddenly turned her amorous attentions on him. "Me? Why?"

"Yes, why?" I added. I'd rip her hair out if I had to. I didn't want to, us being family and all, but as Ainsley said, you don't go stealing another girl's man.

But *huh*. He wasn't quite mine, was he? He was open for the stealing.

The thought made me slightly queasy.

Hazel rolled her eyes and set her hands on her curvy hips. "I came for Dylan because he's the law, and I'm in need of a lawman. I've been burgled!"

≈≈ Chapter Five ≈≈

Dylan used my phone to call for an additional deputy, and then as the four of us trooped across the road to Hazel's inn she explained that one of her guest rooms had been broken into and ransacked. My witchy senses were acting up again, and I didn't need Hazel to tell me whose room had been violated.

The Crazy Loon was a long white gorgeous two-story home with attic dormers and eight guest rooms. A wraparound porch dripped with healthy ferns, wind chimes, and a feeling of hospitality. The expansive garden reflected Hazel's eccentric personality, with its vibrant colors, whirl-igigs, and unusual sculptures.

My aunts might be odd, but they were savvy business-women, and Hazel knew just how badly a break-in could affect her inn's reputation.

"Nothing is missing, and my guest didn't even want the break-in reported, but I can't be having none of that." Hazel led the way across the road.

I had just stepped off the sidewalk when I caught the

scent of cigarette smoke hanging in the humid air. I turned and noticed a rusted-out junker pickup truck parked a little ways down, a woman behind the wheel. She slouched low to keep out of sight, but even though Dinah Perrywinkle Cobb was trying hard to become invisible, she was impossible to miss with her sky-high blond hair and cigarette hanging out the window.

"Carly?" Dylan asked when he noticed I'd stopped walking.

I nodded to the truck. "Katie Sue's mama."

Everyone knew Katie Sue's background. It was a colorful square woven into the crazy quilt that was our town. This was a place with very few secrets. Dylan didn't need to be told what a big deal Dinah's presence was.

A second later the truck made a speedy U-turn out and zoomed down the street in the opposite direction. The cigarette was tossed onto the road, a parting shot.

"Miss Hazel, was Kathryn Perry staying in the room that was broken into?" Dylan asked, apparently making the same conclusion as my witchy senses.

Hazel's glittery gold eye shadow sparkled in the sunlight as her eyes grew wide. "How'd you know? Do you know her? She looked mighty familiar to me, but I couldn't place her face."

"Kathryn Perry," Eulalie said, trying the name on for size. "Hmmm. Nope, I never heard of her, and you know I have a deep recollection of names. It's a talent of mine," she said to Dylan specifically. "All great actresses have to have a good memory. And I never forget a name. Not ever."

Hazel huffed and started up the steps. "I wasn't asking *you*, Eulalie."

My gaze followed the truck as it disappeared around the corner. What I wanted to know was how Dinah knew Katie Sue was here. Had the note Katie Sue sent to Jamie Lynn been intercepted? Or had she told her mama about it?

Dylan whispered to me, "I'll be sure to pay a visit to the Cobbs."

"Can I come with you?" I asked.

"No."

"Couldn't hurt to ask," I murmured with a smile.

The double front doors led into a spacious reception area with a fireplace inset into a wall covered in white wainscoting. Hazel's personality was reflected in brightly colored furniture and unique knickknacks, but the area was kept neutral enough not to scare off guests. Katie Sue sat on a striped turquoise, purple, and green armchair, and she was busy sticking what looked like a whole book of stamps onto the coffee-stained manila envelope I'd noticed in her purse earlier while she was at my shop. As we filed into the room, she rose and quickly stuffed the envelope into the outgoing mailbox attached to the reception counter. I thought I heard her groan when she finally took stock of us all.

"I've gone and fetched the law," Hazel announced, bounding over to Katie Sue and grabbing her hands. "Don't go worrying any. We'll get this sorted out."

Eulalie bumped Hazel aside. "Eulalie Fowl," she introduced herself as she took a long look at the newcomer. "We haven't met before, have we? You do look a mite familiar. . . ." Before she could get an answer, she thumped her small chest. "*My* inn is across the street, and I'm right pleased to say that nothing of this kind has ever happened *there*. I hope this incident doesn't taint your stay in Hitching Post." She lifted a thin eyebrow at her sister. "It's truly a lovely little town despite the sudden jump in the crime rate."

Hazel tugged her sister toward the door. "Shouldn't you be getting back, Eulalie?"

Katie Sue smiled as though just now remembering how odd my aunts could be, and for a split second she looked like the girl I used to know. I stepped up beside her. "Kathryn, you remember Dylan Jackson, right? He's a sergeant with the Darling County sheriff's office now." I took stock of his thin T-shirt and shorts. "He's, ah, off duty right now."

"Hey, Dylan." She leaned in to me and whispered, "Is this the complicated situation you mentioned?"

I felt heat rising up my neck. "Complicated doesn't begin to cover it."

He strode closer. "I heard you were a doctor now, Ka—Kathryn."

Katie Sue peeped at me. "Word travels fast around here."

"I have a big mouth," I said, shrugging.

Dylan glanced around. "This probably isn't the homecoming you were expecting."

Hazel interrupted her displacement of Eulalie, and her gaze bounced from face-to-face. "Y'all know each other?"

"Obviously they do," Eulalie said. "Have you gone daft, sister?"

Before Hazel threw a punch, I said, "You two surely remember— *Ow!*"

Katie Sue had stomped on my toe. I glanced at her,

and she was shaking her head. She didn't want me to tell them who she really was.

"Remember what?" Hazel said.

The sound of a siren shifted our attention. A sheriff's cruiser had arrived and double-parked in front of the inn's gate.

"Oh no," Katie Sue murmured. "Honestly, Miss Hazel, could we just forget this ever happened, please?"

"Heaven's no," Hazel said. "I need to file a report with the insurance company for the damage to the room."

"Damage?" Dylan asked.

"Lawdy, yes," Hazel said. "I'll show you."

"I'll pay for the damages," Katie Sue said. "No problem. I don't want to make a big deal out of this."

"Pshaw." Hazel led the way up a wide staircase. "That's what insurance is for, honey."

I was fascinated by the way Katie Sue wanted to sweep the matter under the rug. Why?

Katie Sue's guest room was on the second floor, at the end of a long corridor. The door stood ajar. Dylan instructed us all to remain in the hallway while he stepped inside the space. We crowded the doorway, except for Katie Sue, who hung back a ways.

"My housekeeper, Dotsie Mayhew, was in here at noon and said the place was clean as could be when she left," Hazel said.

"Did she lock the door behind her?" I kept tight hold of my locket as my gaze swept the doorframe and noted that it didn't look like any force had been used on it. The lock was a simple one—nothing a good credit card or hairpin couldn't bust open if one knew what they were doing.

Hazel adjusted her top. "She says she did, and I believe her."

Inside the room, my breath caught at the damage done. The bedroom had been thoroughly and meticulously searched and destroyed. The pillows had been sliced open, the mattress. Floorboards had been jimmied. Curtains shredded. Dresser drawers had been emptied onto the floor, and furniture had been pulled away from the walls.

Dylan came out and said, "Appears as though someone was looking for something specific." He glanced at Katie Sue. "Are you sure you aren't missing anything? Jewelry? Credit cards?"

"Nothing of mine is missing. The only jewelry I brought is what I have on."

A diamond watch, the pink sapphire ring, and simple gold-hooped earrings.

Eulalie gasped and grabbed Katie Sue's hand. "My lord, child. Look at that stone."

Katie Sue tried to pull her hand back, but Eulalie was having none of it. "Is that real?"

Tact was not a word in the Fowl family vernacular.

"Of course," Katie Sue said, her chin lifting in a strange defensiveness.

"It's *gorgeous*." Eulalie cooed to the ring, "You're gorgeous."

Katie Sue pried her hand away. "Thank you. It was a . . . gift."

Eulalie fanned her face. "Sister," she said to Hazel with a teasing smile, "why don't you buy me gifts like that? I'm sure you have an extra fifty thousand dollars lying around. I deserve it."

"Fifty thousand?" Dylan asked, his jaw dropping.

Katie Sue fidgeted. "It's insured for eighty."

Shoo-ee. A gift that cost eighty thousand dollars? It had to come from someone with deep pockets. Someone like Warren Calhoun.

"I'd say that's just cause for someone to break in here," he said.

"I would break in to steal that ring," Eulalie said. Then she looked around at our stunned expressions. "Did I say that out loud?"

"I'm sure the break-in was random." Katie Sue twisted the ring nervously. "I never take the ring off."

The break-in didn't feel random to me. It felt . . . personal.

A deputy loped down the hallway. Eulalie immediately forgot the ring and began fanning her cheeks with her gloves again, all the while batting her eyelashes and cocking a hip to give her thin rectangular shape some curves. She was in full-on flirt mode. I guess she hadn't been kidding about finding a man.

Dylan said, "Why don't all y'all wait downstairs? I'll be down in a bit."

Eulalie kept batting her lashes, and Hazel said, "You got dust in your eyes or something?"

"Maybe so," Eulalie retorted. "You should do a better job of cleaning this place."

"I never!" Hazel cried.

"Obviously!" Eulalie countered.

"Go on with the two of you," I said, giving them a push.

They rushed ahead, still quacking at each other.

I fell in step with Katie Sue. "What do you think that was all about? Your room, I mean."

"Not sure," she said.

"And you don't know what someone was looking for?"

She looked me dead in the eye. "No. I'm sure it was random."

I didn't believe her. And that realization took me by surprise. She *had* changed—more than her looks. It was best I kept that in mind. "I saw your mama outside when I came in. Did she come by for a visit?"

She stopped short. "My mama? You're sure?"

I nodded.

"I haven't seen her since I left town ten years ago. No one knows my new identity . . . How'd she find me here?"

"Maybe your letter to Jamie Lynn got back to her?"

"Maybe," she murmured. "Or more likely someone tipped her off."

"Someone like who? No one knows you're here."

She didn't answer me, and instead asked her own question. Her voice shook slightly as she asked, "Was Cletus with her?"

Cletus Cobb was Katie Sue's no-account stepdaddy. I studied Katie Sue and felt a surge of her fear. Latching on to my locket, I wondered what he'd done to her. Fear like that didn't come from threats alone. It came from pain. Physical pain. "Not that I saw."

"Well, where she goes, his special kind of crazy follows," she said, "so he's probably lurking around here somewhere."

"You don't think they could have . . ." I hitched a thumb over my shoulder, indicating the torn-up room.

"Carly, they're capable of just about anything."

"What did he do to you?" I asked.

Her eyes flared. "What do you mean?"

"He's hurt you."

Pain flashed in her eyes, and she must have realized it was fruitless to deny it to me. "Let's leave the past in the past."

"But if he was responsible for what happened in your room, then it's not the past. It's the present."

"I don't think he did that," she said. "It was . . ."

"Random. Yes, I heard."

She gave me a thin smile. "One way or another this will all be settled by Saturday, and I'll be leaving town. Give it a week and no one will even remember I was here."

We'd reached the upstairs landing, which looked down on the reception area below. Her gaze narrowed on something downstairs.

Not something.

Someone.

Warren Calhoun stood in a shadowy corner of the small library adjoining the reception area. His arms were folded, his brow drawn tightly as he locked eyes on Katie Sue.

I glanced at her, and I couldn't help but notice the murderous look in her eyes as she glared straight back at him.

≈ Chapter Six ≈

Breaking the tense eye contact, Katie Sue started down the steps, her fists clenched at her sides but her chin held high.

Well, wasn't that interesting? If she had been his mistress there certainly was no love lost between them right now.

As I followed her across the room, I noticed the whole Calhoun family had gathered. Aunt Hazel stood with matriarch Louisa, animatedly explaining what had happened. Cassandra sat in her wheelchair near one of the wide windows overlooking the gardens listening to Eulalie tell her that this sort of thing never happened at *her* inn. Groom-to-be Landry Calhoun stood near the fireplace. He was staring at his feet as though he wished they had wings that could fly him far, far away. But Hermes he was not.

Mercy, but he was a handsome man, tall with long, light brown hair and soulful eyes. I wondered how it came to pass that he was being forced to marry Gabi. He was a grown man, after all, surely capable of saying no to his daddy.

I noticed two bulky men lurking in the hallway, keeping a watchful eye on what was going on. They looked a lot like private security.

It hit me then why they were all here. "Are the Calhouns staying at this inn, too?" I asked in a whisper as Katie Sue and I sat on a settee near the front door. I was shocked Hazel hadn't mentioned this little fact, and realized the Calhouns must have had her sign a confidentiality agreement or something. Because, otherwise, Hazel would have taken out a billboard in Eulalie's front yard.

Up close and personal, the Calhouns seemed quite glamorous and the picture of Southern high society. Mother and daughter, Louisa and Cassandra, looked very much alike, with medium-length chestnut hair, blue eyes, and pearls at their necks. Cassandra wore a vibrant blue silk pleated top with sheer panels with white capri pants, and her mother wore a prim bouclé tulip skirt and cream blouse. Warren had a high forehead, deep set mischievous eyes, strong chin, and the reputation as a playboy. Silver streaked his dark wavy hair. His gaze had shifted from Katie Sue to Hazel as she blathered on.

"Yes, they rented out the whole inn for the family," Katie Sue ground out. "They all arrived this morning."

For the family. Katie Sue wasn't family yet she was staying here. . . .

"They're your friends in high places?" I asked, referencing something she'd said earlier.

"It's more like they're keeping their enemies closer, Carly."

The familiar saying echoed through my head. *Keep your friends close and your enemies closer.*

"And you're the enemy?" I asked.

"Yes."

"Why?" I hoped she'd admit, flat out, that she'd been having an affair with Warren. But no such luck.

She tucked a lock of blond hair behind her ear. "Warren's a puppet master, Carly, and he's pulling a whole host of strings." Her eyes glittered. "Right now I'm the enemy because I'm armed with a pair of metaphorical scissors. I'm done playing his games, and he knows what will happen if he doesn't start playing mine."

I recalled what Caleb had said about her playing with fire, and realized it wasn't just fire . . . it was an inferno.

Someone was bound to get burned. But who?

"What is this all about?" I asked.

Her eyes glistened. "Love."

Dang. She *was* his mistress. My gaze shot to Louisa, who had been staring our way, a calculated look in her eye. A shiver went up my spine. Then I glanced at Warren. The *nerve* of him to set Katie Sue up in the same inn as the rest of his family. It was like a slap in his wife's face.

I gripped my locket. "I don't know what's going on exactly, but I sensed danger around you from the moment you walked into my shop this morning."

"I know what I'm doing," she said firmly. "I have plenty of ammunition and a plan to use it to get Warren to see things my way. Love is worth fighting for, Carly, even if I have to fight dirty."

"Ammunition?" My jaw dropped, and I kept my voice

low. "Have you resorted to extorting Warren, Katie Sue?"

I could only imagine the kind of mementos a mistress could collect during an affair. Mementos he wouldn't want seen by anyone, especially when he was about to launch a presidential campaign. I doubted that threatening him would endear her to him, but she seemed determined.

"Shh!" Grabbing my arm, she added, "It's not extortion. I'm not asking for money. I'm asking him to do the right thing, that's all."

I glanced at him—he'd been looking this way but abruptly turned away. "Do you have evidence against him that you're using to get the outcome you want?" I asked her.

Biting her lip, she nodded.

"Then, money or not, that's extortion!" I whispered fiercely. What exactly was Katie Sue's plan? Was she trying to get him to leave his family? To divorce Louisa and marry her? I couldn't very well ask her here and now. "It might be emotional extortion, but still."

"Then so be it," she said, shrugging. "You don't understand what I'm going through, Carly. I'm doing what I have to do."

"Tell me. What are you going through?" I asked, feeling her heartbreak.

Moisture filled her eyes, and she looked upward until it receded. "I can't talk about it right now. You have to trust me, though, that I'm doing the right thing for the right reasons."

"I don't doubt that, Katie Sue. I don't. But I'm worried for you. Do you understand the danger?" Warren wasn't one to be told what to do. If Katie Sue had simply been a dalliance—and she'd read more into it—he might not be too keen to play her games. He might just want to get rid of her altogether.

"I'm not in danger as long as I have that ammunition, and I've ensured the family can't get their hands on it."

The whole family knew of this plan? *Mercy!* "The ransacking upstairs? Was that someone looking for your so-called ammunition?"

"Probably," she admitted. "Too bad for them I had it with me. She who holds the information holds the power."

I stared at her. Was she kidding? She didn't seem to be. She'd done made up her mind to get what she wanted and wasn't backing down.

Sighing, I said, "Maybe you should tell Dylan what you're up to. It might be safer for you that way. And hire your own bodyguard just in case."

"I'll think about it."

Which meant no. My word, her stubborn streak hadn't changed at all. I tried to tell myself to let it go, that she could make her own choices, but the healer in me, the fixer, didn't want to see any casualties in this mess.

Dylan came down the steps, the deputy on his heel. He made quick introductions of himself to the Calhouns. Even though he wasn't in uniform, his stern voice told them all they needed to know about who was in charge.

"I have a few questions," he said. "If you can gather around, it'll just take a minute."

Cassandra wheeled her chair closer to Landry, and their parents sat on the sofa near the hearth. My aunts sat across from them and Katie Sue and I stayed put.

Dylan ran through a series of questions that quickly led nowhere. Everyone but Gabi had been here during

the time frame of the break-in but no one had seen or
heard anything. Hazel had been in the garden, Louisa
and Warren had been lunching on the back deck (being
watched over by the bodyguards), Landry had been in
his room on the phone with someone from his record
label, and Cassandra had been napping and didn't know
anything had happened until her mother had come in
and woken her.

Dylan glanced at Hazel. "We'll dust for fingerprints and
write up a report, but there's not much else we can do."

She patted his arm. "That'll do for now."

Outside, the sound of squealing tires and raised voices
caught our attention. Cassandra wheeled to the front
window. "The press have arrived."

Eulalie perked up. "Really?"

Dylan nodded to the deputy and he slipped outside to
corral the crowd.

Cassandra turned her chair around. "We should give
them a quick statement," she said. "They're not bound to
leave until they get one."

She had a beautiful mellifluous voice, soothing yet
strong at the same time. Probably the result of being
raised by a Southern politician.

Louisa positively glowed with pride as she looked at
her daughter. "You should do it, Cassandra."

Warren nodded. "Good idea."

Excitement flashed in Cassandra's eyes. "Do you
think I'm ready?"

Warren walked over to his daughter. "You were born
ready, darlin.'"

Landry glanced up from his feet long enough to roll his
eyes. His shenanigans in law school had pretty much ru-

ined his chance at public office for many years to come, but it was no secret that he'd always been first choice to run for Warren's senate seat when the time came. Cassandra's appeal had only become clear after the accident. When her popularity soared with voters, the family immediately took advantage. Never ones to let opportunity pass by, that's when they began grooming her to take Landry's branch on the family's political tree.

A better option, in my opinion. Except for being a male Calhoun, Landry had done nothing to deserve public office, but Cassandra had been quietly serving in political trenches since graduating from college. Volunteering, fund-raising, working tirelessly to fight injustices big and small ... Given time I thought she had a fair chance at becoming more popular than her father.

"Might as well wait until all the media outlets arrive," Louisa said, rising. Her hand went to her pearls, and she tightly held a bead between two fingertips. "It'll save you from repeating yourself."

Cassandra rolled to the front window to keep an eye on the crowd.

Dylan walked over to where I sat with Katie Sue. "You'll have to find another place to stay," he said to her. "I'm sorry."

Hazel gasped. "But there are no other rooms, between the family and their security. . . ."

I saw a smile flit across Louisa's face before it disappeared into a mask of faux concern. It had me wondering if this consequence wasn't the intended result of the break-in in the first place: To get Katie Sue out.

Had Louisa really been lunching with Warren the entire time during the break-in? It seemed to me that any

of them could truly be to blame. Well, except Cassandra—
there was no elevator in the house so she couldn't have
made it upstairs.

"You can stay with me," I said. "Hopefully you don't
mind a little dust and cat hair."

"A *little* dust?" Dylan said, smirking.

"Hush now." I gently elbowed him.

"I don't want to impose," Katie Sue said.

"You hush, too. My door is always open to friends."

Her eyes softened. "Thank you, Carly."

"Good," Warren boomed. "It's settled then. Perhaps
we can get on with the rest of our day. There's much to
do with this upcoming wedding if I'm not mistaken."

Landry looked ill, his face ashen.

Color rose to Katie Sue's cheeks. She stood up. "Warren, may I have a word with you? Outside?"

Louisa's fingers twisted the pearls so tightly I thought
the string would break. She said, "I don't think that's a
good idea."

Warren, however, waved her concerns away. "A few
minutes won't do any harm." He also waved off the private security guards who started to follow them.

All eyes were on them as they stepped onto the back
patio until Earl Pendergrass came barreling through the
front door amid shouts from the reporters, successfully
capturing our full attention. The mail carrier straightened
his shirt and adjusted his bag as he took a deep breath. "A
pack of wolves out there. Pack of wolves. Afternoon," he
said to us all as he tipped his hat. Deep crow's feet wrinkled the skin around his eyes as he smiled. He was near
to retirement age, but loved his job and didn't have any
plans on hanging up his mailbag anytime soon.

We all murmured hellos, while Hazel rushed over to the outgoing mailbox and gathered its contents. "Earl, you be safe heading out there now, you hear?"

Cassandra added with a teasing smile, "They'll eat you alive."

She was quite beautiful when she relaxed and showed some humor. I had the feeling that when she ran, she was going to win the Senate election by a landslide.

"Don't I know it," he said, laughing, his white teeth flashing against his dark skin. He took the mail from Hazel and gave her an extra sweet smile. "Seems you have your hands full, Miss Hazel."

She laughed and gave him a playful shove. "Always, Earl. Always."

As Eulalie primped in front of the mirror for her big debut with the press, I noticed how Louisa's eyes flared when she spotted a manila envelope in Earl's hands. Her gaze flashed to Landry, then Cassandra, then back to the mail—straight to the coffee-stained envelope on top of the pile Hazel had just handed to Earl.

She obviously knew what it was, and it was causing her much distress if the sudden pounding of her heart was any indication.

That envelope had to contain Katie Sue's *ammunition*. I'd bet my witchy senses on it.

I grabbed my locket to try to block Louisa's emotions. This happened sometimes when I was in a crowded room—I couldn't block energy no matter how hard I tried. It kneaded my soul, pushing and pushing until I finally gave in to the pressure.

Louisa stepped toward Earl, and before I could fully reconcile what was happening, she tripped and lurched forward, catching Earl's arm on the way down. The mail went flying, but Earl caught Louisa before she hit the ground. He set her to rights.

At the same time, Cassandra had rolled forward to help her mother and accidentally knocked over an end table. As everyone but Eulalie (she was too busy peeping out the window) scurried forward to help with the situation, Louisa bent down to scoop up the mail. We reached for the coffee-stained envelope at the same time, each grabbing an end.

Anger flashed in Louisa's eyes, a direct contrast to her syrupy voice. "I have it."

"No, I do." I yanked hard, pulling it from her grasp. The motion sent her reeling backward, and she landed flat on her rump. Everyone gasped and glared at me.

"Sorry," I said and quickly handed the envelope off to Earl, who tucked it—and the rest of the mail—into the bag slung over his shoulder. "I don't know my own strength."

One of the bodyguards helped Louisa up, and her mask slipped as she stared at me. "You should be more careful."

"As should you," I countered. "Tripping over invisible obstacles and such."

One of her perfectly plucked eyebrows lifted as she glared. There was nothing but steel magnolia in her countenance, and I suddenly wondered who was really in charge of this family.

They had already proven that they'd go to great lengths to protect each other—and apparently if Louisa was willing to steal that envelope, she had chosen shielding her husband over outing him for his affair. I couldn't understand that depth of loyalty after being betrayed and had to wonder if it was more a matter of preserving the family name for the sake of her children than anything else.

"Now, now," Hazel said, rushing over. "All's well. There, there," she clucked, awkwardly pushing Cassandra's wheelchair away from the table, which Dylan put back in place.

Landry gave his mother's cheek a quick peck and said, "I have a bit of a headache. I'm going to rest for a few minutes." He headed for the stairs.

A bit was an understatement. His head was pounding. I didn't offer him a headache potion, though it would have cured him in an instant. I wasn't feeling too friendly toward this family right now.

I needed to get out of this house. My ability to block energy, even while grasping my locket, was fading. *Headaches, pounding hearts, excitement, anxiety, fear, happiness, love, maliciousness* . . . It was too much. I'd planned to wait for Katie Sue, but surely she could find her way across the street on her own.

Earl said, "I should be getting back to my route." He tipped his hat. "Y'all have a good day. Try to stay out of trouble, Miss Hazel." He winked at her, and she giggled.

I urged him to hurry. To get that envelope far away from here. As he started for the door, I kept a close watch on Louisa to make sure she didn't have any more *accidents*. She had her hands on her pearls and determined eyes on Earl.

Anger. Boredom. Frustration. Infatuation. Stress. Hatred.

Dizzy, I swayed. My palms turned clammy, and I felt

the color drain from my face. I was losing control and had to get away before I was completely overwhelmed with the energy in the room. Dylan leaned and whispered in my ear, "Are you okay, Carly?"

I shook my head and said softly, "I need to leave."

Loudly, he announced, "I'll be in touch. Carly and I are going to head out now, too."

I said, "You'll send Kathryn over to my place, Aunt Hazel?" I suddenly worried about Katie Sue's change of address and her note to Jamie Lynn—but Hazel would know to send Jamie Lynn across the street if Katie Sue didn't reach her first.

Patting my hand, concern filled Hazel's eyes. She knew what was happening—she'd seen it before. "Sure thing, sugar. Hurry on your way now."

Dylan put an arm around me. My head buzzed and I felt queasy—and I still had to make my way through the crowd of reporters. I braced myself as best I could. But as Earl held the door open for us, a shotgun blasted the air, shattering the last threads of my control.

Chapter Seven

I hit the floor with a bone-jarring *whump* after having been tackled by Dylan. Energy swirled around me, flooding my senses. Tears leaked from my tightly closed eyes as I tried to fight against the waves. I was drowning.

Confusion. Stomach hurting. Pounding pulse. Fear. Head aching. Hopelessness. Infatuation. Happiness. Knee hurting. Jealousy. Annoyance.

Warmth settled on my cheek—Dylan's hand. "It's okay, Care Bear. Look at me."

"I—I can't."

"Come on now," he said, his lips so close to my ear that his breath stirred my hair. "What kind of quitter attitude is that?"

Quitter? Did he just call me a quitter? *Oh hell no.* I cracked open an eye.

"That's my girl. Now the other one. Look at me, come on."

His face was blurry through the haze of my tears, but I could still see the flecks of blue in his green eyes, his long dark lashes, the light scar beneath his right eyebrow. He lay half on top of me, half on the floor. Protecting me. Not just from random gunshots, but from things he didn't really understand but accepted without question nonetheless.

"Focus on me. Just me." His hand caressed my face, spreading heat from my cheek to my jaw and back up again. "Remember that time I wanted to make you a special breakfast and I burned the toast, undercooked the eggs, and forgot to put the pot under the coffeemaker? And you scraped the toast, pretended to eat the eggs but actually fed them to Poly on the sly, and sopped up the spilled coffee with paper towels and wrung them over your Professor Hinkle mug so you could still get your caffeine fix? Those were some good times, weren't they?"

A tear slid down my cheek as I managed a smile. It had been right after our engagement, and I'd been over the moon in love with him. "The best." I sighed. "I loved that mug." It had broken into many pieces a year ago when a shelf collapsed in the kitchen. Things were forever collapsing in my house.

Laughing, he said, "I know." His thumb whisked away another teardrop snaking down my face.

Slowly everyone else's energy began to seep away, tide waters receding, leaving me drained and spent and limp as tattered seaweed. All that remained was one solitary emotion.

Love.

I wasn't sure if it was mine or his. I suspected both.

"Thank you," I whispered.

He pressed a kiss to my nose. "Anytime, Care Bear, anytime."

I turned my head and finally took note of the others. The bodyguards were gone—I assumed to the back deck. Eulalie peeked out from behind an armchair, and Earl was atop Hazel on the couch—and looked to be enjoying himself quite a bit. I suspected the infatuation I'd been feeling came from him. Louisa crouched next to Cassandra's wheelchair, which she'd pulled behind an overturned table.

Landry came flying down the stairs. "What the hell was that?"

"Someone's shooting," Cassandra said.

I glanced at Dylan. "Marjie."

"Undoubtedly," he said with a smile. To everyone, he said, "I don't think it's anything to worry about, but hang tight and I'll go check it out."

"What do you mean, you don't think it's anything to worry about," Louisa snapped. "Does this sort of thing happen often around here?"

"Yes," Eulalie, Hazel, and I said at the same time.

At a loss for words, Louisa just shook her head and threw a glance at the liquor cart as though wishing she were sipping on a large gin and tonic.

I levered onto my elbows and said to Dylan, "I'll come with you. I wouldn't want Marjie to shoot you."

For a split second, he looked about to argue but thought better of it. He knew Marjie well. "Good idea." He stood and reached for my hand. I slipped my palm into his feeling safe, secure.

Loved.

In one smooth move, he helped me from the floor but kept hold of my hand. Because I still felt spent, I didn't mind him toting me along.

"Everyone stay put for a minute," he said.

"Okay," Earl said with a toothy grin.

Hazel giggled.

"For land's sakes," Eulalie muttered. "She has two and I can't even get one."

Undoubtedly, hers was the jealousy I sensed. I smiled. I loved my family. Outside on the deck, the two security guards had pig-piled atop Warren. Each had a gun drawn and didn't look the least bit afraid to use it.

"Crazy lady next door is shooting up the place," one said.

I glanced around for Katie Sue and found her ducking behind a bush, left behind to fend for herself by the two lug nuts protecting the senator. Her eyes were wide with caution but she wasn't hurt.

I glanced next door. Hazel had tried her best to camouflage Marjie's unkempt yard with a row of arborvitae and a six-foot privacy fence, but Hazel's deck was high and gaps between the evergreens revealed glimpses of the mess. Marjie stood on her should-be-condemned back deck, a shotgun on her shoulder, a target in site.

"Aunt Marjie, for heaven's sake!" I shouted. "Put the gun down."

"Ain't my fault they can't read," she said loudly. "Says plain as day TRESPASSERS WILL BE SHOT. It serves them right to be popped full of holes. Out with you now, you hoodlums. I ain't got time for this. I have a *hike* to be taking."

She said hike with all the enthusiasm of someone going in for a colonoscopy.

Two Darling County deputies stood at the gate—safely on Hazel's property—smiling ear to ear. They were familiar with Marjie's antics and how she took trespassers seriously. There were at least a dozen No TRESPASSING signs on her land.

There was no movement in Marjie's backyard. Apparently the intruders didn't realize she was deadly serious.

"I'm going to count to ten; then I start shooting again," she said. *"One!"*

"Miss Marjie, you don't want to have to clean up all that blood," Dylan said, trying to reason with her.

"It's good for the plants," she said. *"Two!"*

Someone squealed and came running out, a long-lens camera in hand. A reporter. A foolish, foolish reporter.

"Well, that's one of them," she said. *"Three!"* Another reporter went running, tripping on weeds as he tried to navigate Marjie's overgrown yard.

"Four!" she shouted.

No movement.

"Five! . . . Six! . . . Seven!"

Dylan looked at me. "The paperwork alone . . ."

Marjie shouted, "You always were a stubborn coot, Cletus Cobb! Get your ass out of my yard! *Eight!"*

I glanced at Katie Sue. She'd gone pale at the name. Her stepdaddy.

"Fine!" a man shouted. "You always was batshit crazy, Marjie Fowl!"

"I should shoot you just for that, but can't fault a man for tellin' the truth, even if the man is you." She laughed manically, and said, *"Nine!"*

Cletus came scurrying out of the scrub, hitching up his sagging pants as he did so. A long scraggly beard covered most of his gaunt face, and greasy hair hung to his shoulders.

Katie Sue sank back farther into the shadows of the bush.

Marjie lowered her gun. "Carlina Bell Hartwell, get yourself over here, child. I want a word."

I glanced at Dylan. "Want to come with me?"

He shook his head. "I'll stay here and let everyone know that it's all clear."

"Chicken."

"*Bawk,*" he said.

I rolled my eyes and said, "You should probably also make sure Warren hasn't been suffocated and that Katie Sue comes out from under that rhododendron."

I noticed how she trembled and wondered again what Cletus had done to her. Anger bubbled, my hands clenched, and I willed myself not to go after Cletus with my pitchfork.

Taking steadying breaths, I scooted around the reporters and deputies, high-stepped over weeds, and made my way to Marjie's deck. She jerked her chin upward, motioning for me to climb the rotted steps.

The first one broke as I stepped on it. "If it's okay with you, Aunt Marjie, I think I'll stay down here."

"Suit yourself." She stood there for a minute, her gaze scanning the horizon, the look in her eye scaring people away from her fence line.

"Did you need me for something?" I asked, shooing away a wasp that was getting a mite too friendly.

"I do believe there's something over yonder that belongs to you, if what I saw in your shop earlier is any indication."

I leaned back to see where she was pointing. In a corner of her yard, I could see a pair of feet underneath a malnourished shrub. Girly feet if the sandals were any indication.

"I'll give you a minute to get her and sneak out the back. And don't let it be gettin' around that I didn't shoot her on the spot, got it?"

Baffled, I said, "Got it."

"Now git! Your time's tickin'!"

I jumped off the step and quickly bushwhacked my way through the backyard jungle toward the trespasser. "Hello?"

No one answered, but as I neared the bush, I heard her say in a small voice, "Don't shoot me."

"I don't own a gun, but you probably have thirty seconds or so before Marjie loses her good will."

"Carly, is that you?"

I rounded the bush and my eyes widened as I recognized the intruder. "What are you doing here?"

"Is she really batshit crazy?" Gabi Greenleigh asked.

"Yes," I said, grabbing her hand and yanking. She didn't budge. "And she will shoot you if you don't get moving."

"I—I can't. I'm so scared my legs are like jelly."

I put an arm around her and said, "Lean on me. Come on."

"This is so embarrassing," she muttered.

I half dragged her to the loose slat in the fencing. I'd ducked through this opening more times than I cared to admit. "What are you doing here?"

"I got to thinking about Landry possibly having another woman and thought I'd sneak over and check it out. There's a good view of his bedroom balcony from here."

"You were spying on him?"

"Is that bad?"

"I'm not one to judge." I nudged the slat aside and pushed her through. I quickly followed.

Breathing hard, Gabi leaned against the fence, a twig stuck in her long hair. "I can't believe she was really going to shoot."

"Marjie takes her privacy seriously."

"She didn't shoot you."

"I'm family. I get a two-minute warning at least."

We stood there for a second picking thorns from our clothes and assessing the scrapes and bruises. Gabi had a long thin scratch running along her arm that was going to be hard to cover with makeup. Hopefully the wedding photographer could airbrush it out. But then I remembered Delia's dream and my heart sank. Would there even be wedding pictures? Why had Gabi been covered in blood?

As I tried to get a sticky burr out of her hair, we turned at the sound of a nearby fence picket sliding out of place.

Gabi shrank a bit. "She's not coming after us, is she?"

"That's Hazel's fence."

"Is she crazy too?"

"Yes," I said, "but not in a gun-toting kind of way."

"Dang. Your family is something."

"I know."

A leg with a familiar gold shoe stuck out of the gap, and then a body shimmied through. Katie Sue gasped when she turned and saw us. Her cheeks immediately flamed as she righted her dress, smoothing it into place. "I had to get out of there," she mumbled.

"Are you avoiding the reporters like I am?" Gabi asked.

Maybe so, but it probably had more to do with Cletus.

"Yes, the reporters," Katie Sue said quickly.

"Have we met?" Gabi asked, sizing her up. "You look mighty familiar."

"No, but we've been to some of the same events," Katie Sue said in a strange, strangled tone. "Calhoun events."

"Right, right," Gabi said thoughtfully. "I think I've seen you with Warren a time or two."

Katie Sue's hands were fisted. "Just a loyal supporter," she said through clenched teeth.

"Do you live around here? Or are you in town for the wedding?" Gabi laughed. "I barely know most of the guests."

Katie Sue said, "I won't be at the wedding."

There was a tremble to her voice that had me studying my old friend. And when she didn't offer Gabi good wishes on her upcoming nuptials—good manners, pure and simple—I let down my guard to feel her energy.

White hot anger so fierce it felt as though my skin were on fire. Someone had ticked her off but good. Had it been a result of her conversation with Warren on the patio?

All that came from Gabi was bewilderment and that soul-searing sadness. I held my locket and blocked it all out again.

"Ah. Well, I should get going to get cleaned up." Gabi

turned to face me full-on. "Thanks for the help, Carly, and if you don't mind, I'd like that potion we talked about earlier after all. I can pick it up in an hour or so."

"I don't mind at all, and I can save you the trip. I'm headed to the chapel to help out my mama, so I can stop by the shop on my way."

"Great. Thanks." She flashed a bright toothy smile at Katie Sue. "'Bye!"

Katie Sue responded only with a halfhearted smile. With fists still clenched, she watched Gabi hustle down the sidewalk. "Bless her heart."

"You don't like her?"

"I don't *not* like her. She's just so perfect, isn't she? Perfect upbringing, perfect skin, perfect manners, perfect everything."

I shrugged. "No one's perfect." Sometimes I wished others could have a fraction of my empathetic skills. If Katie Sue could feel Gabi's sadness, maybe she'd have a different opinion of Gabi's "perfect" life.

Before she could say anything, a fancy black SUV with tinted windows pulled up next to us. One of the rear windows powered down, and Warren's twinkling eyes appeared. "Pardon the interruption, ladies. Kathryn, we should finish our conversation." He wasn't asking, he was telling.

One of the lug nuts jumped out of the front and opened the back door for her.

She gave a quick nod and turned back to me. Her eyes were filled with cold calculation. "Well, despite her *per-fection*, I actually feel bad for Gabi because she doesn't have any idea that her perfect little world is about to fall apart."

A chill went down my spine. "What do you mean? How so?"

"I've got to go, Carly."

With that, she turned, the lug nut helped her into the SUV, and they were off. A second later, brake lights flared red as they turned the corner headed away from town, leaving me with Katie Sue's shocking words ringing in my ears.

Chapter Eight

"What did she mean about Gabi's world?" Ainsley asked, her violet eyes wide with astonishment. She sat on a stool behind the counter at Potions, her *Southern Living* magazine abandoned as soon as I came racing into the store. I'd already checked in with Dylan, who'd dispersed the reporters after Cassandra Calhoun gave them a quick statement and was getting ready to finish up the bathroom framing. He promised to lock up my place when he left. Aunt Hazel had a key to my house, so I knew Katie Sue could get in just fine.

As I went into the mixing room for Gabi's love potion, I said, "I don't know." With Katie Sue now staying with me we'd have lots of time to talk—and I hoped she'd tell me what was going on in her life.

Ainsley poked her head through the pass-through. "Maybe she's jealous of all Gabi's hair."

"That's just you, I think."

Ainsley chuckled. "Maybe so. Think I should grow mine out?"

Love potions were my easiest to make. I used a funnel to add one part lavender infusion to four parts distilled water to a beautiful red potion bottle—the only color bottle I used for love potions. I folded a rose petal and fed it through the top of the bottle. Now for the magic. I opened the handcrafted floor-to-ceiling cabinet my granddaddy had made decades ago. It had many secret compartments, and from one of them, I lifted out a beautiful silver flask etched with lilies.

The Leilara was cultivated from the dewdrops of a pair of magical entwined lilies that bloomed only once a year. There was a small window of time when the lilies cried, releasing the drops that made my potions . . . potent. Cultivation was nothing short of a nightmare due to the lilies' location, and there was a finite number of drops. They had to last me the whole year, so I tended to use them sparingly.

"Grow it out? Don't you remember the last time?" During one blow-dry, her hair had gotten so tangled up in a round brush that it had to be cut free.

I inserted a dropper into the flask and withdrew one tiny dewdrop. It was all that was needed for this love potion. As I let the droplet fall into the beautiful red potion bottle, I wondered what my great-great-grandparents would think of their legacy.

Leila and Abraham's romance was legendary in these parts. Her goodness trying to overcome his darkness. It was a troubled relationship that ended in tragedy after Abraham was bitten by a poisonous snake, and Leila, an empath, had felt his agony and tried to suck the venom from his wound. They'd died wrapped in each other's arms in the exact spot the magical lily bloomed every year. Would they be enchanted to know their magic helped people find true love? I hoped so.

"A slight mishap." Ainsley fluffed her bob. "I think I'll give it another go."

"I give you three months, tops."

A sparkling tendril of white vapor swirled into the air above the potion bottle before dissipating. I quickly boxed the potion, placing it into a purple gift box, and hurried back out front.

"I'm more stubborn than that," Ainsley said.

"I factored in your stubbornness. That's why I said three months instead of two."

"We'll just see, won't we?" she said with a smile as she flipped a page of the magazine. "You think Katie Sue is aimin' to hurt Gabi? Maybe that explains Delia's dream."

"Maybe. Nothing's making a lick of sense." I glanced at my watch and was surprised my mama hadn't started calling around looking for me. I was late. Really late. "Everything okay here? Any calls?"

"Nope. It's just been me, the potions, and my magazine hanging out. Nothing as exciting as an inn room being ransacked or Marjie on a shooting spree. You have all the fun. But oh!"

"What?"

"Lyla Perrywinkle Jameson strolled by earlier, giving me the stink eye as she did so."

"You think she knows about the note to Jamie Lynn?" It might also explain why Dinah and Cletus Cobb had been stalking Katie Sue at the Crazy Loon.

"I called up Francie right off. She said no one but Jamie Lynn was home when she delivered the note, and that Jamie Lynn swore up and down she'd keep the secret. Ripped up the note, too, right in front of Francie, so we know no one found it by accident."

Maybe Katie Sue was right and her family had been tipped off by another source. Either way, the whole Perrywinkle family apparently knew Katie Sue was in town.

Which wasn't a good thing.

"Francie also said that Jamie Lynn broke down bawling when she realized the note was from Katie Sue." Ainsley leaned on her elbows. "I could just cry myself."

Me, too. Their separation had been so unjust that my heart still ached for them.

Ainsley said, "Jamie Lynn's older now, and can make her own decisions. Maybe after this reunion they'll stay in touch?"

"Maybe," I said. "But I have the feeling it's not going to be that easy. Lyla will put up a fight and we all know she fights dirty."

"Oh, I know." She rolled her eyes. "In addition to what she did to Katie Sue, I hear all the time about how Lyla cheated in the cooking contest at the Darling County Old Thyme Herb Festival last year by making those savory hand pies."

It had been quite the uproar when Lyla showed up with meat pies instead of sweet pies. But after scouring the rule book, no one could find a specification that it had to be a sweet pie entered. She won by a landslide, garnering her a big trophy and a cash prize. Francie Debbs and her buttermilk pie had finished second, taking home a red ribbon and a bunch of resentment.

Rumors lingered to this day that Lyla (gasp) bought her herb plants from online nurseries instead of raising them from seeds, but I knew from experience that her big garden was lush and beautiful. She might be a cold cruel woman, but she had quite the green thumb.

Ainsley frowned. "Francie also said that Jamie Lynn looked like she was wasting away. Whatever she's got, it's bad. I was thinking . . ."

I smiled. This was always how her schemes began. "Mmm-hmm?"

"That it wouldn't be a bad thing if you happened upon their meeting. It'll probably be at your house now that Katie Sue's been displaced from the Loon. Perfectly reasonable that you should be there. And if you happen to be able to feel Jamie Lynn's energy . . ." Ainsley innocently examined her fingernails.

"I'll try to get back, but my mama has a to-do list for me a mile long."

"What's more important, Carly Bell Hartwell?"

"Don't get all indignant with me. You're not the one who has to deal with my mama."

She stared.

"I'll *try*."

"Try real hard."

"Yes, ma'am." I grabbed up the bag and headed for the door.

"Oh, and Carly?"

I turned.

She grinned. "If you could call me as soon as you know what's going on with her . . . I'm mighty curious."

Rolling my eyes, I headed out into the heat. I squinted against the bright sunshine as I followed the Ring around to Dèjá Brew. A few treats would soften my mama's blow about me being so late.

Jessamine "Jessa" Yadkin smiled when she saw me. "The usual, Carly?"

The usual: a cup of coffee and a cookie. "Plus some." I eyed the dessert case. "I need to take the edge off my mama's anger."

She snapped her fingers. "I've got just the thing. Odell just pulled a chocolate hazel torte out of the oven. That'll sweeten Rona up but good."

Her happy raspy voice was just the balm I needed right now. I was feeling out of sorts with this Katie Sue business.

"Perfect," I said. Odell was the finest baker I knew, and his chocolate-anything was hard to resist.

"I heard about that business at the Loon," Jessa said, leaning in. "I can't believe Katie Sue Perrywinkle is back in town. I never thought I'd see the day."

Never underestimate the speed in which gossip traveled in this town. Katie Sue may have wanted to keep her presence here a secret, but the news had already made the rounds. "How'd you hear?" I asked.

Pursing her lips, she said, "Dinah and Cletus are spreading the news all over town. As I live and breathe, I've heard it from five people in the last half hour. Oh, and that she's now staying with you after her room at the Loon was burgled. Do you know why she's back?"

I groaned. "Not yet. I hope to find out more when I see her later."

Looking disappointed that I didn't have gossip to share, she said, "I'll be right back with that torte." She pushed through a swinging door into the kitchen. I was still peering in the dessert case when my witchy senses sent a shiver down my spine. I turned around just in time to see Lyla Perrywinkle Jameson storming through the doorway, the snap of her flip-flops sounding like gunshots.

She marched right up to me, poked my shoulder, and said, "I've been looking for you, Carly Bell Hartwell."

"Poke me one more time and you'll wish you hadn't found me," I fired back, trying to keep my temper in check.

"You have some nerve," she said, her body tense as a bull ready to charge.

If not for the bad attitude that shone in her every pore she might pass for pretty. With sun-streaked brown hair, sun-kissed skin, and pink cheeks, she was medium height, thin and wiry, but strong. Wearing a white tank top, cutoff shorts, flip-flops, and clenched fists, she looked ready for a fight.

"Me? I think this"—I gestured to her stance—"is pretty nervy."

The healer in me tried to find the good in her. After all, she hadn't had it any easier growing up than Katie Sue. She'd been raised by the same parents, suffered the same stepfather. Married at seventeen, she was widowed at twenty-six, just a year after Jamie Lynn came to live with her. Her gardens were her main income, and she worked harder than just about anyone I knew to make ends meet.

I wanted to like her because a part of me admired how she had pulled herself out of the muck and refused to be a victim. But that being said, it was hard to muster any compassion for her, knowing how she had hurt Katie Sue.

"Don't be turning this back on me, Carly. I heard you were putting up Katie Sue at your house."

Her and everyone else in town. "You may have also heard she needed a place to stay after her room at the Loon was ransacked."

Her stubborn chin jutted. "She made that bed. Now she has to lie in it."

"You sound like you know exactly what happened," I prodded. "Maybe you heard it from your mama or Cletus?"

Blue eyes narrowed on me. "I have no idea what happened."

"Did Cletus tear that room apart?"

"I ain't going to stand here going round and round with you. I came to have you pass a message on to Katie Sue. Tell her to stay away from Jamie Lynn." She looked about to poke me again but thought better of it and drew her hand away. "The same goes for you, Carly." Her voice caught as she added, "Jamie Lynn doesn't need another upheaval in her life right now. She has more important things to worry about."

The raw, desperate emotion in her voice caught me off guard. It was rare to see Lyla show any emotion but irritation. "But what if we can help her get better?"

"What? Because now Katie Sue's some barely graduated doctor? And you with your phony potions? I don't think so. Jamie Lynn has real doctors in Huntsville takin' care of her. Like I said before, stay away from her. The farther, the better."

With that, she turned and stormed out, much the way she'd come in.

"What was that about?" Jessa asked, stepping up behind the counter. A cardboard cup of coffee, its lid askew, was balanced atop the pastry box in her hands.

"A warning to stay away from Jamie Lynn Perrywinkle," I said, taking the goodies from her.

Jessa's messy bun wiggled as she tipped her head back and snorted. "That Lyla Jameson doesn't know you so well, does she, Carly?"

I paid for the order and tightened the lid on the coffee. "What makes you say so?"

"Tellin' you to back off, darlin', is like an invitation for you to butt on in. A big gold-embossed invitation with swirly lettering and no need to RSVP." She wrinkled her nose as she handed me my change. "Give my best to your mama."

As I walked out of the coffee shop, I was already trying to figure out how I could sneak out of my mama's later on so I could catch up with Katie Sue and Jamie Lynn.

No need to RSVP indeed.

Chapter Nine

My mama's chapel was just a hair outside the Ring, on a winding picturesque brick lane that eventually dead-ended at the river walk. Lamplights and soaring elm trees with their trunks wrapped in twinkle lights lined the sidewalk. Large public parking lots at the north and south ends of the Ring kept most vehicle traffic off the road, adding to its charm.

Across the street, Without a Hitch looked like a glistening diamond amid its leafy backdrop of towering shade trees. Bright wildflowers bloomed around the fieldstone foundation, contrasting beautifully against crisp white clapboards. Sunlight glinted off tall arched windows, but a semicircular gable canopy above wide arched double doors shaded the front steps. A short spire was the cherry atop this sundae.

The gardens were my daddy's pride and joy, and I secretly wondered if he spent as much time as he did tending them as a time-out from my mama. After all, she was a handful on her best days.

Flowers spilled over both sides of a broad stone walk-way that meandered around the property, leading to the gazebo in the clearing where the Calhoun wedding was to be held and behind the chapel down to the footbridge that spanned the creek just in front of the small cottage where my mama and daddy lived.

Down the lane a bit, two wooden posts marked a gravel path that led into the woods behind the chapel—the Lover's Leap trail—and beyond that stood Johnny Braxton's chapel, the Little Wedding Chapel of Love. His place was night to Mama's day but (I hated to admit) just as lovely. Done up with rustic timbers, stained glass windows, and topped with a quaint bell tower, his chapel was set back into the woods, and was surrounded by stunning landscaping, including ponds and rock water-falls.

One chapel was bright, the other dark. Much like their owners. However, both chapels thrived, and were the most successful among the dozen or so in town.

I glanced again at the trail and wondered whether Marjie and Johnny had set off on their "hike" yet. And whether one or the other had been pushed off a bluff.

Along one side of Without a Hitch, three hundred white wooden folding chairs were sitting on rolling racks, waiting to be set up in front of the gazebo—one of the many jobs I'd been assigned by the loveable tyrant known as my mama.

The dictator herself was standing in the gazebo with Landry and Gabi, Warren and Louisa. She was busily pointing here and there, and bustling to and fro. My mama, the whirlwind.

I guessed Warren had finished his conversation with

Katie Sue. I just hoped he'd delivered her safely back to my house when he was done with the little chat. I had to admit Caleb's earlier teasing about missing mistresses worried me a bit.

Louisa's arm was linked with Gabi's, and I had to wonder if their close relationship was the source of Katie Sue's dislike of Gabi. And, as I watched, I wondered how difficult planning this wedding had been for the young woman, without her own mama to help out. I'm sure Louisa had done her best as a surrogate, but these nuptials had to bring up a whole slew of emotions for Gabi to deal with.

As Gabi smiled at Louisa, suddenly her wanting this marriage to Landry to work out—despite the fact he didn't love her—made a lot more sense. Maybe she did love him. But I suspected she loved the idea of having a family again a whole lot more.

As I headed up the steps into the chapel to drop off the goodies and put the love potion in mama's office, I picked up on a strange noise coming from somewhere nearby. It was a low sound, guttural, followed by an undercurrent of cuss words that would make even my mama—who was fluent in foul language—blush.

Curious, I backtracked down the steps and poked my head around the corner. The right wheel of Cassandra Calhoun's wheelchair had gone off the stone pathway, and had become mired in the spiky grass covering the embankment of the lily pond. She was tipped precariously, and trying her best to use her body weight to get her wheel unstuck. Apparently she thought using every cuss word she knew would help her prevent an afternoon swim with the resident bullfrogs.

"Need help?" I asked, unsure if her sense of pride would be put in front of her sense of self-preservation.

She jumped in her seat at the sound of my voice. Her chair wobbled, and she let out a squeal. Quickly, I set my packages on a nearby bench and grabbed the handles of the chair. I gave it a good yank, back onto the safety of the walkway.

Her hands immediately went to the pearls around her neck, and she nervously rolled beads between her fingers. "Thank you." She eyed the pond she'd almost toppled into and smiled wryly. "I don't look good in algae."

Her smile transformed her sullen features, crinkling her eyes and brightening her whole countenance.

"Not many can pull off that shade of green," I said. "Are you okay?"

"Fine, fine," she said. "Just a little rattled."

"I heard. It's a colorful vocabulary you have."

She had the grace to blush. "You pick up a lot of words while working with politicians."

"Mostly from outraged constituents, I imagine."

Laughing, she said, "Fortunately, I don't get much of that. Ever since leaving D.C., my work has been more . . . charitable." Her gaze softened.

I thought about the time she's spent with a group that raised money to help feed hungry children. Not too long ago, there had been a photo of her getting a hug from a little girl whose family had been helped by the program. There had been tears in Cassandra's eyes. Sincere ones.

"Hugs from little kids are much better than cusses."

Smiling, she said, "Infinitely. But I'd trade those hugs in a hot second to stop the reason why I'd gotten them in the first place. No child should ever go hungry."

I watched her closely. It sounded like such a spiel, but I could tell she meant every word. "If you become a senator, maybe you can help make that happen."

Her eyes flashed with determination. "That's the plan ... eventually." Her nose wrinkled. "I grow more impatient every day. There's so much I want to do. To change."

I wondered if she could truly make changes. Seemed like politicians had to jump through a hundred hoops to get anything accomplished these days.

"You were at the Crazy Loon earlier, right? Kathryn's friend?" She held out her hand. "I'm Cassandra Calhoun."

I shook. "Carly Hartwell." I didn't think it necessary to verify that I'd been at the inn—Cassandra had gotten a good look at me. "Do you want me to fetch your mother to come over here? I just saw her over at the gazebo."

"No!" She tucked a strand of hair behind her ear. "No, thanks. I don't want to hear the lecture about how I should have been more careful in unfamiliar terrain." She eyed the pond. "Fortunately, I'm a good swimmer. I spent many hours in the pool after my accident, building upper arm strength. That was quite the hullaballoo earlier," she said.

I wasn't sure which hullaballoo she referred to. The break-in or Marjie's trigger finger. "It was," I said, agreeing on both accounts.

With a bemused smile, she added, "This is an *interesting* little town."

It was true. We were nothing if not interesting. Movement at the back of the chapel caught my attention.

Katie Sue stuck her head around the corner, gave me a finger wave, then disappeared again.

My first thought at seeing her was that I was glad she survived the car ride with Warren. My second thought was *mercy sakes*. What was she doing here, skulking around the chapel? Her presence most certainly wouldn't be welcomed by the Calhouns.

"Do you need help back to the gazebo?" I asked Cassandra. Maybe if I could waylay Katie Sue, I could avoid any more drama today.

"No, thanks," Cassandra said, "I think I'll explore a lit—"

Her words were cut off by the sound of a man's voice calling her name. "Cass? Cassie!"

"Over here!" she said loudly.

Landry Calhoun rounded the back corner of the chapel, and rolled his eyes when he spotted her. "I've been looking everywhere for you."

To me, she said, "He always was the worst at hide-and-seek. When we were little it would take hours for him to find me sometimes."

He winked at me. "She still hasn't figured out that I hadn't been that keen on finding her."

"Hey!" she said, giving him a playful shove.

"What?" he asked slyly. "You were such a bossy thing. It was good to have a break from you ordering me around." He nodded his head toward me. "I'm Landry Calhoun. I think I saw you earlier at the hotel."

I introduced myself again. "How's your headache?"

He grinned. "It would be better if my mama wasn't harpin' on me to find where Cass wandered off to."

Shoo-ee. His smile could knock a girl's knees out from

under and make her throw her caution—and panties—
to the wind if she weren't careful. Fortunately for me I
always had my guard up around people. For a little extra
protection, I grabbed my locket. Just in case.

"Well, these days I'm not all that hard to find," Cassandra said, smiling at her brother. She patted her wheelchair. "I can't get very far in this thing."

"You kiddin' me?" he said. "You could roll plumb
down to the Gulf if you wanted."

"The Gulf sounds nice right about now," she said, her
eyes glinting with mischief. "If we leave now . . ."

"Don't start," he said, his voice taking a harder edge.

Seemed as though Cass wasn't too happy about her
little brother getting hitched. I had to wonder why. Because she knew he wasn't in love?

"And on that note," he added, "you hiding from the
planning isn't going to stop the wedding from happening.
You're Gabi's maid of honor. You should be over at the
gazebo with us and not hiding here with the lily pads."

It was like they'd forgotten I was standing there.

"At least over here I don't have to bear witness," she
said, folding her arms across her chest.

"Cass."

"Landry."

As much as I was enjoying this little show . . . "Ahem,"
I said, clearing my throat.

Both their gazes snapped to me.

"I should get going," I said. "I have a lot to do to set
up for the wedding."

Both their brows crinkled, and I could easily see the
family resemblance in their confused expressions.

"The wedding?" Cassandra asked.

"Oh, didn't you know?" I asked. "This is my mama's chapel. I'm helping with the wedding set up. There are three hundred chairs calling my name." And a potion to deliver to a certain bride.

"Your mama's chapel? Doesn't your aunt own the inn where we're staying, too?" Cass asked.

Even though it was probably only good manners—and a desire for public office—that kept her from saying, "Are you crazy people everywhere?" I could practically hear it in her tone.

"Miss Rona is your mama?" Landry asked, another one of those knee-knocking smiles gracing his face.

"That's what I'm told," I said, "though when I was little my aunties, the Odd Ducks, also told me that my mama found me floating in a basket on the river while gigging frogs, felt sorry for my sad self, and brought me home to spear my daddy since she didn't catch any frogs that day. Can't tell you how long I believed that story."

Landry tipped his head back and laughed.

Hoo-boy. Even holding on to my locket, the man made my knees wobble a little.

Cassandra's lip twitched in humor.

"You think your mama would adopt me?" Landry asked. "I could get used to this town right quick."

"I wouldn't bring it up to her," I said, "or you'll have adoption papers on your pillow by bedtime." I was kidding. Mostly.

Cassandra looked at him and pouted. "You'd be lost without me."

He tousled her hair. "That's a fact. I'd have no one to boss me about."

I laughed. "Oh, my mama would have that covered in no time."

"Whoa, then," he said, holding up his hands. "I best stick with the bossy mama I already have. And besides, who'd find Cass when she goes hiding?"

"I *swanee*!" a woman cried from nearby. Louisa Calhoun stood at the curve of the walkway, her hands on hips. Color was high in her cheeks as she said, "How long does it take to find your sister? She can't go very far."

"I told you so," Cassandra said.

"Lands sakes," Louisa went on. "You think I was the one getting married for all you care about this wedding."

I noticed her words slurring a little and had the feeling she'd indulged in an afternoon tipple. Or two.

"Come, come," Louisa said. "Get a move on, you two."

"Nice to meet you, Carly," Landry said. He grabbed hold of Cassandra's wheelchair handles and started up the walkway.

"Wait," she said. "Turn me around."

He did and winked at me. "See what I mean about bossy? I'm double-teamed."

"Shush," Cassandra said. "You wouldn't have it any other way."

"Oh, I don't know," he said. "Now that I have options . . ."

"Landry! Cassandra! Now!" Louisa said, one octave shy of shrill.

She'd definitely been drinking if she was behaving this way. Usually Southern mamas threatened by dropping voices not raising them.

Cassandra twisted and said, "One moment, Mother." She turned back to me and said, "I just wanted to say thanks for saving me from the algae, Carly. I truly appreciate it."

"No problem. Thanks for the vocabulary lesson."

Smiling, she said, "Anytime."

"Vocabulary lesson?" I heard Landry ask as they disappeared around the back of the chapel.

I thought about the upcoming wedding and how it seemed to be causing nothing but stress and strife. Then, of course, there was Delia's dream to worry about.

As I headed to set up those chairs, I couldn't help but wonder if this wedding was going to happen at all.

Chapter Ten

"This here row's a little crooked."

I wiped sweat from my eyes with blistered hands and found Dylan sitting in one of the chairs I'd just unfolded. "I think your eyes might be a little crooked."

I'd been out here in the sun for hours now, and I was ten chairs away from being finished with this horrendous task. The last thing I wanted to hear was that one of the rows was crooked. I just wanted to be done, go home to take a cold shower, and have a heart-to-heart with Katie Sue to find out what was going on with her. I never did find her after her game of peek-a-boo behind the chapel. I hoped she'd gone back to my house to lie low for a while.

Laughing, he said, "I brought you a milk shake. Chocolate." He held it aloft and wiggled it.

I lunged toward him, grabbed the shake, and planted myself next to him. It felt good to sit down. "I take back every bad thing I've ever said about you."

"You've said bad things? I'm shocked. Just shocked."

I talked around the straw. "A time or two."

Or twenty. Out of anger. Of sadness. But as I looked at him now, I realized that all those old feelings had just about disappeared. My heart was healing. *I* was healing. The time we'd spent together lately had helped. I was getting to know him again. Seeing him through new eyes. And lord help me, I liked what I saw. Which made me wonder what would become of us this time around. Could we be "just friends"? Were we destined for another trip down the aisle? Or would we split for good?

I held up the drink. "Thanks for this."

His dark eyebrows dipped into a concerned V. "What happened to your hands?"

Icy bits of chocolate slid down my throat, making me hate the past three hours a little less. "Two hundred and ninety chairs is what happened."

Taking hold of one of my hands, he inspected my blistered palm. "No gloves?"

"In this heat?"

"Better than blisters."

"Says you. A little marigold cream mixed with some Leilara and I'll be good as new in no time."

He hadn't let go of my hand. I tried pulling it away, but he held tight.

"What?" he asked with a twinkle in his eye. "Don't you like holding hands with me?"

Truth was I liked it. A lot. Blisters and all. This line we were walking between being friends and dating was quickly disappearing. "I'm sweaty and dirty and blistery. This is no time for hand-holding."

"Says you," he said, throwing my words back at me. "I like you this way. All mussed up." He gently kissed my palm. "But I don't like when you're hurt."

His kiss sent a sizzling sensation straight to the pit of my stomach.

"Better?" he asked.

I held the paper milk shake cup to my cheek, hoping the cold would freeze me from the inside out. "A little," I admitted.

"There's more where that came from."

"Milk shakes?" I asked innocently.

"As many as you want, Care Bear," he said, playing along, making me want him more than I already did.

Good Lord Almighty, I had zero willpower. I sucked so hard on my straw I wouldn't have been the least bit surprised if I swallowed my tonsils.

Fortunately for me and my lack of discipline, Dylan let go of my hand, stood up, and grabbed a chair from the rolling rack. He went about setting it in line with the others.

"I didn't just come bearing milk shakes," he said, "but a bit of bad news, too."

"Nothing happened to Gabi, did it?" Last I'd seen of her, she'd headed off to supper with the Calhouns, the love potion tucked tidily into her purse.

"Not that I know of, but Carly, Earl Pendergrass was attacked today."

I went cold—and it had nothing to do with the shake. "What happened?"

"Someone jumped him at the tail end of his mail route. Knocked him upside the head, stole his bag."

"Is he okay?"

"Doc Hamilton diagnosed a concussion and gave him nine stitches to the back of his head where he hit the sidewalk."

Suddenly, my shake was sitting like lead in my stomach. "The Calhouns are behind this. They're after the envelope Katie Sue mailed." I'd already told him about the "ammunition" Katie Sue said she had and how she'd resorted to some form of extortion—which Dylan could do nothing about as a lawman unless the Calhouns reported it.

"Louisa had been hell-bent on getting her hands on that envelope earlier. I bet she had Warren send one of his lug nuts after it."

He set another chair in the row. "That's what I figured, too, but there's just no way to prove it. No one saw anything. Wait. Lug nuts?"

"The private security thugs? But they'd probably just vouch for each other."

"Lug nuts," he repeated, chuckling under his breath.

"It fits."

"Suppose so," he said, setting another chair. "Worst of all for Earl, the attack was for nothing."

"Why's that?"

"Earl had already dropped off the mail he collected from his morning route at the post office."

I wondered if Katie Sue sent the package to her home address—and suddenly worried that her local mail carrier would be attacked, too. Hopefully, she wasn't that naïve, and had sent the package to a neutral party.

Dylan grabbed another chair—he was much faster at this than I was. "You'll never guess who Earl called to drive him home from Doc's."

"Who?" I asked.

"Your aunt Hazel. I think he's sweet on her. Last I saw, she was fussin' over him and he was smilin' ear to ear. Him getting conked on the head might be the best thing that happened to him all year."

"Hush," I said, but I couldn't help but smile, too. Maybe Hazel's affections could be swayed from the very young John Richard Baldwin to the very age-appropriate Earl . . . *Hmm*.

"Well, me-oh-my! Looks like my Carly girl got her delegating skills from her mama!" My mama, Veronica "Rona" Fowl, fanned her face with her hand as she toddled in three-inch heels over to where I sat. "You did good, baby girl. Real good."

"You're going to make me blush, Miz Rona," Dylan said.

My mama's hair color of choice this week was a nice sedate fire engine red. Little plumes of hair stuck up like flames all over her head. The pixie cut suited her spritely personality, but I could blink and she'd have extensions—she was forever changing her mind about styles.

She wore a zebra-printed wraparound dress that clung to her full-figured body, and even with her heels she barely came up to my chin.

"Did y'all hear about Earl Pendergrass?" she asked as she sat next to me. Her eyes, complete with false lashes, widened when she spotted my shake.

"It's gone," I said, mourning the empty cup.

"Damn shame," she said.

"About Earl or the shake?" I asked with a smile.

"Don't go puttin' me on the spot like that, Carly." She leaned in and whispered, "The shake. Earl's going to be just fine."

I laughed and rested against her. She was all kinds of

crazy, but I loved her more than words could say. "I did bring you a torte from Dèjá Brew. It's in your office."

She patted my leg. "I forgive you about not sharing your shake with me. Dylan, sugar, you're hired. I have a whole trailer full of flowers arriving tomorrow morning to cover that there gazebo, and well, someone actually needs to cover the gazebo with the flowers."

"Sorry, Miz Rona. I'm full up with jobs." He grabbed another chair. "Between the sheriff's department and Carly working me to the bone at her house . . . I will, however, put this rack back in the shed before I have to leave for my night shift."

We watched him walk away, rolling the chair rack toward the back of the property.

"To the bone . . ." Mama nudged me. "You're a chip off the old block."

"He looks good with no shirt on, too. An added perk."

Mama laughed. "Well, I'll just have to get your daddy to do the flowers. I'll let him keep his shirt on, though. You know how easily he burns."

Thank goodness for small favors. "Isn't he working tomorrow?" My father was director of the Hitching Post library.

"He *was*," Mama said, her eyes sparkling. "But this wedding takes precedence. Have mercy on my soul, it's going to be the death of me."

The reminder of death had me thinking again of Delia's dream about Gabi . . . and if it involved Katie Sue somehow. "Mama, have you seen Katie Sue Perrywinkle around here this afternoon?"

"Shut your mouth, Katie Sue's back in town? No, I haven't seen h—" She bolted upright and faced me head-on. "Wait a blessed second. I met a friend of the Calhouns today—Kathryn Perry—and couldn't help but think I knew her somehow. We chatted about her shoes and how much I wanted to snatch them off her feet and keep them for myself. Was that . . . ?"

I smiled. "That was Katie Sue."

"No!"

"Yes. She changed her name—and she's a full-fledged doctor now." I gave her a partial rundown on Katie Sue's reappearance, the break-in and how she was staying with me now, and how Lyla had threatened me to mind my own business.

"Well, I'll be." She shook her head. "She has great taste in shoes. Those gold sandals would make a right good birthday present." She batted her eyelashes at me.

Subtle was also not a word in the Fowl family vernacular.

"Noted," I said, laughing. "What time did you see her?"

"Round about four or five. I haven't seen her since. What's she doing mixed up with the Calhouns?"

"Nothing good," I said. I didn't mention how I suspected Katie Sue and Warren had something doing on the side.

"She ain't planning on sabotaging this wedding somehow, is she? Because I won't have none of that."

Katie Sue was due to meet with Jamie Lynn any minute now, so it was high time I moseyed home to see what I could overhear. Standing, I stretched, feeling each and every kink in my neck and shoulders. I needed to find Dylan and tell him that I was leaving. "I don't know what she has planned, Mama. But I aim to find out."

Chapter Eleven

The last time I'd seen Jamie Lynn Perrywinkle was a brief run-in at the local movie theater nearly a year ago. Back then, she'd been a vivacious nineteen-year-old out with friends. She'd looked healthy and happy and ready to take on the world.

It was a far cry from what I saw now as I found Jamie Lynn sitting in a wicker chair on my front porch. Thin brittle-looking brown hair had been scraped back into a mousy ponytail, and dark circles colored the pale skin beneath her eyes. Her simple T-shirt and jean shorts hung loosely. With hollow cheeks, bones jutting, and a sickly complexion it appeared as though the whole world had crashed down on her.

"Hey, Jamie Lynn," I said as I started up the steps and pushed open the screened door.

"Miss Hazel sent me over. I hope it was okay to wait out here until Katie Sue gets back," she said. Perspiration dotted her hairline and two forearm crutches rested at her sides.

I sat in the chair next to hers, still unable to believe the changes in her appearance. "More than okay." My brow furrowed. "Where'd Katie Sue get off to?"

I glanced across the street, toward the Loon. There was no sign of the Calhouns, and I wondered if they were still at dinner, and if Gabi had slipped Landry the potion.

"This was taped to your front door." Jamie Lynn handed over a note.

JL, had to run out. V. important. Will be back by 6:45. xo

I wanted to crumple the paper and toss it in the gutter. Jamie Lynn should have taken precedence over everything, no matter how *important*. It seemed to me that Katie Sue had her priorities all kinds of mixed up.

A lightning bug flashed as it fluttered near the newly planted rose bushes in front of the porch. I handed the note back to Jamie Lynn. "I'm sure she'll be here soon." It was only a little past that now. "She really wanted to see you."

A bit of hope flashed in her tired eyes. "Really?"

I nodded. "She's missed you."

Jamie Lynn's lower lip trembled. "I couldn't hardly tell."

I wasn't sure if she meant because Katie Sue ditched her to run an errand or if it had been the years and years she hadn't seen her sister. Either option fit, I supposed.

I could have told her about all the letters Katie Sue had written and Lyla sent back unopened, but I didn't really want to make trouble. Surely Katie Sue would tell her all about them. "It seems that way, doesn't it?"

She nodded.

"But not everything is always as it seems."

"I s'pose not."

One thing that was exactly as it seemed was her health. I tapped the arm strap of the crutch closest to me. "How long have you been using these?"

Lifting slim shoulders in a slight shrug, she said, "A couple months now. My legs—they don't work so well." Her laugh, a sweet tinkly sound, reminded me that she used to be an effervescent teenager. "Nothing on me seems to work so well anymore. The doctors don't quite know what's wrong yet, but they're working on it." She slid me a shy look.

"Do you want me to read your energy?" I asked, knowing I was going to do it anyway, with or without her permission.

"My family wouldn't like it much. They don't believe in your kind of magic."

"Who's they?" I asked. "Lyla?"

"And my mama and Cletus. They call you a devil child." She bit her lip. "No offense."

I smiled. "None taken." I'd been called worse— sometimes if people didn't understand something, they believed it best to file it under "evil" and leave it there. As long as they let me be, I let them be. "It doesn't surprise me much, but I thought Lyla of all people would understand the healing elements of nature."

"She's stubborn."

An understatement if I ever heard one. "So, you're spending time with your mama and Cletus?"

"About once a week. Don't tell Lyla, okay? She doesn't

know and would flip her lid if she did. She banned me from seeing them a long time ago. But, you know, they're family?"

Her last sentence ended in a questioning lilt, as if asking my approval. I slid my locket back and forth along its chain. Even though I was an only child, I had family aplenty, so I couldn't understand what it was like for her to have had only Lyla to lean on for a good part of her life. But I could definitely understand why Lyla had cut Jamie Lynn out of her mother's life—to protect her.

"Sometimes DNA doesn't a family make," I said softly.

She bit her lip. "But, my mama's . . . my mama. And it might be silly, but I still have dreams about all of us back together, being a big happy family."

I wasn't the least bit surprised she felt that way about her mama. It was a bond that was near impossible to break, even when it should have been long shattered, the pieces buried.

"Obviously I believe in second chances," she added. "Or I wouldn't be here."

I figured Dinah Perrywinkle Cobb had to be on her eleventh or twelfth chance by now, but bit my tongue. People *could* change. I just hoped with all my might that Dinah had. For Jamie Lynn's sake.

She rocked slowly. "I want to hear what Katie Sue has to say for herself. It's probably stupid of me, opening myself up to her again. But . . . family's family." She drew in a deep breath.

I wasn't sure who she was trying to convince. Me or herself.

"Well," I said, "while we're waiting, how do you feel about getting a reading?"

She glanced at me. "When I was little, Katie Sue would be cooking up supper and telling me all kinds of stories about your grandma Adelaide, and about how plants and herbs could heal people. And I'd beg her to tell me again and again about the story of Leila Bell and Abraham and how their kin inherited their magic, and I'd just sit there in awe, soaking it all in."

The legend of my great-great-grandparents Leila Bell and Abraham was well known around town, and could easily be recited by any local. It was a tale of love and loss. Of right and wrong. And the dangers of following your heart instead of your head.

After their tragic deaths, most of my ancestors abandoned practicing magic all together, but there was no abandoning the magic that remained within us — and the magic the two left behind. The Leilara drops, the magical lily nectar that made my potions so powerful.

My great-great-grandparents had certainly left their mark on this tiny town.

And on their descendants.

Jamie Lynn said, "Mama and Lyla say that story about your grandparents is all made-up foolishness, just a way to make your shop more interesting to folks. They say there is no such thing as magic. But Katie Sue ... She always believed. She said she didn't necessarily understand it, but she knew it was real."

Shades of pink and orange blurred the blue sky, the first hint of sunset. "What do you believe?"

She twisted her fingers, and looked me in the eye. "Carly, I don't know what I believe, but at this point all I have left is hope. And I hope with every breath I take that magic is real ... and that you can fix me."

I felt for this young woman. I could see the pain in her eyes, hear it in her voice. Not just physical pain, either. As we sat here, I was reminded of gym class in high school, playing tug of war. A thick line drawn in the sand, two teams, and a heavy rope that bit into tender skin. In the middle of that rope was tied a red flag. That flag would jerk left, right, left, with every pull as the teams battled each other.

Jamie Lynn was that flag. And she was being pulled apart by the family she knew ... and the sister who'd left her.

"I could try to see what's wrong," I said. "Then we could go from there."

"Okay." She nodded, her brows furrowed.

Though she said she had only hope left, I could see by the look on her face that she was trying hard not to get her hopes too high. I took a deep breath, let down my guard, and was immediately overwhelmed with pain.

Pain everywhere. My head. My stomach. My legs. Lord have mercy, my legs. They were dull and heavy, yet tingling and burning. And something was wrong with my heart—it beat irregularly.

My pulse thrummed as I searched and searched for a source. Cancer. A genetic deformity. Any kind of abnormality. And finally realized my nervous system was under attack.

I grabbed hold of my locket, took a few deep breaths, and finally said, "Have you seen a neurologist?"

"Not yet," she said. "Just a general internist, a cardiologist, and a gastroenterologist. Why?"

"Something's attacking your nervous system."

Her eyes widened. "Like what?"

"I don't know. It's not multiple sclerosis—I'd have known that. Or Parkinson's or ALS." I gave my head a shake as my legs went back to feeling like normal. "It's something I've never seen before."

Her hands shook. "Can you cure it?"

"I don't know, Jamie Lynn," I said softly, honestly. "We can work on the symptoms first, until you see a medical doctor. Then once we know for sure what it is, we can go from there."

She slumped, looking crestfallen. "I suppose it's a start."

I felt horribly that I couldn't give her tried-and-true answers. But I didn't have them. I had no idea what was causing the trouble in her body—and that bothered me. It was an unusual situation.

"Where do we start?" she asked. "Can you fix my legs?"

Mine ached with phantom pain. I needed a potion that would protect her nerve fibers from further attack. "I think I have something, but I need to look in my recipe book, which is back at the shop. We can go now . . ." I glanced at her legs. "I can drive." My Jeep was in the garage. I rarely used it, but there was no way I'd ask Jamie Lynn to walk to my shop.

"Okay," she said, giving her head a firm shake. "Let's do it."

"I'll just grab my keys . . ." I stood up and wobbled a bit—my legs still not fully recovered from reading her energy. She was fitting her arms into her crutches. "Jamie Lynn, how come you're not using a wheelchair?" She had to be in agony, making her way around with only the crutches.

"It's not that bad," she said softly.

Only I knew it was. Before I could debate the issue with her, the sound of a ringing phone carried easily through my single-paned windows.

Hope filled Jamie Lynn's eyes. "Maybe that's Katie Sue?"

I shoved my key into my front door lock, mourning the days I could leave the house open, threw aside the door, and dashed for the phone, past Roly and Poly who fled as I blew by.

I grabbed up the phone on the fourth ring, and said a breathy, "Hello!"

The voice on the other end of the line was high and thready, on the verge of panic. "Carly Bell, is that Katie Sue Perrywinkle there with you?"

"Mama?" My stomach immediately started churning. My mama was often dramatic, but rarely was she the type to raise alarm without merit.

"Is she there?" Mama asked, more insistent.

"No, I haven't seen her in a few hours. Why? What's wrong?" Because something was.

"I . . . I'm not sure. It's just that I found her shoes, you know the gold ones I'd been admiring so? But she's no-where to be found."

"Her shoes? Where?"

"In the wedding gazebo . . ." Her breath hitched. "We need to find her."

I glanced toward the porch. Jamie Lynn stood in the doorway, her eyes transformed from hopeful to cautious. "Why? What aren't you telling me?"

"There's ..." Mama's voice dropped, as though she didn't want anyone to hear what she was about to say. "There's some blood on the shoes. And on the gazebo. There's ... blood droplets everywhere."

I sucked in a breath. "Call Dylan. I'll be right over."

Chapter Twelve

"What's wrong?" Jamie Lynn asked as soon as I hung up the phone.

I didn't know what to tell her. Certainly not the truth. Not yet. "There's a problem at my mama's chapel. I have to go. I can make your potion first thing in the morning and deliver it to you, Jamie Lynn."

"No, no." She nibbled her lip. "I don't want Lyla to catch wind of this. I'll come by and pick it up. Is that okay?"

"More than okay. I'm sorry I can't stay. I left the house unlocked in case you need to use the phone or anything. Just lock up when you leave."

"I can't stay much longer, either," she said, glancing toward the horizon at the setting sun. "A friend of mine will be here soon to pick me up." Moisture filled her eyes. "I think I expected too much. I think she's made it clear what's important to her. I should have known better."

Her. Katie Sue.

My mama's voice rang in my ears, her panic. What

happened to Katie Sue that there was blood on her shoes? "Let's not jump to conclusions just yet, okay? Maybe she just . . . got caught up in something." Jamie Lynn shrugged as I heard a siren in the distance. I needed to go. I gave her arm a gentle squeeze. "I'll be in touch soon. Stay here as long as you need."

She sank back onto the chair, deflating before my eyes. "Thanks, Carly."

I hated to leave but gave her a wan smile, ran to my bike, kicked up the stand, and pedaled as fast as my legs would move toward my mama's chapel. The whole way I kept thinking about the danger I felt around Katie Sue. I had a bad feeling about that blood my mama found.

The horizon blazed with the fiery colors of the sunset. My palms were slick as I bumped along brick roads, dodging cars, tourists, and my growing anxiety. A sheriff's cruiser was parked in front of my mama's chapel, its lights sending blue streaks across the white siding. A small crowd had gathered, necks craned, but there wasn't much to see. My mama and daddy stood next to Dylan, who looked formidable in his uniform. Mama's arms waved as she gestured, and I could hear the nervous high pitch of her voice, but not her words. A deputy carefully walked around the gazebo, using a flashlight beam as a spotlight. He placed small flags at uneven intervals. My stomach dropped. He was marking blood spatter. My gaze zipped to all the little flags. A dozen at least.

I jumped off my bike before I came to a full stop, set the stand, and jogged over to my parents. My daddy's thin face was drawn and pale, and my mama's was so full of color it nearly matched her scarlet hair. Dylan gave me a dark look. A look that clearly said "be prepared for the worst." No need for him to worry about that—I'd been expecting this anvil since Katie Sue walked into my shop this morning.

This morning.

It felt ages ago.

"Do we know what happened yet?" I asked as streetlamps flickered on one by one.

"Not really," my daddy said. Augustus Hartwell rarely looked anything other than studious. But tonight... tonight there was fear in his eyes.

"Last I saw of her," my mama said, "she was going at it with that sister of hers but good."

"Lyla?" I asked. Certainly not Jamie Lynn, because she'd been sitting at my house a good while now.

"Fighting like hellcats, they were." Mama pressed her hands to her cheeks.

"About what?" Dylan asked.

"Sounded like it was about money," Mama said. "I was just about to turn the hose on them when Lyla up and stormed off. When I checked on Katie Sue, she was crying. I asked her to come inside for a spell, but she said she had somewhere to be and just needed to collect herself."

Somewhere to be. Her meeting with Jamie Lynn, no doubt. "What time was this?"

"Oh, about six thirty, I think. Around about there."

I wondered if seeing Lyla had been the reason Katie Sue didn't meet with Jamie Lynn on time. I had a hard time believing that, though. Katie Sue seemed like she didn't want to communicate with her family—other than her baby sister—while she was in town.

"I let her be. The next thing I know, she's gone, but her shoes are still sitting there."

"Still?" I asked.

"She'd had them off during the fight with Lyla—for a bit there I was thinking she might use one to stab her sister."

"The fight was that bad?" Dylan asked.

Mama said simply, "Yes."

I let out a breath. The two of them took the term "bad blood" to a whole new level.

"Did you notice anything unusual, Augustus?" Dylan asked.

My daddy tugged on his chin. "Rona called me over at the library and had me rush home after she found the shoes. I saw two things that were out of place. I wouldn't think to mention them at all, but in light of this situation . . ."

"What's that, Gus honey? What'd you see?" Mama asked, her eyes going wide. Everyone but my mama called Daddy by his given name. Mama's always called him Gus—it was a name usually reserved for her and her alone.

The rubberneckers slowly dispersed, maybe figuring this was a domestic issue and that there wasn't anything else to see. No other sheriff's cruisers had arrived, no fire trucks, no ambulance. I was glad to see them go, but I was worried that the worst was yet to come.

"First thing odd was that on my way home, a jogger ran past me, nearly knocking me over, no apology or anything."

"That's just rudeness," Mama said, waving him off. "Which is not all that unusual unfortunately."

"Bad manners are something to which I've become accustomed," my daddy said, raising an eyebrow at my mama. "It was the manner of dress that was unusual."

"What do you mean?" I asked, trying not to smile at my father's oh so proper way of speaking. My mama, thank goodness, didn't seem to notice the playful jab he'd thrown her way.

"The jogger wore sweatpants and a heavy sweatshirt, with its hood up, and also had on gloves."

"In this heat?" Dylan asked.

Daddy nodded. "As I said, unusual."

"Was it Delia?" I joked. No one found it amusing but me. I frowned and said, "What was the other unusual thing?"

"Dinah Perrywinkle Cobb was sitting in her truck, parked just around the corner. Unusual since I haven't seen her since her release from prison."

We all turned simultaneously toward the spot Daddy mentioned. No one was parked there now. Dylan's jaw set. I recalled what Katie Sue had told me earlier. That wherever her mama went, Cletus was sure to follow. He had to have been around here somewhere. And he was bad, bad news.

"The jogger," Dylan said, "man or woman?"

Daddy's forehead crinkled as his eyebrows dipped. "I'm unsure. Medium height, medium build. I didn't get a good enough look at the runner to be able to identify a gender based on gait. Could have been either. I admit I was more focused on getting home—and distracted by the jogger's clothing."

"Dylan, do you think the jogger had anything to do with whatever happened here?" Mama asked.

"I don't know, Miz Rona. Sometimes little bits of information come together to make a big picture. But right now, all those bits are looking like confetti. First things first. We need to see if we can find Katie Sue," Dylan said.

Mama pressed a hand to her forehead. "I need to sit down."

"Rona, honey, why don't you go inside?" my daddy said. "We'll get this sorted out."

She didn't need to be asked twice. She scurried up the steps of the chapel—and I figured if she hadn't dug into the torte yet that it would soon be decimated. Food has always been Mama's choice of therapy. Part of me wished to join her—I also tended to eat away my troubles—but another part of me, the healer, wanted to find out what happened to Katie Sue. The healer always won.

"We should search the grounds," my daddy said. "If she hurt herself, she could be wandering around, delirious."

I noticed Katie Sue's gold sandals on the bottom step. They'd already been placed in an evidence bag. Rusty splotches flecked the shoes, marring the brilliant gold color. Perspiration popped out on my forehead and dampened my T-shirt. It was just a little after seven thirty now, so whatever had happened had taken place during a very small window of time.

The deputy near the gazebo started flagging a path that led toward the woods. If Katie Sue had been disoriented, she could be lost in the thick brush.

Dylan was stuck between a rock and a hard place. A potential crime scene was at risk, but he needed the manpower we offered. He finally nodded and said, "If you find anything suspicious, don't touch it. Call out for me right away."

We fanned out. My daddy headed in the direction of

his and mama's cottage, and I headed toward the Lover's Leap trail. Dylan went to speak with the deputy.

I half jogged toward the trailhead, my eyes open wide to the environment around me. Looking for any sign Katie Sue had been through here. But I didn't have a flashlight, and twilight was making it near impossible to see anything other than shadowy silhouettes.

Mosquitoes buzzed, crickets chirped, and I heard the first croak from a bullfrog in my mama's pond. Which reminded me of Cassandra Calhoun. Which reminded me of how much the family seemed to hate Katie Sue. And how they probably wouldn't offer sympathies if something *had* happened to her.

Then I thought about Katie Sue's family. Her mama. Cletus. Lyla. None but Jamie Lynn seemed too pleased that Katie Sue was back in town.

I heard footsteps and looked behind me. Dylan loped toward me, a flashlight in his hand. "You'll most likely need this."

He was right. Twilight was quickly turning into darkness. "Thanks."

"Remember," he said. "Anything suspicious, just holler. I'll come running."

"I'll remember."

He gave a nod and turned away, his own flashlight sweeping side to side. I flicked on the light, pointing it toward the trailhead. I'd been on this trail more times than I could count, but never had I been filled with such dread.

The bullfrog croaked again, spurring me into action. I started forward, alternately hoping I'd find Katie Sue and hoping I wouldn't.

I'd taken two more steps when I stopped, picking up a sound.

Adrenaline surged as I realized it was someone crying. I took off running toward the noise and just as I was about to enter the trail, a woman stumbled toward me. "Help!" she wailed. Tears streaked her dirty face. Twigs and leaves were tangled in her hair.

Gabi.

I gasped as I realized she was covered in blood, absolutely soaked in it. All the injuries I could see were a jagged cut on her face that had crusted, and she held one of her hands against her chest as though it was hurt. It wasn't enough to explain the amount of blood ... and I kept searching for other wounds.

But before I knew what was happening, she rushed toward me and flung her arms around me, crying and wailing, her body convulsing against mine.

I held her tightly, trying to catch my own breath, as I again spotted movement at the trailhead. Johnny Braxton appeared, carrying a bloodied and battered Katie Sue, who looked like a limp doll in his strong arms. My aunt Marjie hobbled along behind him, using a branch as a crutch.

I suddenly realized whose blood it was that had soaked Gabi's clothes.

Drawing in the deepest breath I could manage, I hollered, "Dylan!"

"Your dreams suck," I said.

Delia glanced my way, a pale eyebrow lifted. "You're cranky. Don't forget that my dreams saved your life not that long ago."

"Yeah, yeah," I grumped, then mumbled an apology.

"Accepted," she said. "But only because you had a bit of a traumatic night."

Bit was an understatement.

"Otherwise," she added, "I might have had to put a hex on you."

"You wouldn't."

She smiled a wicked smile. "Dare me."

Part of me really wanted to, because I was feisty that way, but I was also smart enough to know she'd actually do it. "I'll pass this time."

"That's what I thought."

"No need to gloat."

She laughed—a sound I didn't hear very often. Despite her Gothic flair, she was really quite reserved. But

the more she let me into her world, the more I saw that
her outward appearance was a wall she'd built around
herself for protection. From what, I still didn't know. But
I was grateful that she trusted me enough to glimpse
small peeks of who she truly was.

We sat on my mama's front porch in comfy white
wicker chairs, padded with deep cushions, while dual
ceiling fans circulated humid air and the scent of citronella candles. Delia's little black dog, Boo, stretched his
leash as he sniffed around the porch, the bushes. She'd
adopted him from a local animal rescue group that didn't
know his exact age or breed. They guessed he had a lot
of Yorkiepoo in him, but none of that mattered to Delia.
She'd taken one look into his jet-black eyes and fallen
head over heels. I didn't blame her. There were times I
wished I could steal him out from under her, but doubted
I could get away with it for long. She'd definitely put a
hex on me then.

We were lucky, Delia and me. Tucked safely away in
this little nook, with a light breeze blowing, the water in
mama's fountain burbling, and the stars glittering in the
dark sky. On any other day, we'd probably be telling stories or swapping gossip and sharing deep thoughts.

But not tonight.

Tonight we were waiting.

Waiting to hear word on Gabi and Aunt Marjie—
they'd been whisked off to the hospital, my mama and
daddy going with them. Waiting on Dylan to finish
speaking with Johnny Braxton. Waiting for the call that
my mama's done had herself a nervous breakdown because her wedding venue was draped in police tape.
Waiting on the county coroner to come collect the body

under the white sheet that lay near the gazebo. Waiting for all hell to break loose when word got out that Katie Sue Perrywinkle was dead.

Delia had arrived at the same time as the ambulance, and had taken my hand while Dylan transferred CPR duties on Katie Sue over to the EMTs. When they finally stopped their efforts and called the coroner to come pick up the body, Delia put an arm around me and guided me here, away from everyone. Away from the throng and all their *emotions*. We were especially vulnerable in crowds, and it was best to view this situation from afar.

The *situation*. Katie Sue was dead.

The anvil had fallen, crushing me with the guilt that maybe I could have somehow prevented this outcome.

Delia had made me change into one of Mama's T-shirts (DANGEROUS CURVES was stamped in bold white letters across my small chest, which would have made me laugh on any other day) and cleaned me up the best she could, scrubbing dried blood from my arms, my chin, my cheeks. She'd been extra careful with my hands, still blistered and raw. My normally suntanned skin had been beet red by the time she'd finished, but I wouldn't have minded if she kept on scrubbing. I had the feeling I wouldn't feel clean for a long, long while.

"Do you really think she jumped off Lover's Leap?" Delia asked.

The woods behind us buzzed with critter chatter, the night song of cicadas, crickets, katydids, owls, and frogs. It was quite the symphony they had going on, and every once in a while, quiet would reign, making me wonder what had spooked them into a moment of silence before their song swelled once again. But it was a secret the woods would keep. I just hoped that it wouldn't also keep the secret of what had happened to Katie Sue.

From what we knew so far, when Marjie and Johnny had come across Gabi yelling for help and trying to carry Katie Sue up the narrow trail that snaked from the river to the top of the bluff, Katie Sue was still alive. Barely. By all appearances, Katie Sue had jumped off the bluff, but instead of landing in the water, she'd hit the rocks below her. They knew they didn't have time enough to get out of the woods and call for an ambulance, so Johnny had picked up Katie Sue and carried her as fast as he could. But somewhere on the trip out of the woods, she'd died.

I closed my eyes against the memories of her injuries. The gaping head wound. The broken bones jutting at odd angles. The abrasions, cuts, and bruises.

The talk of suicide had grown along with the amount of gawking tourists gathering on the sidewalk, filling the street with their nosiness. Gossip flowed faster than the swirling waters of the Darling River after a soaking rain, picking up dribs and drabs as it went. *That her boyfriend had dumped her; that she was distraught from fighting with her family; that she'd taken to the bottle like her mama; that she'd let her demons get the best of her.*

I had to admit, it looked like a suicide. There had been others in that same spot over the years. Usually a casualty from a breakup, a soul too brokenhearted to realize that true happiness was found within—not with somebody else. It was as though throwing oneself off that cliff was proof positive that there were no happy endings. It was ultimate happily *never* after. However, I kept thinking of Katie Sue's shoes. The flecks of blood on them.

And the danger I'd felt around her. I'd bet my witchy senses that this wasn't a suicide. "No," I said. "I don't."

"Me either." Delia stretched her long legs. Boo came over to her and gently pawed her knee until she lifted him onto her lap.

I glanced at my cousin, who looked both angelic with her snowy blond hair and her fair complexion, and also devilish with her dark clothing and cape. "Why? You didn't have another dream, did you?"

"Just a feeling," she said darkly. "Katie Sue came into my shop earlier; did you know?"

"For a hex?"

She nodded. "She was quite mad at someone. She wanted a little . . . revenge."

I easily recalled the anger she'd been emanating when Gabi and I bumped into her behind Marjie's house. "Mad" was too mild a description. But I still didn't know who was at the receiving end of all that rage. Had it been Warren, who she'd just been meeting with? Or someone else?

"Did she say who the hex was for?"

"No, but I have the feeling we'll know soon enough. It was my baldness hex, the weak version. Whoever she gave it to, well, their hair is about to fall out. But, because it's the weak variety, the hair will grow back." Moonlight fell across her face as her lips twitched into a half smile. "Someday."

I blinked, amazed how casually she could talk about causing someone to go bald. "What if it had been extra-strength?"

"Cue ball for the rest of their life."

"Dang."

"I rarely sell that hex," Delia said, scrunching her nose. "When someone asks for that strength I need all the particulars, a full rundown on what the hexee had done to deserve that kind of revenge."

I was glad to hear she had some kind of moral barometer.

"Take Dixie Perrault for example," she said.

"No!" I could easily picture the hair stylist who'd suddenly started wearing wigs about a year or so ago before she up and moved out of state.

"Oh yes."

"What'd she do?"

"The question isn't what she did. It's *who* she *didn't* do."

I swatted away a moth. "Hush your mouth."

"Let's just say that a lot of upset wives suddenly understood why their husbands had developed an affinity for fancy salon hairdos. The wives banded together, came to see me, and told me the whole sordid tale."

When Dixie left Hitching Post, I'd joked with Ainsley, asking her if Dixie had been making Carter cinnamon rolls . . . Little did I know how close I had been to the true reason the hairstylist left town. "Why not give the baldness hex to the husbands?"

"Oh, don't worry none about them," she said softly, her gaze focused in the distance on something I couldn't see. A memory.

It was probably a recollection I *never* wanted to know about.

Drawing one leg up onto the chair, I wrapped my arms around it. I set my chin on my knee. My role in life was to fix people. It seemed Delia's was to exact revenge. But try as I might, right here, right now, I couldn't find fault in what she'd done to Dixie. Or to the husbands who strayed.

Tomorrow, maybe, I could find some measure of judgment. By then I might have some wits about me and remember why I didn't make hexes. Why I chose to focus on healing, not harming.

But not right now.

Because right now, as I kept staring at that white sheet, I felt the need for revenge. It rose inside me, fighting to be let loose. It clawed at my soul, slicing open the very heart of me. Ripping to shreds everything I had ever stood for.

I hated it. Yet I embraced it. It gave me purpose. I had to find out who did this to my old friend. Had to find out *why*. Maybe then I could understand. I could put it in a neat tidy compartment in the back of my mind, tucked away as a painful lesson. I could go back to seeing the light.

Delia said, "When she was with me, despite the revenge hex, she seemed . . . hopeful. She wouldn't go jumping off a cliff. Not willingly."

I had a flash of someone making her walk to the bluff and forcing her to jump. Heavens above, I hoped that hadn't been the case. Tears stung my eyes, and I took hold of my locket, squeezing it until my knuckles ached. "Hopeful about what?"

"I don't know exactly, but when I read her energy, I felt happiness."

I watched the flame flicker on the citronella candle as I said, "What time was she at your shop?"

Delia tipped her head side to side, thinking about it. "Round near one-ish."

After Marjie's gun-toting incident and the car ride with Warren Calhoun, but before I'd seen her poking her head out at my mama's chapel.

It made me wonder what had happened in that car with Warren. Had they made up? Had he agreed to whatever ultimatums she'd laid down before him? *Hopeful.* I didn't question Delia's observation. She had the same empathy skills I did—she'd know hopeful if she felt it.

Which made Katie Sue's death that much more tragic.

Again, I wondered about her secret ammunition. . . . It was still out there, somewhere. That ammunition might have just turned into evidence. Hopefully, it would point to who was responsible for her death.

I needed to put together a timeline of her whereabouts during the day. Who had she met with? Who'd received the hex? And what had she been fighting about with Lyla? Old family problems? Or something new?

My gaze skipped to all the people gathered around. Familiar faces, most of them. On the fringes, I spotted one of Warren Calhoun's lug nuts. He was standing completely still, intimidating in his size and demeanor. There was no way he could see me watching him, not from this distance, but I could have sworn for a second there that our gazes met. The next thing I knew, he turned and threaded into the crowd, disappearing from sight.

I searched for any other sign of the Calhouns, but I didn't find any. Were they oblivious to what had happened here? Or were they on the way to the hospital to meet up with Gabi?

Gabi, who'd been covered in Katie Sue's blood. Gabi, who'd "found" Katie Sue on the rocky riverbank. Her presence raised the question of why she'd been on the trail in the first place. Alone, at that. And how she'd come across Katie Sue.

My gaze once again swept the crowd, and a flash of metal caught my eye. Lamplight gleamed off one of Jamie Lynn's crutches. By now she had to have learned who was under that sheet, and it showed by the look on her face. Then Lyla appeared behind her, put an arm around her shoulders, and led her away.

I couldn't help but wonder what would happen to Katie Sue's estate. With her kind of money, she must have had a will. Would it all go to Jamie Lynn? I wasn't sure how to figure it out, and hoped Caleb could help me.

I also needed to have a talk with Lyla. The sooner the better. I wanted to know exactly what she was arguing with Katie Sue about—and if she knew why her mother had been spying on her sister.

"Here comes Dylan," Delia said, nudging me.

I hadn't noticed him walking over—I'd been too fixated on Katie Sue's next of kin. The world around me seemed to fall into a hush as our gazes met, and most of my anxiety seeped away. He was the only one who could soothe me with just a look. I'd missed that ability when he moved away after our last breakup. I'd missed *him*.

"Sap," Delia whispered.

"Stop reading my energy."

She laughed. "Stop being so overwhelmingly lovey-dovey, and maybe I wouldn't have picked up on it at all."

I was just glad that Dylan couldn't sense what I was feeling, too. Heaven's above, that would cause all kinds of trouble I didn't need right now. I set my foot back on the ground as he crossed the small bridge over the creek, his footfalls echoing on the wooden planks. He came up the steps, and leaned on the porch railing. Boo wagged his tiny tail, let out a happy yip, and leaped down off Delia's lap to sniff Dylan's feet.

I was envious of the little dog's joy.

"Nice shirt," he said, eyeing my chest.

"What did Johnny say?" I asked, ignoring him—and the urge to cross my arms. "Anything interesting?"

"Basically, he gave the same account as Gabi," Dylan said. "He and Marjie came across Gabi trying to get Katie Sue up the path from the riverbank."

"What happened to Marjie's leg?" Delia asked. "Did he say?"

Dragging a hand down his face, he said, "Apparently the two were taking an evening hike and picnic. When they were headed back, Marjie tripped on something and fell, hurting her ankle."

Had she really tripped? Or had she been pushed?

"But about the same time," Dylan went on, "Johnny was overtaken with some sort of stomach bug. So he kept having to make pit stops in the woods, while Marjie went about fashioning herself a crutch from a broken branch. By the time they came across Gabi, they'd been in the woods going on three hours."

I wondered what Marjie had given Johnny to cause the "stomach bug." Because I was sure as heck certain she'd done something. There were plenty of plants in those woods that would cause intestinal distress. Certain leaves, berries, and sap were poisonous to varying degrees. She could have easily slipped something into his picnic food. Heck, she had plenty of those things in her own yard and could have packed something in the picnic basket. From pokeweed to milkweed, azaleas, mountain laurel, hydrangeas, oleander . . . and many, many more. Aunt Marjie had her pick of poisons.

As I tried to block the mental image Dylan had just painted of Johnny dashing in and out of the woods, Delia said, "Do you think Katie Sue's death was a suicide?"

"Not sure right now," Dylan said, his lips pressing into a grim line. "All I know is that things aren't adding up."

"Like what kind of things?" I hoped he'd elaborate.

"Just things." He evaded like a pro. "But I will tell you this . . ."

Moonlight grew brighter, throwing shadows throughout Daddy's gardens. Delia and I eagerly leaned in like moths drawn to Dylan's flame.

He dropped his voice a notch. "Johnny said he saw one other person on the trail."

"Who?" My guess was Cletus. With Dinah parked nearby, he had to have been around here somewhere when all this went down. But how close had he come to Katie Sue?

"As Johnny put it, 'a crazy-assed runner' dressed all in black, head to toe."

"Wasn't me," Delia said quickly.

I laughed. They stared. "Sheesh," I said.

Somberly, Dylan added, "We need to find that runner. At the very least, that person's an eyewitness."

"At the most?" Delia asked.

"That person could be a killer."

A shiver rippled through me at the thought. "You should check on Cletus's alibi."

"Already on it, Carly. I sent a deputy over to his and Dinah's trailer to question them."

"You sent someone?" I asked. "Don't you think *you* should go?"

"You two might as well head home," he said. Apparently it was his turn to ignore me. "It'll be a late night here. There's a lot we need to get done still, and then I have to head to the hospital to interview Gabi."

"Oh?" I wouldn't mind going with him.

"You can't come with me," he said.

He had always been able to read me well. I countered with, "I'm sure my aunt Marjie would want to see me."

Delia snorted.

I didn't dare look at her, or else I wouldn't be able to keep a straight face. Marjie hated hospitals, and I wouldn't doubt if she was currently biting the heads off everyone who came near her.

"Marjie's being released soon," Dylan said. "Apparently, she's been yelling at the doctors since she got there, and they are more than happy to let her go."

I bit my nail. "I'm sure Gabi would like my company."

"The Calhouns are on their way to be with her, and there's a guard watching the door, keeping out anyone who's not approved."

"I might be approved . . . Gabi likes me."

His eyes darkened. "Be that as it may, Gabi's a person of interest in this case. No one's talking with her until I do."

"But maybe she'll tell me—"

"Carly." He cut me off.

"Dylan," I echoed, using his same serious tone.

"Let it go, Carly," he said. "Go home, get some rest. Nothing's going to happen tonight."

"Fine," I lied, leaning back, not wanting to cause another scene for the tourists to witness. There was no way I was letting this go. I was too involved. From the moment Katie Sue walked through my door this morning, to when I left Jamie Lynn on my porch . . . I was in it up to my eyebrows.

Suspicion clouded his features. "You're not going to let this go, are you?"

Nuts, I knew I shouldn't have agreed so easily. "I just said 'fine.'"

He stared.

I stared back.

Letting out a resigned sigh, he said, "*Fine*. I need to get going." Turning, he walked away, his strides long and sure.

I smiled at his retreating form. I knew his "fine" meant that he would turn a blind eye and deaf ear to my snooping.

Delia looked at me, a mischievous knowing twinkle in her eyes. "I can't imagine why you two never married."

"Hush," I said.

What I really wanted to say was, "Never say never."

But I had the feeling she already knew.

As much as I hated to admit it, Dylan may have been right about one thing. There wasn't much I could do tonight to figure out what happened to Katie Sue. It was too dark to trek into the woods to see where she'd gone off the cliff; the area around the gazebo was cordoned off with a deputy keeping watch; and Johnny, Marjie, and Gabi were otherwise occupied. I'd have to bide my time where they were concerned. I ultimately decided to go home, but I doubted very much that I would rest.

As Delia and I had parted, she promised to let me know if she came across anyone who'd suddenly gone bald, and I—much to her surprise and a little of mine as well—threw my arms around her and hugged tight, thanking her for cleaning me up and for just . . . being there. Happily, she didn't shove me away, but hugged me back.

It made me think about families and second chances. Maybe Jamie Lynn Perrywinkle was right. Maybe her mama did deserve another shot.

I'd made a quick stop at Potions to make an ointment for my hands, and then pedaled home. As I coasted down the street, I noticed Marjie's inn cloaked in darkness and wondered when she'd get back. My gaze quickly skipped to the Crazy Loon with its welcoming lights shining softly through the windows. Dylan said the Calhouns were on their way to the hospital, but I spotted Warren and one of his lug nuts smoking cigars in Hazel's garden. I wondered if it was a celebratory cigar now that Warren's problematic lover was dead. Had he cared for her at all? Or had he been the one to put an end to her threats? I debated whether to go over there to confront him about his relationship with Katie Sue but hesitated. I didn't quite know what to say, and before I could think of anything, the pair turned and went back inside the Loon.

I took that as fate's way of telling me to let it go. Fate, apparently, had been chatting with Dylan.

For tonight, I *would* let it go.

But tomorrow . . . all bets were off.

I parked Bessie Blue next to the garage and climbed the back steps of my house, ready to face the wrath of the cats. I'd been gone most of the day, and they weren't ones to suffer hunger patiently. Especially Poly. I fully expected to hear his outraged cries as I opened the back door, but oddly they didn't greet me there.

I made kissy noises to call the cats as I kicked off my shoes in the mudroom and set my lotion on the kitchen counter. As I started toward the living room, I suddenly froze at hearing a strange noise, one I couldn't quite place. A surge of adrenaline shot through me.

I waited for the tingle of my witchy senses, but felt

nothing. All was clear. There was no danger. But just in case, I grabbed my pitchfork from the kitchen pantry and held it at the ready as I tiptoed into the living room and called out, "Roly, Poly!" I made more kissy noises.

A head popped up from the other side of the sofa.

"Eeee!" I screeched, startled.

"Don't fork me!"

I grabbed my heart. "Ainsley Sage Debbs! You just took a year off my life at least."

"You're telling me! I wake up to kissing noises and come face to prong with your pitchfork. *Hell's bells!*"

Ha! Now that I knew she'd been sleeping, the noise I heard was easily recognizable as her snoring.

"I mean I'm used to kissing sounds from Carter and all, but that pitchfork is a whole other thing." Her eyes narrowed and she giggled. "You been raiding your mama's closet?"

I glanced down at the dangerous curves T-shirt. "Long story. Carter makes kissy noises? I don't believe it."

Grinning, she tucked her hair behind her ears. She had changed out of her flirty sundress into sweatpants and an oversize Oscar the Grouch tee. "Once in a while. Don't tell him I told you."

I couldn't even imagine that conversation. Carter and I rarely talked about anything but the weather. "My lips are sealed." Smiling, I set the pitchfork aside. "What are you doing here?"

"Well," she said and took a deep breath. "I'd just got the kids down for the night when the phone started ringing off the hook with news about Katie Sue Perrywinkle being dead and all. I felt just horrible after joking about it earlier. I never imagined it might actually happen."

I wish I'd felt the same. I'd known something bad was going to happen—and hadn't been able to stop it.

"Of course I wanted to know what went down, and knew the best source for getting the news, so I left Carter and set off to find you, but I couldn't even get close to your mama's chapel for the crush of people there. So I came here to wait you out, but I must've dozed off. Getting the Clingons into bed is enough to do me in. *Shoo.* Those kids . . ."

I sat next to her on the sofa. "They're just like their mama. Unless they go around making kissy noises. In that case I'd say they take after their daddy."

She laughed. "Hush now."

"What's all this?" I asked, taking note of the items stacked on my coffee table. A pile of folded clothes. Toiletries. A cell phone. "You moving in?"

"Not me . . ." Heat colored Ainsley's cheeks. "Since I was here, I decided to poke around some and check out the work that you've been doing—the place is coming along nicely, by the way—and when I peeped in the guest room, I saw the overnight bag on the bed and . . ." Shrugging, she scrunched up her face. "I went through it. I mean, that's not too terribly wrong, is it? She couldn't possibly care at this point, right?"

Overnight bag? I was puzzled for a moment, before it clicked. "Katie Sue's bag."

Ainsley nodded. "I don't even know what I was looking for necessarily, but I can tell you there was nothing to find. Just some clothes and makeup and her phone, which might be helpful if I could figure out the code to get the thing unlocked. There are probably some juicy text messages stored in there."

"How long did you try?" I picked it up. I had very little know-how where cell phones were concerned.

"An hour."

"I'm surprised you gave up so easily," I teased.

She elbowed me and leaned over the side of the couch to haul up Katie Sue's handbag as well. "Nothing of interest in here, either."

I peeked in the bag. Goose bumps raised on my arms. It felt strange going through her things. I opened Katie Sue's wallet and found plenty of money, credit cards, her driver's license and hospital I.D. She worked at Birmingham Memorial—one of the best hospitals in the state. I couldn't help but think of her lifelong goal of being a doctor—and how unfair it was that she wasn't going to be able to live that dream.

"So, tell me what happened with Katie Sue? Did she ever meet with Jamie Lynn?"

I set the bag aside. "Let me feed the cats, and then I'll tell you all about it."

"Already fed them. They're passed out on your bed in a tuna stupor."

"Tuna? They're never going to want you to leave."

"It is kind of nice here," Ainsley said, rubbing the sofa arm. "So quiet."

I laughed. "You'll be missing Carter and the Clingons soon."

"Maybe," she said, her violet eyes gleaming. "Or maybe not. I should sleep over, like the old days."

"You won't last till ten."

"Try me."

"You're on."

As I checked Katie Sue's clothes, I filled in Ainsley

about the night's events. Katie Sue had packed enough for two more days. There was no ammunition I saw, no diary with Mrs. Warren Calhoun written inside a heart shape. No hint as to why she'd died tonight.

Ainsley tucked her legs beneath her. "You couldn't tell what was wrong with Jamie Lynn?"

"No, it's the weirdest thing. I'm going to do some research in my medical books tonight." I had quite the assortment of textbooks, collected throughout the years. Even though I could *feel* someone else's ailment, it was important for me to understand how that translated into a diagnosis. With all the reading I'd done, I was probably as well schooled as Katie Sue had been. But there was always room for improvement—as Jamie Lynn's case proved.

"Did you talk to Jamie Lynn after Katie Sue's body was found?" Ainsley asked.

"No, but I saw her from afar. She looked crushed."

"I can imagine."

In light of what happened to Katie Sue, I felt even more pressure to help Jamie Lynn. Regaining her health certainly wouldn't bring her sister back, but it would give her future a brighter outlook.

"Do you think Cletus and Dinah had something to do with Katie Sue's death?"

I sank into the sofa, feeling the weight of today's events. "Katie Sue was afraid of Cletus, so we have to take that into account. Plus, his whereabouts during what happened to her are still a mystery." Shaking my head, I sighed. "I should have been able to stop her death."

"Oh, Carly, you tried. You told Dylan. You warned her. You're only one person."

I had tried. But it hadn't been enough. What good

were my witchy senses if I couldn't prevent tragedies when warned in advance?

I was well on my way to quite the pity party when headlights lit the front windows as someone pulled into my driveway. A second later, a car door slammed. Then another. Raised voices carried as I pulled open the front door. I found my father trying to help Marjie up the porch steps.

"I can do it myself," Marjie snapped, hopping up the steps on one leg. The other leg was bent out of the way, a white cast covering most of the lower half, from just below her knee to the top of her foot. Only her toes peeped out.

Behind her, my father stuck out his tongue as he carried a pair of crutches.

"Fancy seeing you two here," I said, glancing between them.

Marjie looked over her shoulder at my father, who quickly stuck his tongue back into his mouth. "You didn't call her?"

"Why would I do that?" he asked.

"To let her know I was coming?" she said in a tone that made me want to go back inside the house, shut off the lights, and pretend I wasn't home.

"Why would I warn her like that? She'd pretend she wasn't home."

My father knew me well.

Marjie harrumphed and hopped past me into the house. She plopped onto the couch next to Ainsley and growled at her. Ainsley growled back—she had the Clingons, so not much scared her.

I thought I saw Marjie smile. Twice in one day. It was

some kind of record. I blocked my father's entrance. "What's going on?"

He eyed my shirt. "Isn't that . . ."

"Yes. Yes it is."

He shook his head and asked no more questions. "Marjie's going to be staying with you for a while."

"What?" I asked. "Why?"

"The doctors have advised Marjie that she should have some help while her broken ankle heals, at least until she gets used to getting around on crutches." He shoved the pair of them at me.

I looked over my shoulder. "Help usually means a home nurse or aide."

"No," Marjie cut in.

"What about Johnny?" I asked. "I'm sure he'd move in to help for a few—"

"No," Marjie snapped.

"Where's Mama?" I asked with a hint of whine, looking around my father, trying to see into the car.

"I already dropped her off," he said. "The doctors gave her a tranquilizer, so she'll be out until morning at least."

"Lucky," I murmured.

"Don't I know it," he said. "Anyways, Marjie insisted on staying with one of the family, so we drew straws, and you lost. Sorry and good luck." He turned and ran down the steps. He was already slamming the door of the car and peeling out before I could even think to stop him.

I slowly twirled around. Marjie had her casted leg propped on the coffee table, a scowl on her face, and Ainsley was beaming ear to ear.

Marjie said, "Is that shirt a statement of irony or wishful thinking?"

I grabbed my locket. "You know, my parents have a couple of guest rooms. . . ."

"This house is just fine. I can't do stairs yet, so I'll sleep down here."

"Here where?" I asked. "The couch is too small to stretch out on."

"You'll have to bring down a mattress from upstairs."

I jerked a thumb toward the front door. "I'm sure Hazel or Eulalie would love to have you. . . ."

"They have inns full of guests. Here is fine, I said. That's it. End of story. I'm staying." Glancing around, she bent down, and picked up a dust bunny made of mostly cat hair. She glared at it. "When's the last time you cleaned around here?"

I set my hands on my hips. "Said the woman who has tumbleweeds for a lawn."

Her lips pursed. "Don't sass. Go get the mattress. I'm tired. It's been a long day."

Ainsley popped off the sofa. "I'll help bring it down."

A half hour later, the mattress was down the steps, fresh with new bedding, and Aunt Marjie was in the downstairs bath, getting ready for bed. I'd scrounged up an extra toothbrush, and had given her one of my nightshirts to wear. I'd offered to run to her house to pick up some of her things, but she'd declined.

"Why do you think she doesn't want you in her house?" Ainsley said loudly as she fluffed a pillow. "Do you think she has a collection of dead bodies in her parlor or something?"

"I heard that!" Marjie snapped.

Ainsley said, "You were supposed to! Come on, Miss Marjie. Why all the secrecy?"

Marjie hopped into the living room. She'd yet to use the crutches. "I like my privacy. Now leave it be."

"For now," Ainsley said, a devious hint in her tone. She looked at the wall clock. "I suppose I should get home."

"Yes," Marjie agreed. "Yes you should."

Glancing at the time, I smiled. "Nine fifty. I win."

"It's only because Marjie is here," Ainsley said, slipping into her sandals.

"Sure, sure." As much as the Clingons gave her fits, she adored them.

She lovingly flipped me off and strode out the door.

Marjie pulled back the sheet on the makeshift bed and said, "I like that girl."

I laughed. "Can I get you anything? Water?"

"I'm not an invalid." She lowered into the bed, letting out a *whoomph* as she did so. "I know where to find the sink."

I couldn't imagine this was a better setup than staying with my parents. Not wanting Johnny around, I understood, but not my mama—especially when she was drugged up. "All right then." I went around locking the doors and turning off lights. I grabbed the lotion for my hands and headed for the stairs.

"Carly?"

"Yes?"

"I don't suppose you have a gun around, do you? I don't sleep too well without my gun."

"No guns. I can go down to your house . . ."

"No, no."

Why didn't she want anyone in her house? I always thought it was because of her cantankerous personality, but now I truly wondered. In all my years, I'd never set foot farther than her front porch. "I have a pitchfork," I offered.

There was a beat of silence before she said, "It'll have to do."

I tucked the pitchfork next to her mattress, and I saw her hand sneak out from under the sheet to grasp the handle.

"Just holler if you need anything else. Good night, Aunt Marjie."

She grunted. "What's so good about it?"

I glanced back at her as she settled in, her eyes squished closed, her grip tight on the pitchfork. Lordy be, but I loved my family. I was smiling as I clicked off the last light and headed up the stairs.

~≈ Chapter Fifteen ≈~

Early the next morning, I woke with a start, shooting upright in bed. My chest pounded. Sweat dampened my hair and my thin tank top. My pulse thudded in my ears.

The cats didn't seem the least bit bothered by my abrupt awakening as they lazily yawned and stretched. I glanced around. Listened. The only noises were the whirr of the air conditioner, the hum of ceiling fan blades, and the purrs from Roly. Nothing seemed out of place, but I felt ... out of sorts. Like there was something important I should remember.

"It must have been a dream that woke me up," I said under my breath. But try as I might, I couldn't remember a dream. I couldn't even remember falling asleep, but sometime during the night, I had. My light was still on, and the medical textbooks I'd been reading when I climbed into bed last night were still piled next to me.

I'd had no luck finding an ailment that matched all of Jamie Lynn's symptoms. I was looking forward to seeing her today when she came by for her potion. I wanted to read her energy again—see if there was anything I had missed. And I wanted to know her reason for not using a wheelchair, because she needed one. Putting undo stress on an already failing body wasn't going to do her any good.

I checked the palms of my hands and smiled. They were mostly healed, the skin still tender but no longer raw and weeping. Another dose of the potion and they'd be good as ever.

The first thing on my to-do list at work today was to make Jamie Lynn a potion. I needed to check the grimoire—the book of herbal recipes—to see which would be best for her symptoms. The Leilara made the potion work, but the mixture had to have the right ingredients.

In high doses, the Leilara could cure just about anything on its own, but the issue was that the drops were in limited supply. There were only so many tears before the entwined lilies shriveled for another year. Combining the drops with herbal remedies allowed me to help many people, not just a few.

As I slid my locket back and forth on its chain, an orange glow tinted the window shades, the first hint of sunrise. I had a lot to get done today. Besides working, I wanted to see if Dylan had learned anything new about Katie Sue's death, talk with Caleb about finding out if she had a will, and track down Lyla Jameson. And I'd promised to help my mama at the chapel, too, and wondered what would happen with the Calhoun wedding. Would it be postponed? The cut on Gabi's face wouldn't heal in time for her to walk down the aisle, and would she want her wedding to be held in the same place Katie Sue had died?

It seemed unlikely.

Which meant my mama was going to need a whole crate of tranquilizers.

But if there was no wedding, would the Calhouns pack up and leave town today? The thought alone made me mad enough to spit nails. What if one of them had something to do with what happened to Katie Sue? I imagined Louisa was happy as could be right now. I hoped she wouldn't have wished Katie Sue dead, but as a woman scorned . . . I wouldn't put it past her. Or be surprised if she'd orchestrated the death.

I glanced at my bedside clock. It was a little past six in the morning. I stared at the bright red numbers and gasped when I remembered what had woken me up. It hadn't been a dream at all—it had been a memory. A memory of a lifeless, bloodied body.

Reaching over the stack of books, I grabbed up the phone from my nightstand and dialed a number I knew by heart.

"Yeah," a sleepy voice answered.

"It's Carly. Sorry to call so early." I heard the rustling of covers and could easily picture Dylan sitting up in bed, rubbing his eyes, swiping a hand through his hair. He'd be shirtless, of course, because he slept only in a pair of old gym shorts. I could picture his chest, too, and could practically trace the contours of his muscles with an imaginary fingertip.

I gave myself a good shake.

"What time is it?" he asked.

"A little after six." Poly inched his way up the bed, stretching as he did so. One step, *streeeetch*. Another step, *streeeetch*. At this rate, he'd make it to my chest by noon.

"Wrong answer. You were supposed to say it's time for us to elope. Today's the day. Do I need to pack a bag, Care Bear?"

Have mercy on my soul, I almost said yes. "Don't you remember the last time we did that? It didn't work out so well."

"Ancient history."

"History tends to repeat itself."

"Well, it's time we rewrote it—don't you think?"

My palms grew damp. "I don't think rewriting history is possible. What happened is what happened."

"Maybe so," he said softly. "But that doesn't mean we can't glue back together what was broken. Rebuild on what was a solid foundation."

Broken. It was a good description of what had happened to our relationship. Our hearts.

"Glue, you say?" I asked, wanting our relationship to end happily-ever-after with an ache so fierce I almost groaned.

"Really good stuff. Thick. Gooey. Stuff that'll never so much as crack again."

"Does that even exist?"

"It does if we want it to. Do you want it?"

He was asking so much in that one little question, but I was too scared to answer honestly. I didn't want my heart broken again. "Maybe."

"It's a start." I could practically hear his smile as he added, "So what's on your mind this early if not to elope with me? Booty call? I can be there in ten minutes. Five if I use my lights and siren. Four if I don't bother getting fully dressed."

Poly head bumped my arm, looking for attention. I scratched under his chin as his purrs grew louder and louder. "You've given this some thought."

"Care Bear, you have no idea how much."

It was suddenly very hot in my room. "Lights and sirens would be a bit much."

"No, no they wouldn't."

"My aunts would surely take notice."

"They take notice of everything anyway. Might as well give them something to really talk about."

"Well, Marjie would surely be interested, considering she's sleeping in my living room."

There was a moment of silence, of mourning what almost was. "What?"

I explained how my father had dumped her on me.

He let out a deflated sigh. "Why'd you call, Carly?"

I suddenly felt ashamed for flirting and forgetting why I'd rung him in the first place. "It's about Katie Sue."

"Did you find out anything?"

"Not really. I just remembered something about Katie Sue's body." Poly flipped onto his back so I could rub his tummy. Roly preferred getting her beauty sleep.

I heard him stifle a yawn as he said, "What's that?"

"Did you notice her jewelry was gone?" It was what had woken me. I must have been thinking about her subconsciously when I realized her ring, her watch, and her earrings had been missing when Johnny Braxton laid her on the ground next to the gazebo last night.

"You're sure?"

I'd spent many long, long minutes scanning her body for signs of life while Dylan attempted CPR. I could easily picture her lying on the ground, and in that image, there was no sign of her jewelry. "You can double-check with the coroner's office but I'm sure. What I'm not sure about is why. What happened to it?"

"I'll be seeing him this morning. If the jewelry is missing, this may be a case of a robbery gone wrong," he speculated.

Maybe. Or Warren Calhoun didn't want his investment wasted when he had Katie Sue killed. "Did you learn anything else overnight? Could you tell if Katie Sue jumped off that cliff or if she was pushed?" Knowing that for certain would send this case in very different directions.

"Neither, Carly."

"What's that mean?"

"It looks like the initial attack on Katie Sue was at the gazebo, and then someone dragged her through the woods to Lover's Leap."

My hand trembled as I held the phone. "And?" I asked. I knew the worst was yet to come.

"She didn't jump off that bluff, Carly. And she wasn't pushed either. She was *thrown*. Katie Sue was murdered."

Murdered.

Long after I'd hung up with Dylan, the word played on repeat in my mind. I couldn't stop thinking about what he had said and felt an overwhelming sadness for what my friend had gone through.

I wished I could have saved her. Wished it with all my heart. I swiped a tear from my eye and pulled myself together. I could sit here all day wallowing, or I could do something to bring about justice for Katie Sue.

Tossing off my blanket, I slipped on my robe. I'd shower, get dressed, and get going. I'd just opened my closet when Poly suddenly leaped off the bed and skidded toward the door, pawing it open (I always left it open a crack for the cats to come and go). Confused, I looked at Roly, who quickly followed the same path as her brother. What in the world?

Sticking my head out into the hallway, I picked up the aroma of bacon in the air. Ah. Now their behavior made sense. Nothing got them moving like the possibility of bacon.

Sniffing again, I picked up another scent. I hightailed it down the steps—nothing got *me* moving like the possibility of coffee.

I found Marjie in the kitchen, sitting on an old wooden stool next to the stove. Bacon sizzled in a cast iron pan, and two fluffy cats sat, ever hopeful, at her feet.

"Morning," I said, heading for the cabinet where I kept my mugs. "Sleep okay?"

As I pulled open the cabinet door, and saw the mugs all lined up, the memory of a day when another shelf of mugs had come crashing down on me slipped into my mind. Dylan had helped me clean up ceramic shards, and we'd laughed and kissed and made plans about how we wanted to renovate the kitchen. At that moment in time, I never dreamed that our relationship would end up collapsing as well.

Could we rebuild?

I didn't know. But I'd be lying if I said I didn't feel a little seed of hope bloom deep in my heart at the thought.

"Heard you yapping on the phone. How's a woman supposed to sleep with that kind of racket?"

I reached in for a mug. "You've been up since five, and you know it." She was always up at five on the dot. Shortly after which she usually speed walked the neighborhood, scaring birds from the trees, but with her casted ankle, today the birds were safe. I, on the other hand, was not.

The coffeepot was blissfully full. I filled my mug, added a little milk, and took that first sip. "Good stuff. Thanks for making it."

Marjie harrumphed. I took that as a "You're welcome." She hopped over to the fridge and pulled out a carton of eggs. "Scrambled okay?"

"I can do that. Why don't you—"

She spun and glared.

"Scrambled is good."

"I thought so." She turned back to the stove and pulled down another frying pan from the rack, the hem of the nightshirt I'd lent her riding up. I didn't think I ever noticed how strong she was before now. Her arms and legs were toned and firm—no wiggle jiggle to be seen. No wonder she could hop around with no difficulty at all. Speed walking did her body good.

I cleaned the cats' dishes, and then filled them with food and fresh water. Both ignored them, in favor of the bacon.

Leaning against the counter, I watched my aunt cook. Her movements were sure and swift—not an ounce of energy wasted. Her hair was a mess—I could see three tangles from where I stood. I didn't dare ask her if I could help with it. I needed to ration my questions, and right now there were more pressing matters than her hair. "Can I ask you a question, Aunt Marjie?"

"Depends on the question."

I took another sip of coffee and wondered why it always tasted better when someone else made it. "What did you slip into Johnny's food yesterday on that picnic hike?"

She'd been reaching for an egg when her hand stilled. Slowly, she turned to face me. "I'm sure I don't know what you mean."

"Stop smiling like that. You're scaring me." A Grinch-like grin was plastered to her face.

She chuckled. *Chuckled!* Grabbing the egg, she whacked it against the lip of a bowl, cracking it clear in half but not letting a bit of the white drip onto the counter. She cracked three more eggs the same way. *Whack, whack, whack!*

I winced each time. The cats were unfazed.

She grabbed a fork and set to whisking the eggs. "Don't you worry none about ol' Johnny."

"It's not so much Johnny I'm worried about. It's you. This time it's a broken ankle, but what about next time?"

"I tripped on a tree root."

"If you say so." I set out two plates, forks, and napkins. "Did you see the jogger on the trail last night, too?"

"Of course. I ain't blind."

"Did you see anything about the jogger that could help with an identification? Man or woman? Facial features?"

For once, she didn't give me a flippant answer. "Blazed by so fast my head was spinning so I didn't see much. But," she said, "I did see a bit of hair."

This was news.

"Brownish. Longish."

"Longish and brownish like Cletus Cobbs' hair?"

She swiveled. "You think he has something to do with this?"

"Dinah was parked nearby, so we're speculating that Cletus had to be around somewhere."

Her gaze narrowed. "Wish I could say for sure it was him, but I can't. The runner was the right size for sure, but I'm not certain Cletus could run that fast given his history of smoking anything that lit up."

She had a point, but I also knew the body was capable of just about anything when adrenaline was involved.

She glanced over her shoulder. "Now git with you. I can't abide talking in the morning . . . or hovering. I'll call you when it's ready."

I went over and planted a kiss on her cheek.

"Ugh," she said, wiping it off and pushing me away. "Git!"

Laughing, I headed for the front porch, and when I glanced back at Marjie, my heart warmed at the small — genuine — smile on her face. I slipped outside before she noticed that I saw.

Birdsong filled the morning air, and the humidity promised another hot day. Across the street, I noticed Hazel in her garden, bustling about with a pair of pruning shears. I glanced at the Loon and noticed someone looking out one of the upper floor windows. Louisa. She spotted me about the same time I did her and quickly swished the curtain closed.

I was wondering how Gabi was faring and if I'd get a chance to speak with her today when I spotted her running down the street. Her dark ponytail flew out behind her, and a pink cast covered her left forearm. A line of stitches ran along her jawline near her ear.

Her concentration was so fierce, her steps pounding, that I had the uneasy feeling that she was trying to out-run some demons. She pulled to a stop in the middle of the street and walked in circles, shaking out her legs as her chest heaved from exertion.

Abruptly, as though she realized she was being watched, she glanced toward my house. I said, "Should you be doing that? You know, running with a broken arm?"

Her pained gaze landed on me, and I saw her take a deep breath. At which point, she burst into tears.

❧ Chapter Sixteen ❧

"I'm sorry," Gabi said, carefully avoiding the stitches on her face as she swiped at her eyes. "I can't seem to stop crying on you."

I put my arm around her and led her into the house, hoping she wouldn't notice the pigsty that was my living room. Between the mattress on the floor and Katie Sue's belongings on the table, and the pitchfork leaning against the TV stand, this looked more like a country flophouse than a home. "I won't melt."

Marjie poked her head out of the kitchen, gave me a questioning look, then disappeared again.

I led Gabi to the sofa, and went to grab a handful of tissues. Her wedding was tomorrow. It was supposed to be the happiest day of her life . . . If I were in her gym shoes right now, I might be sobbing, too.

Sniffling, she said, "It's just been so . . . surreal. Like I'm living a bad dream."

Sitting next to her, I handed her the tissues. "This is definitely nightmare material."

"When I found out my parents died in that plane crash it was the worst day of my life." She pressed tissues to her leaking eyes, nose. "This is a close second. I feel like I'm losing everything, but then I think about the poor woman who died and wonder how in the world could I be so selfish? At least I'm alive." She sniffled again and took a few deep calming breaths.

The poor woman. Katie Sue. My heart ached.

The scent of bacon filled the air, but I'd lost my appetite. I was sure Roly and Poly wouldn't mind getting my share of breakfast. "Katie Sue—Kathryn—was an old friend of mine. She grew up here in Hitching Post before moving away about ten years ago."

Confusion flashed across Gabi's eyes, then sympathy. "I'm so sorry. I didn't know her well at all—we were passing acquaintances at best, but I guess it makes sense now that she was around if this was her hometown. I couldn't figure out why she was here if it wasn't for the wedding."

I still wasn't sure why Katie Sue had come back. That answer might have gone to the grave with her.

"I wish I could have helped her more," Gabi said. "Maybe if I'd come across her lying there earlier . . . I tried so hard to get her up that trail."

"Is that how you broke your arm?"

"Wrist," she said, eyeing the cast. "I fell backward while trying to pull her up the trail. I broke the fall with my hand."

"Ouch."

"And then I fell again, and cut my cheek on a rock. It was . . . terrifying."

"Why didn't you just run for help?" I asked. Especially knowing she could run really well.

"I knew I didn't have time. By the time I made it to a phone, called for help, and that help arrived . . ." Her brow furrowed and she shook her head as though trying to erase bad memories. "When I found her, her pulse was so weak I wasn't even sure she was still alive at first. I was never so grateful in my whole life to get an answer to my shouts for help."

Glancing behind me, I spotted Marjie standing in the doorway to the kitchen, listening to our every word.

"What were you doing on that trail in the first place? Weren't you supposed to be at supper with the Calhouns?"

"Oh my word, that supper." She closed her eyes. "A fiasco."

"What? Why?"

"Where to start? I mean, the restaurant, the Delphinium, was lovely, and they'd gone above and beyond meeting our needs for a private room and it was such a beautiful table setting and the food was wonderful . . . But Louisa was drunk and Warren was outright angry— they'd been fighting earlier and I think they carried their disagreement to supper."

"Fighting about what?" I could only guess that it had been about Katie Sue—maybe she had been seen at Mama's chapel earlier. Perhaps it had something to do with why Katie Sue was so happy. Had Warren agreed to her demands?

"I'm not sure. I could only hear their raised voices. And Cassie was so distracted by her parents that she wasn't even making her usual comments to Landry that it wasn't too late to change his mind."

My nosiness demanded that I cut in. "Why's she so against the wedding?"

Her bottom lip jutted. "She wants Landry to marry for love, not because his father told him so."

Ouch. The hits kept on coming for Gabi.

"Warren and Louisa are the only ones on my side." She frowned. "I'm not stupid, Carly. I know that Warren only wants this wedding because he believes that Landry and I as a couple can win Warren the younger voters in a presidential election. We're America's hottest couple," she said scathingly. "We both have large social followings, and Warren wanted to tap into that."

A puppet master, Katie Sue had called him. An accurate description, it seemed.

"And Louisa?" I asked.

Biting her lip, Gabi said, "Part of it is the votes for Warren—in that family, politics comes first— but she's also hoping that one day Landry will use the popularity he gained as a musician and run for governor. But I also think she loves me like a daughter and wants me to be officially part of the family, to fulfill my mama's wishes for looking after me."

I sighed. It sounded to me like Gabi was being used, plain and simple. I think she knew it, too, but didn't have what it took to walk away from the situation. She loved Landry. She longed for a family. The high price of a loveless marriage was one she was willing to pay. It made my heart hurt.

"The worst part of the dinner," Gabi went on, her eyes filling with tears, "was Landry. He was awful."

"How so?"

"He totally ignored me and kept getting up, pacing, using the restroom, going outside for a breath of air." She shifted toward me. "I'd already slipped the love potion into his water at that point, but his behavior made me second-guess giving it to him, so I switched the glasses at the last second and 'accidentally' knocked the love potion over," she said, using air quotes around the word "accidentally." "I couldn't go through with it. Landry ended the meal before we'd even had dessert and took off. Everyone else headed back to the house but I ..."

"What?"

"I was suspicious. So I followed him." Her brow knit. "He went back to your mama's chapel, but then I lost sight of him. I checked the chapel and the grounds but he wasn't to be found."

"Did you see Katie Sue at the chapel, in the gazebo?"

She looked confused again.

"Kathryn?" I corrected.

"No, no sign of her. Or Landry either. So then I thought maybe he'd gone on the trail, to Lover's Leap— we'd talked about that spot earlier, and how romantic it sounded. So I went in after him. I thought ..."

"You thought he might be meeting someone."

She nodded. "I was grasping at straws, trying to come up with an explanation for his behavior other than the obvious."

"Obvious?"

"That he had a bad case of cold feet. Even though I knew he didn't really want to marry me, I never dreamed he'd go against his daddy's wishes and break the deal they'd made. But"—her nose wrinkled—"I'd sensed the change in the air. He was going to walk away." She laughed—there was no humor in the sound. "Not walk. Run. Run away, fast as he could."

Her comment struck me hard. "Does he jog, too?"

Swollen eyes grew wide, and she sniffled again. "Oh, I didn't mean *literally* run."

"I know." I smiled. "But does he run? Jog?"

"Yeah. A few miles a day usually. Why?"

That was interesting. He also had longish brownish hair. Had he been sent to do his father's dirty work? "He headed toward the chapel directly after supper?"

She nodded. "Why?"

"There was a jogger on the trail last night that the police are trying to find. That person could be an eyewitness." Or a killer, I silently added. "But I don't think it could have been Landry because he wouldn't have had time to change into running clothes. Did you see a jogger?"

"I didn't see anyone until I looked down that bluff and saw a body on the rocks." She drew in a deep breath. "It was just awful."

I let my guard down to read her energy and felt absolutely no deception. As suspicious as it was for her to have found Katie Sue, for Gabi it had in fact been a matter of being in the wrong place at the wrong time.

"What was Landry's excuse for his behavior?" Gabi might have a good excuse for being where she was, but where had Landry been? Did he have an alibi?

She shrugged. "I haven't spoken with him. I haven't even seen him since last night when I followed him to the chapel."

Shocked, I said, "He didn't come see you at the hospital?"

"No. Apparently, no one could find him."

"Is he missing?" Lordy, what was going on with the Calhouns?

"No, I heard him arguing with Warren late last night, so he returned from wherever he went. I couldn't hear specific words, but I imagine it was about the wedding and Landry's cold feet." Tears filled her eyes again. Tipping her head back, she inhaled deeply, trying to get hold of her emotions. Her cheeks puffed as she let the breath out. "I haven't cried this much in years. I'm not usually a cry baby."

"Nothing wrong with tears," I said. "You've been through a lot, and I'm guessing you're wrestling with some hard decisions." If she took back the love potion, she must be having second thoughts about the wedding.

"I got to thinking about what you said yesterday, about borrowing trouble." Picking at the tissue, her voice grew louder, stronger as she said, "I love Landry, I do, but if I had a sister or a friend who was willing to marry a man who openly admitted he didn't love her . . . I'd knock her upside the head. What kind of weak-willed woman would marry a guy like that?"

I stretched my legs. "Probably a woman who desperately wants a family again, and is willing to risk her heart to get it. I'm not sure I'd call her weak-willed. In a way, it's actually kind of brave."

She dropped her head and kept picking at the tissue. Shreds of it littered the floor. "But it's a completely foolish thing to do."

"It is at that."

Her gaze snapped to mine, as though she couldn't believe I'd just agreed with her. I took hold of my locket.

"What that woman didn't understand is that marrying a man who doesn't love her is opening herself up to a world of hurt. A hurt so powerful that it pales to the grief she's been carrying around at the loss of her own family."

Pain filled her eyes. "I . . . I don't want to lose Landry."

Softly, I said, "Seems to me you never really had him."

"I know," she whispered. "Lord, how I know."

Her jaw quivered before it clenched so tightly my teeth hurt in sympathy without even doing a reading on her.

She said, "Louisa and Warren have asked me to make a decision this morning about postponing the wedding. They need advance notice to hold a press conference."

"Postponing?" I asked, holding my tongue about the press conference. "Or calling it off?"

"I . . . I need to think about it. I don't want to disappoint Louisa and Warren. I have to think about my future, too. All my plans were tied into being with Landry."

A pot clanged in the kitchen, and she jumped a bit, as though suddenly realizing we hadn't been alone. "Oh! I didn't know you had company."

"Not company. A squatter."

Marjie appeared in the doorway. "You can damn well make your own coffee from now on, Carlina Bell Hartwell."

"Did I say squatter?" I smiled. "I meant my beloved houseguest."

Marjie glared.

Gabi stood. "You . . . you're the woman from last night."

"Gabi, this is my aunt, Marjie Fowl."

Gabi's gaze flew to me. "The one with the gun?"

I laughed. "Yes."

Marjie rolled her eyes.

"Are you okay?" Gabi asked her. "How's your leg?"

"Blessed ankle is broken."

Gabi held up her wrist. "I know the feeling."

Marjie narrowed her gaze. "Your face ain't looking too good, either."

It was my turn to glare.

Marjie said, "What?"

Raising her hand to her face, Gabi's lip quivered. "It's okay, Carly. I know how bad it looks. The doctors said I could probably get plastic surgery to cover the scar."

"You don't need plastic surgery. Stay right here." I dashed up the stairs and grabbed the potion I'd used on my palms. Back in the living room, I handed it to her. "Use this on it twice a day. In a few days' time you won't even know there was an injury. And come by the shop later, too. I have a potion that helps speed the healing of broken bones."

"I could use a little of that myself," Marjie said, lifting an eyebrow.

"But who would make my coffee?" I asked with a sweet-as-sugar smile.

"Sass," Marjie snapped.

Gabi said, "Thanks, Carly. And thanks for just . . . listening."

"Anytime."

"I should go. I'm sure everyone's wondering where I've gotten off to. Thanks for your help last night, Miss Marjie. And thanks for not shooting me yesterday in your yard."

Marjie folded her arms across her chest. "Don't make me regret that choice."

Gabi tipped her head. "Why would you?"

"Because, child, I can't abide a fool. If a girl like you decides to marry into that family, you're too stupid to live."

≈≈ Chapter Seventeen ≈≈

A couple of hours later, I came down the stairs to find Marjie sitting on the couch, poking away at Katie Sue's phone. She was trying to figure out the pass code.

"Might as well do something useful while I'm sittin' around here," she said.

I stood next to her, picking cat hair from my dark shorts. Hazel and Eulalie had already been by, quacking over Marjie's injuries and rehashing the news of Katie Sue's death—I'd eavesdropped on the conversation from my room, not in the mood to join the conversation.

Over bacon and eggs, Marjie and I had chatted about Katie Sue's case and her return to town. I told Marjie everything I knew, from Katie Sue's possible affair with Warren to her seeking a hex from Delia. I spilled the tea about my run-in with Lyla and how I'd promised to help Jamie Lynn. And I revealed how I knew Cletus had hurt Katie Sue before, because I'd read it in her energy.

Marjie had remembered Katie Sue well—including the switching she'd given her that one time. She hadn't recognized her last night, but I didn't know if that was because of Katie Sue's transformation into Kathryn Perry . . . or if her injuries had been too severe.

It felt good to let it all out—and I knew Marjie wouldn't go shooting off her mouth, either. Her gun, maybe. But not her mouth. She'd kept quiet when my other aunts went on and on about poor Katie Sue—and didn't so much as taunt either when both suddenly claimed they had known who Katie Sue was the whole time and weren't fooled by her phony name.

My aunts hated having anything pulled over on them.

"It'll be a miracle if you figure it out," I said, nodding to the phone.

"I don't believe in miracles. If I figure it out, it'll be from sheer will."

"Don't you mean stubbornness?"

"Patience," she corrected, pursing her lips.

I couldn't help but smile. "I have a couple of errands to run, but I'll be at the shop after that. Just call if you need anything."

She harrumphed.

I whistled to the cats. It was time to go.

"They can stay," Marjie said. "I'll keep an eye on them."

I narrowed my gaze. I didn't come out and accuse her of actually *liking* the cats, but I could tell she did. "Don't let them take advantage of you. Especially Poly."

"Don't worry none. Go on with you now. And don't forget to bring me back that bone potion."

I'd just picked up my purse when a shout from the street caught my attention. I strode to the front window and pulled back the curtain. Reporters filled the lane, curb to curb. Warren Calhoun stood on Aunt Hazel's front porch and was trying to calm the crowd with grand arm gestures. Everyone stilled.

I blinked. Until now I never fully understood the power that man held over people. But I saw it now.

"What's going on?" Marjie asked.

"Looks like Warren is giving a press conference," I said, pulling open the front door. This I had to hear.

I leaned against the porch pillar and wasn't the least bit surprised when Marjie followed me out, nightshirt and all.

She hopped over, and used the railing for support. "He's a fine lookin' man, isn't he?" she said. Then *tsk*ed. "The devil in disguise."

I glanced at her. "Not many can see through him."

"I'm not one who's ever been blinded by charm."

Truer words had never been spoken.

"Thank you all for coming on such short notice," Warren boomed. He didn't need a microphone for his voice to carry.

A reporter shouted, "Is it true one of Landry and Gabi's wedding guests was found dead last night?"

"Who was the woman?" another yelled. "A friend of the bride or groom?"

Warren held up a hand again, silencing the questions. "It is with a heavy heart that I tell you one of this family's dear friends, Dr. Kathryn Perry, had an unfortunate accident last night. While partaking in a nature hike, she slipped and fell off a cliff. Though she initially survived the fall, she later succumbed to her injuries. Louisa and I offer our deepest and heartfelt condolences to Dr. Perry's family."

Family friend? Unfortunate accident? I gasped at the

expert way he'd spun what happened. It had been no accident. His *mistress* had been murdered. My breakfast churned in my stomach.

"Can you confirm that Dr. Perry was drunk when she fell?" a reporter shouted.

I fumed. I hadn't smelled alcohol. Clearly this was just another rumor.

Warren's deliberate hesitation was a silent affirmation. However, he followed it with, "I'm unaware of her condition at the time of her death."

I wanted to shout out at the way he was manipulating everyone, making them truly believe she'd been drunk and had fallen. I couldn't, however, without hurting Dylan's investigation.

"But didn't Dr. Perry eat dinner with your family last night before her walk?" A reporter glanced at his notes. "At the Delphinium restaurant? A waiter places her there at the same time your family was dining. Surely you'd notice if she was intoxicated."

I stiffened. Katie Sue had been at the Delphinium? Why had she been there? It had to have been around the time she was supposed to have been meeting with Jamie Lynn.

Warren's jaw jutted. "If Dr. Perry was at the restaurant, it was merely coincidental. She didn't dine with the family."

"Is it true Gabi was the one who found her?" someone asked.

"Yes. In a selfless attempt to rescue Dr. Perry, Gabi herself was injured, breaking her wrist and suffering a facial wound. She's been released from the hospital and is doing well this morning."

There was a flurry of questions about the severity of the wounds, and if she'd be permanently scarred.

Marjie mumbled something under her breath. I was glad I couldn't hear what she'd said.

"What of the wedding, Senator Calhoun?" someone asked. "Is it still being held tomorrow evening?"

Warren dipped his head and steepled his fingers under his chin. Drawing in a dramatic breath, he lifted his face and said, "In light of this unfortunate incident and Gabi's injuries, the wedding is postponed indefinitely. Louisa, Cassandra, Landry, Gabi, and I will be leaving this afternoon to have Gabi seen by her personal doctor back in Shady Hollow. We request your cooperation in honoring our privacy as Gabi heals. I'm sure you all understand."

There was another round of questions, mostly about the wedding and when it would be rescheduled. Warren simply brushed the questions off with a "Too soon to know." He answered a few more questions, then ducked back into the Loon. The reporters left with a front page story to file.

I was left filled with disgust.

"The Calhouns might not have been notified yet that Katie Sue's death was a homicide," Marjie said. "That'll change their plans right quick. They're not going anywhere until Dylan has a chance to question them."

Time was ticking.

I just hoped I figured out exactly what happened to Katie Sue before the Calhouns got the all clear to leave.

Because if any of them had something to do with her death, and the longer it took to solve the crime, the more time they had to fabricate alibis and bury all the evidence.

*   *   *

"Any news for me yet, Carly Bell?"

I was in the middle of watering Mr. Dunwoody's flowers when Aunt Eulalie called over the fence that separated the two yards. It took me a second to remember what kind of news she'd be looking for.

Then I remembered. A man. She wanted me to find her a man.

"Not yet. But I'm working on it," I lied. If I'd told her I hadn't had the time to even think about looking I wouldn't have heard the end of it. "I want to make sure I pick some good candidates. These things take time. You don't want any ol' man off the street."

Beneath the brim of a large straw hat, one of her eyebrows lifted in skepticism.

Hmm. Maybe any ol' man would do after all.

"How long?" She wore a prim sixties-style pink dress. Capped sleeves, white belt cinched at her narrow waist, and an A-line skirt. Yet she was walking around her yard in bare feet.

I tipped the watering can, drenching a flower bed. Beautiful pink petals drooped under the assault. "Hard to say." I tried to buy myself some time. "A week, maybe two."

She *tsk*ed.

"You deserve the very best, don't you?" I asked, playing to her vanity. "The best takes time to find."

"Yes, yes I do." She fluffed her hair. "The best deserves the best. But if you could hurry the process, I'd appreciate it. Marjie has Johnny. Hazel has John Richard and now Earl as well. I have . . . no one but myself." Pressing her hands to her chest, her voice rose. "And though I'm simply fabulous on my own, I think my fabulousity should be shared with a fabulous companion."

"That's a lot of fabulous."

"I know, Carly Bell," she said earnestly. "I know."

"How's Earl doing?" I asked. I hadn't heard much after initial word of his attack.

"Lapping up Hazel's attention like a thirsty dog at a watering hole. The fawning"—she shook her head—"is positively nauseating."

"Is Hazel thinking of cutting John Richard loose?" Finally? *Please-oh-please.*

"Heavens, no. She loves having the attention of two men." Lifting her nose in the air, she sniffed. "I think it's shameful."

Shameful only because it wasn't Eulalie the men were fawning over. If that were the case, it would be perfectly acceptable.

Her blue eyes flared. "She's done moved Earl into the Loon until he's recuperated."

She did? "I didn't think she had any rooms left." It was, after all, why Katie Sue was supposed to stay with me.

"She has him splayed on her pullout sofa in her suite like they're at some kind of campout. People will talk. It's not decent."

People. Meaning Eulalie. Her words, however, reminded me of my conversation with Dylan this morning. Of how my aunts would talk if he showed up at my place using lights and sirens. I ducked my head so she wouldn't see my smile. One of these days I might just take Dylan up on that offer.

But then other parts of our conversation seeped into

my thoughts. Of Katie Sue and her jewelry. What had become of it? Had it been a robbery gone wrong? Or made to look like a robbery gone wrong?

I couldn't help but feel, deep down, that the Calhouns were at the bottom of what had happened to Katie Sue, but it would be foolish of me not to consider that Katie Sue's own family had something to do with her demise. Cletus, especially. All that expensive jewelry would have been an added incentive to get rid of his stepdaughter.

Eulalie leaned on the fence. Sunlight slashed across her lower face, highlighting her sharp jawline and the curve of her beautiful cheekbones. Mercy be, but she did look *a lot* like Meryl. "I'm not looking for the kind of man who will fawn on me."

"You're not?" I asked. Because it seemed to me that Eulalie adored fawning. "What kind of man are you looking for?"

"Oh," she said dreamily. "Someone who's highly intelligent, but smart and funny. A man who has his own money and isn't afraid to spend it. A man with some age. I don't have time to train a puppy, if you know what I mean." She wiggled her eyebrows.

I wondered if I could wash my imagination out with soap.

"A man who loves the ballet, a man who doesn't mind when I need my own time, a man who will cook and clean, a man who will buy me pretty sparkly things yet surprise me with flowers from the garden. A man who's grounded but a dreamer as well. A man—"

"Aunt Eulalie," I interrupted.

"Yes?"

"How many traits on that list are must haves?"

"Why, all of them, of course. You just said, the best deserves the best."

I was pretty sure *she'd* said that. "I'm afraid a man like that is going to be hard to find." Especially in Hitching Post, Alabama. The ballet? *Mercy.*

"Don't I know it. Why do you think I've been single all these years? I refuse to settle."

Settle. *My word.* Where was I going to find this perfect man? "It might take me more time than I thought." Like a year or two.

Her lip jutted. "But Marjie and Hazel . . ."

I eyed her suspiciously. "How much of finding this man is because you're looking for love, and how much is because you're trying to keep up with your sisters?"

Hands on hips, she said, "I don't like your tone."

"Because," I said, shading my eyes against the sun, "if you're just competing with Hazel and Marjie, that's a game I can play. But if you're looking for love . . . true love . . . I need to know."

Her lips pursed. "Does it have to be one or the other?"

"What do you mean?"

"I mean I want you to look for Mr. Right, but I recognize that may take some time. In the meantime . . ."

"Any man will do?"

"Not *any* man," she said, shaking her head. "I have *some* standards. But if you could find someone who would make Hazel and Marjie's eyes turn green with envy . . . that'd be perfect."

"Now who's shameful?" I asked, smiling.

She gave me a saucy wink. "Who do you think Hazel learned it from?"

❦ Chapter Eighteen ❧

Déjá Brew smelled like a little piece of heaven as I pushed through the doors, the cowbell clanging my entrance. Odell must be baking something chocolaty, because the oooey-gooey scent permeated the air, making me crave a fudge brownie something fierce.

Jessa glanced up with a welcoming smile as she took an order at a nearby table. I strode to the display case and eyed the goodies.

"I'll get you fixed right up, Carly," Jessa said, heading around the counter.

"Could you please make it a brownie instead of a cookie, Jessa? And throw in a few cupcakes as well. I have some buttering up to do."

"Sure thing, sugar." Jessa went about gathering goodies. "What's the latest on poor Katie Sue Perrywinkle, Carly? I was shocked when I found out who'd died last night."

"I haven't heard too much yet," I said, trying my best not to spill too much. Telling anything to Jessa was like taking out a full-page ad in the local paper. "I think Dylan's meeting with the coroner this morning." I didn't mention that Katie Sue had been murdered. That news would be out soon enough.

"That poor little orphan Gabi, though," Jessa said, shaking her head. "Broken arm, jagged cut on her face, wedding ruined . . . If I were her, I would've went ahead and married that Landry Calhoun. Hooked him but good before he could get away. He's a fine specimen of man." She fanned her face.

"That he is," I said, shifting uncomfortably.

Jessa pushed a pastry box my way with the cupcakes inside, and handed over a bag with the brownie and a cup of coffee. "How's your mama taking the news of the wedding cancelation?"

I tightened the lid on the cup. "I'm afraid to call and ask her."

She tipped her head back and barked out a laugh. "You always were a smart one."

"My daddy's taking care of her—he usually knows just what to do."

"Always has," Jessa agreed.

They were good together, my parents. Loved each other fiercely. I suddenly wondered what it had been like for Landry and Cassandra to grow up with parents who seemed to privately despise each other. I couldn't imagine. *I* had commitment issues, and I'd seen firsthand that love could last. No wonder Landry didn't want to marry.

I paid my tab, said my good-byes, and had just stepped into the Ring when I heard my name being called.

Smiling, I found Ainsley running toward me across the park in the middle of the Ring, her hands pressed to her chest to keep her boobs from bouncing around. I couldn't help but laugh.

When she finally reached me, she bent to catch her breath. "I'm going to regret that come tomorrow," she said.

"Maybe so, but you sure brightened my day."

Smiling, she said, "Well, hold on to your britches, because I've got more news to make your day."

"Like what?" We started walking toward Potions.

"After I heard that press conference this morning with Senator Calhoun, I went straight to work, tapping into every gossip line in town."

"Why?"

"To find out who saw Katie Sue at the Delphinium last night. I figured it'd help you create that timeline like you wanted."

My eyes lit. "Did you find out who it was?"

"Of course I did. No one knows how to work the gossip mill in this town like I do."

"You do have a gift."

"Just be glad I use my powers for good not evil."

"I think the whole town is grateful for that." Smiling, I said, "Who was it? The server?"

"Junior McGee. And not only that, but I've already exacted a promise from his mama to get him to stop by Potions later today to tell you all about it."

I reached out and gave her a quick hug. "Thank you."

She waved a hand dismissively. "It was nothing. Makes me feel better to help out." She reached into her cleavage and pulled out two sets of keys. "I need to give these back to you, too."

"What're these?"

She dropped them in my hand. "Katie Sue's keys."

"They're what?"

Sheepishly, she said, "I might have borrowed them last night from her purse. One set's the original, the other is the copy. I just got to thinking that it couldn't hurt to take a peek inside her house in Shady Hollow, and the police are probably going to confiscate all her things soon."

She was flat-out nuts. "If Dylan finds out . . ."

"No need to go blabbing."

"It *would* be good to see her place. She might have pictures. Or a diary or something."

Eagerly, she nodded. "This is what I'm saying."

"How about tonight?" I asked. "You game?"

"Oh, hell no."

I stopped, stared at her.

"If I ever got caught breaking and entering, Carter would kill me. This is as far as my criminal inclinations go. You're on your own from here on out." She gave my arm a squeeze. "I've got to get back. Call me later!"

I watched as she headed across the Ring, then shook my head and eyed my next destination. Caleb Montgomery's law office. I had a favor to ask, and I was armed and ready.

Cupcakes were his kryptonite, and I wasn't afraid to use them to assure that he'd help me figure out what was going to happen to Katie Sue's estate.

I took a deep breath and pulled open the door to Caleb's office. As soon as my eyes adjusted to the dimness, I blinked repeatedly, thinking I was seeing things.

I wasn't.

"John Richard Baldwin, as I live and breathe. What're you doing here?"

He sat behind the reception desk—a desk that had been vacant for months. Caleb was a perfectionist, and none of the assistants he hired ever lasted long. John Richard's dark hair was smoothed back, and he wore a crisp light blue shirt, the top button undone. He was younger than I was by a few years and was a rookie attorney, only a year or two out of law school.

"Well, if it isn't Broom-Hilda," he said, teasing me with the phony name I'd given him the first time we'd met.

"You can just call me Hilda now, seeing as how we're going to be kin soon." I scrunched my nose. "Uncle John Richard has such a nice ring to it. Hazel's so happy, you know. Winter weddings are simply beautiful." I batted my eyelashes. "Can I be flower girl?"

"Stop," he groaned. "You know perfectly well we're not getting married. We're not even dating."

"I don't think Hazel knows that."

"I keep telling her. She refuses to listen."

"No surprise there. We Fowl women like to hang on to our men." I flashed to an image of Dylan waiting for me at the end of a long aisle. "Most of the time. Every once in a while, we're stupid and let a good one go. Now are you going to tell me what you're doing here? Does Caleb know you're sitting there? Because I think if he sees you behind that desk, I'll be bailin' him out of jail later. He's a bit possessive of his office furniture."

"Yes, he knows I'm here. He hired me."

"I think I should sit down." I pulled up a chair and put the box of cupcakes on the desk. "Say that again."

He rolled his eyes. "He hired me."

My jaw dropped. "As a receptionist?"

"Administrative assistant," he corrected.

"There's a good use of your law degree."

He leaned back in his chair. "I was a little rash in moving here after I was fired from that Birmingham firm. I thought I'd be able to open my own firm right off. . . ."

"You're not used to small towns, are you?"

"I'm like Alice in Wonderland around here."

Wonderland fit. This town was a madhouse.

"Caleb took pity on me, and hired me on. I'm starting out here behind this desk, but if we get on well enough, then he said he'd consider hiring me on as an attorney."

"You're okay with that?"

"Pride goes before the fall, Carly. And I don't like falling. Right now I'm grateful for a paying job."

In this day and age it took a lot of courage to set ego aside. "You're all right—you know that, Uncle John Richard?"

"Aw, shucks," he said. "I'll talk to Hazel about the flower girl gig. Now"—he cleared his throat— "how may I help you this morning?"

"I came to see Caleb."

"Do you have an appointment?" he asked, clicking a few buttons on his computer.

"I don't need an appointment."

He lifted both eyebrows in surprise. "I see. Are you two, you know . . ."

"No!"

The door to Caleb's office opened, and he came out grinning ear to ear. He'd obviously been eavesdropping on us. His light eyes shimmered with humor. "Oh, come on, Carly, you know you love me."

"I do, it's true." But not like that. "I even brought you cupcakes."

His good humor vanished in a flash. He crossed his arms. "What do you want?"

I scooted to the edge of my chair. "Say someone you know just died . . . How soon can you find out the financial situation of that person? Wills and such?"

He tipped his head back and let out a breath. "No."

I stood. "Come on, Caleb. Please?"

"No."

John Richard's head turned side to side as Caleb and I verbally volleyed.

"Don't you think you owe me? After not believing me about how much danger Katie Sue was in and joking about it? I think I remember you saying that I didn't have a sense of humor anymore. Them are fightin' words, Caleb Montgomery, yet I let it go, the good friend that I am."

His gaze met mine, staring, staring, staring, until he finally blinked. "What kind of cupcakes?"

I threw my arms around him. "Thank you."

"Stop with that," he said, wiggling. He wasn't much for affection. "Tell me what you know about Katie Sue's new life as Kathryn Perry. Probate probably won't be filed for a month or so, but I can send out some discreet inquires, see if we can determine who her attorney is."

"Wait a sec," John Richard said, brightening. "Are you talking about Dr. Perry? The one who died last night?"

"Yeah," I said. "You didn't know her, did you?"

"Not personally, but I do know her attorney. I used to work in the same cube farm as him at Doughtree, Sullivan, and Gobble. . . ."

I glanced at Caleb. "Hiring John Richard is paying off already." I grabbed my brownie bag and said, "I need to go. You'll let me know if you learn anything?"

"What is it you're looking for, Carly?" Caleb asked.

I grasped the bag and looked between the two of them. "I want to know what happens to all Katie Sue's money. Does it go to Jamie Lynn? Did she have a change of heart about her mama or Lyla and leave some to them? Because with a fortune like hers, that could be a big motive for murder."

❧ Chapter Nineteen ❧

One of my favorite parts of the day was that quiet time in Potions before I opened. When it was just me and the comforting scents of the shop. I had half an hour before I turned my CLOSED sign to OPEN, and I had a lot to get done.

First things first, I stepped into the potion-making room. I quickly went through the steps to release the grimoire from its secret hiding spot in the tall wooden cabinet my grandfather had constructed decades ago.

I slid hidden panels and lifted secret boxes until I pulled the leather-bound journal from its hidey hole. Taking a seat on a stool, I carefully flipped pages, looking for a recipe that would help with Jamie Lynn's symptoms.

Leila Bell's handwriting was a thing of beauty. Scripted letters that bespoke of a different era when people took pride in their penmanship. That being said, over the years, the book had deteriorated some, and various splashes and spills marred the pages. Some were near impossible to read. I'd been telling myself for years to recopy what I could, but there was something so magical about *this* book, *these* pages, that I hated to put this one away forever.

After a few minutes of searching, I came across a potion to ease muscular aches and pains. I searched another few minutes for something that would help with nerve pain specifically but found nothing. Which wasn't all that surprising considering there probably wasn't much known about nerve conditions when Leila Bell was alive.

I tapped a page and wondered—not for the first time—if I should try concocting my own recipes. I'd always relied on the tried and true, but maybe it was time to branch out.

I let down the leaf in the cabinet, providing me with ample work surface. A counter to my left, below the pass-through window, also had plenty of space and housed a sink.

Sunbeams poked through the front windows of the shop as I gathered ingredients from the baskets and bins of dried herbs, essential oils, and supplements for the potions I needed to make. Agrimony, barberry, bee balm, and a few others for Jamie Lynn's potion, and pine oil and rosemary for the bone-healing potion for Marjie and Gabi. I preheated the oven in the break room and then headed back to the small room where all the magic happened.

As I chopped the agrimony, releasing a lemony scent, I thought about Jamie Lynn's ailments and wished I knew exactly what was causing her nervous system to attack. I racked my brain to match symptoms to diseases and started to wonder if it was a parasite of some sort.

The warm waters of the South were breeding grounds for all sorts of microscopic bugs that could wreak havoc on a body. And it would also explain why I hadn't been able to read the disease right off the bat—I couldn't diagnose what I'd never experienced.

I smiled at the recollection of an old memory, of Grandma Adelaide sneaking me into hospitals in Huntsville to visit "a dear friend," when in reality we'd go from room to room and *feel* what was wrong with the patients. It was how I'd first learned to diagnose. These days, security was much tighter, but back then, those little trips had been more invaluable than medical school would have been.

The phone rang, and I dashed into the front room to answer.

"Carrrrrly," my mama wailed. "The wedding's been canceled."

"I know," I said. "I'm sorry."

She said, "What am I to do with the thousands of dollars' worth of flowers sitting in my chapel? I ask you, what am I to do?"

I winced, having forgotten about the floral delivery. "The Calhouns are still covering the cost, right?" I hated thinking of my mama being on the hook for such a big expense.

"That's not the point, baby girl," she said shrilly. "The point is I can't walk down the aisle of the chapel for the roses, hydrangeas, and peonies filling the place!"

"Mama, take a deep breath." And a tranquilizer. "It'll be okay. We'll figure it out."

She sniffled. "You'll come over and help out your mama like the good girl you are?"

Mama was a good actress, I'd give her that, but when you had been part of her theatrics for thirty years, you knew when you were being played. "You want my help with those chairs, don't you?"

"Oh! Now that you mention it, that'd be wonderful. You're such a sweet girl for offering." Her voice sharpened. "There's three hundred of them that need to be folded up, stacked up, and put up as soon as possible. When can you come by?"

"I'm not sure," I said. "I need to find someone to cover the shop for me."

"If that's more important that your ma—"

I cut her off. "I'll see you when I see you, Mama. I have to go."

"But—"

I hung up. *Mercy.* She could have at least bribed me with cupcakes. It was the only decent thing to do.

After grabbing two potion bottles—fuchsia—from the colorful display, I headed back to my work. In no time at all, I had the herbal part of the recipes done. I funneled Marjie's and Gabi's into the pink bottles and turned my attention to Jamie Lynn's potion. I wanted her to drink it as a tea, so her method of delivery was a little different. I went back to the cabinet and unearthed the Leilara from its hiding spot and twisted the top off the tiny silver flask. I inserted a dropper and sucked up enough drops for all three potions.

Over Jamie Lynn's bowl of herbs, I squeezed in two droplets, for Marjie's and Gabi's just one. White tendrils of magic rose up, swirling and twirling before dissipating. I capped the flask and replaced it and the grimoire back in the cabinet and closed it up tightly.

I added distilled water to the fuchsia bottles and stoppers, then shook them, watching the bits of herbs and oil floating in the liquid. I set them aside and turned my attention to Jamie Lynn's. I scraped the magical concoction onto a baking sheet, then headed to the oven in the break room. I needed the now-wet herbs to dry. I baked the herbs for five minutes, then quickly put the mixture into a tea filter and pulled the drawstrings tightly to close it up. I then placed that tea bag into a purple velvet pouch and set about printing up directions.

I'd just placed the last instruction label on the tags when I heard a knock at the door. I glanced through the pass-through and saw a gangly young man peering into the shop.

Junior McGee.

I owed Ainsley big time for this one.

I wiped my hands on a dish towel and quickly pulled open the door. He smiled broadly when he saw me and said, "My mama sent me over. She says hello, and wanted me to give you this." He handed over some sort of loaf wrapped in foil.

I sniffed it. "Banana bread?"

"She makes the best in town."

"I don't doubt it." I motioned him into the shop and toward a stool at the big worktable. "Thank her for me, will you?"

"Will do." He grinned again.

I bet he made a lot of money in tips. He just had a happy, easygoing way about him. "Thanks for stopping by," I said. "You want a Coke? Some coffee?"

"No, thanks. But, Miss Carly, I'm not altogether sure why I'm here," he said, shrugging.

I tucked my hair behind my ear and said, "I don't really know how to explain it, other than to say you have information I need." I sat next to him. "I need to know all about Katie Sue Perrywinkle's visit to the Delphinium last night."

His eyes flared for a second. "Sure thing. I'm feeling badly for Jamie Lynn. Terrible shocking what happened."

"You know Jamie Lynn?"

"Same graduating class." He shrugged again. "Heard she's been sick, too. Been meaning to pay her a visit, but . . . just haven't yet."

I swung my locket on my chain. "Sometimes it's awkward to see someone you know sick like that, but just remember she's still the same ol' girl underneath."

He didn't look like he believed me.

"I didn't realize it was Katie Sue who'd come in last night—I didn't recognize her or nothin'. She was just acting strange, so she stood out."

"Strange how?"

"Real nervous." He brushed long bangs off his forehead, swooping them off to the side. "Fidgety. Kept getting up, walking around." He ducked his chin and his leg wiggled.

"What else?" I pressed, because he was nervous about something.

"I probably shouldn't say anything, but maybe it doesn't matter, because she's dead? But that's also why I think I should tell you."

"What?" I asked, feeling nervous just from sitting next to him.

"She paid Jimmy Banks five hundred dollars to slip something into someone's drink."

My jaw dropped.

"He couldn't turn down that kind of money, not with his mama just losing her job. . . ."

"What did he slip and into whose drink?"

He shrugged again. "I don't know what it was. It was purple liquid stuff in a little vial."

Delia's hex, no doubt. "Do you know whose drink?"

"All I know is it was one of the fancy women."

Mercy. Had she hexed Louisa Calhoun with baldness? I imagined the matriarch waking up today, losing handfuls of hair. She wasn't going to handle that well at all.

Or had it been Cassandra? Or Gabi?

Oh, that Katie Sue had gumption to spare.

"Where can I find Jimmy?" I asked.

"He'll be working tonight. Starts at four."

"Thanks, Junior, you've been really helpful. You can tell Jimmy I'll be stopping by."

"You're not going to"—he winced—"get him into trouble, are you?"

"Why? Because he spiked a customer's drink with an unknown substance? Could have been poison in that vial for all he knew."

Color bloomed on his cheeks. "When you say it like that . . ."

"But no, I don't aim to get him in trouble," I said, sliding off my stool, "however, I might scare a little sense into him."

But only *after* I found out who'd been hexed.

~∞ Chapter Twenty ∞~

A half hour later, I was contemplating how I could sweet-talk Ainsley into covering the shop for me this afternoon when the door opened and a woman trudged into Potions as though she were wearing cement blocks for shoes, not flip-flops.

I'd been expecting a visit from a Perrywinkle today, but never dreamed it would be this one.

"Lyla?"

Dragging her feet, she tromped to the counter. Cutoff jean shorts accented her toned legs, and her white tee was bright against her tanned skinned. Red-rimmed eyes fixed on my face. "I'm here to get that potion you made up for Jamie Lynn."

I held on to my locket and eyed her suspiciously. "Why?"

"She sent me over."

"Why would she do that? You both told me that you don't believe in my potions."

"Look it here, Carly Hartwell, I'm tired. Jamie Lynn's worse than ever. If she thinks one of your stupid-ass concoctions will help her, then by God, I'm willin' to try it at this point. I don't want to lose another sister this week."

I bit my lip to keep from being snide and saying something about how she'd lost Katie Sue a long time ago—when Lyla chased her out of town. And it was best I ignored the "stupid" comment, too, for my peace of mind.

"She's worse?" I asked. "Is she in the hospital?"

"At home for now. If she gets worse, though, I'll bring her to the ER. The stress of last night took its toll on her."

By the looks of Lyla, it had taken a toll on her as well. "It was a rough night for a lot of people."

"Yeah, well. Life's tough."

Lyla usually looked ready to take on the world, fists swinging. But right now, she looked nothing but deflated.

"Katie Sue dug her own grave," she said. "That girl never knew when to walk away."

The hairs rose at the back of my neck. I wanted to argue, but I was afraid she was right. I decided to take another track. "She did seem over her head with the Calhouns."

"Like I said, she never knew when to walk away."

"A family trait, I think."

Weary eyes flicked to me. "Maybe so."

"What were you two fighting about?" I asked.

"Money, as usual."

I had the feeling her fatigue was the only reason she answered at all.

"I dared asked for a loan, and she turned me down flat. Couldn't get off her high horse long enough to listen to reason."

"A loan for what?"

"Jamie Lynn's legs are bad off, and her arms aren't that much better. I wanted to get her one of those electric wheelchairs, but you could not even imagine the amount of money they cost. A fortune to us. Jamie Lynn said it's no big deal and tries to hide the pain, but I see it in every step she takes."

I knew the pain. I'd felt it.

"I asked Katie Sue to loosen the restrictions on Jamie Lynn's trust fund so we could take an advance." Moisture filled her eyes but she blinked it away. "It was stupid of me to ask, but I'd do anything for Jamie Lynn. Even set my pride aside. All Katie Sue kept saying was that she'd think about it. I told her we didn't have time for her to think about it, but she stubbornly refused to listen. It made me angry. We fought. I ended up walking away."

It didn't escape my notice that she was also medium height with longish brown hair. But as much as I wanted to place her as that jogger, I didn't think she'd have had time to change into a jogging suit, either.

"I've got to get back to Jamie Lynn. Is that concoction ready?"

"I'll get it." I grabbed the velvet pouch off the counter in the potion room and put it on the counter.

Lyla opened it and peeked inside. Making a sour face, she said, "A tea bag? That's your fancy potion? What about the bottles?" she asked, nodding to the display.

"Certain potions call for different methods of delivery. This one needs to be drunk like tea. The directions are on the tag, but basically, you let the bag steep in a cup of hot water for five minutes. Make sure she drinks it all."

"She usually has a cup of hot tea every morning—that's not going to interfere, is it?"

"No," I smiled. "It won't."

"Good. She can't eat much anymore because of her illness, so having the tea makes her feel a little bit like normal. Tea and toast." She shook her head and then carefully read the tag. "She usually likes a little honey in her tea, too. Can she use it with this?"

"I wouldn't mix it. It probably wouldn't hurt, but the honey, especially if it's local honey, could cause a reaction."

"The pollens and such?"

I nodded. "Not many realize that honey is full of pollen."

"I do. I'm allergic to the stuff, but Jamie Lynn loves it, and hers *is* local. Supposed to help her immune system, for all the good that's doing her."

"Are you allergic to the pollens or the honey itself?" As a healer, allergies fascinated me.

"Honeybee allergy," she said. "I had a bad reaction to honey as a kid. The doctor said it was related, even though not everyone who's allergic to bees has trouble with honey."

"Must be hard to avoid the bees in your gardens."

"Honeybees aren't really aggressive, and I always keep my EpiPen handy." She tapped the pouch. "How soon would Jamie Lynn feel a difference?"

"A couple hours at most. But, Lyla, this is only to treat her symptoms. Because I don't know what's causing her problems, I can't cure it. Has she ever been tested for parasites?"

She blanched. "Like what?"

I listed off a few off the top of my head, including the bug that caused Lyme disease. "Whatever she's fighting has invaded her nervous system. There aren't a lot of things out there that can cause problems like that."

"Not that I know of. I'll ask her doctor about it."

"Let me know how it goes."

She gave a short nod. "How much do I owe you?"

"On the house."

"I don't want any charity."

"It's not charity. It's a gift for Jamie Lynn."

Her mouth tightened. "Thanks," she ground out and turned for the door.

"Lyla?"

She faced me.

"Before you go, do you know why your mama was watching Katie Sue last night?"

Her eyes flew open wide. "She was what?"

"Dinah was seen parked in the lot near the chapel. Cletus, however, was nowhere to be found."

She shuddered. "No, I don't know why."

"Would they have reason to hurt Katie Sue?"

"They don't need reasons to hurt people," she said bitterly. "It's in their DNA. But if you're thinking they might have had something to do with Katie Sue's death, I'd follow the money trail. They'd do anything for a dollar."

It's what I'd been thinking, too, especially in light of her missing jewelry. "Is there any chance you can ask your mama if she spoke to Katie Sue?"

"No," she said firmly. "I can't. I don't speak to my

mama. Or Cletus. Haven't for years. Not since the day they killed my husband."

And with that, she walked out the door.

I immediately called Ainsley. Olive was screaming bloody murder in the background as Ainsley answered.

"Is she being torn limb from limb?" I asked.

"I'm trimmin' the ends of her hair."

"With a chainsaw?"

"Go, git, I'm done," she said loudly to her daughter. The silence was immediate.

"She has a gift," I said. "Maybe think about opera lessons?"

"Sweet baby Jesus, I need some chocolate."

"Load up, because Lyla Perrywinkle Jameson just left the shop, and on her way out she dropped the bomb that she thinks Cletus and Dinah killed her husband."

"Hold on, I'm going to lock myself in the bathroom." I heard her hurried footsteps, then a door close. "Killed him? I thought it was an accident."

"That's what I thought, too. Working on his truck, wasn't he?"

"Yeah, and the jack failed, and the truck fell on him."

I shuddered at the thought of it. "How could that have been murder? And why would Cletus and Dinah want him dead? Did you ever hear any gossip about it?"

"It was so long ago," she said. "What? Nine, ten years?"

It was about that. Travis Jameson had died a year after Jamie Lynn moved in with Lyla. He'd been twenty-six years old.

"I can't think of anything," she said. "I just remember being sad to hear about it. I never heard a whisper of murder."

"Me, either. But Lyla sure thinks so. Can you think of anyone who'd have more information?" I didn't think I'd get any more out of Lyla.

"Francie might know something. It was right about that time that Lyla joined the gardening club. I'll call her."

"Let me know," I said. "Oh, and Junior came by." I gave her a quick rundown of our conversation.

"Shut the front door. You're tellin' me that Louisa Calhoun's hair might fall plumb out?"

I glanced up and just happened to see Delia running across the park toward my shop, her cape flying out behind her. "Plumb."

"I'll be damned," she whispered. "I sure do hope no one ever slips me one of those hexes."

"You'd best stay on Delia's good side, or all that hair growing you're about to undertake might be for nothing."

"I'm growing it out, Carly."

"I'll believe it when I see it. I'll talk to you later."

I hung up just as Delia burst through the door.

"What's wrong?" I asked.

"Break-in," she gasped.

I came around the counter. "Where?"

"Your house, Carly. Hurry!"

Chapter Twenty-one

I grabbed my bag and the potions I'd made, quickly locked up the store, and raced home. A break-in. I couldn't believe it. "Is Marjie all right?"

"I think so," Delia said, jogging alongside me. "She's the one who called me when your shop phone was busy."

We were halfway down my street when a sheriff's cruiser sped down the lane, its lights flashing, its siren blaring. It angled to a stop in front of my house, and Dylan stepped out just as Delia and I reached my walkway.

He gave me an exasperated look. "Not the use of the lights and sirens I'd been hoping for."

I tried to catch my breath. "Tell me about it."

The front screen door opened and Marjie barked, "About damn time! How long's it take to get the law around here?"

As Dylan passed by, he gave me another exasperated look and ran up the steps.

Delia said, "The man knows how to fill out a uniform."

I knew. Mercy, I knew.

I glanced around—everything outside seemed perfectly normal. A serene facade to such a violation. I noted that Warren and Louisa had come out onto the porch of the Loon to gawk, and that Louisa still had all her hair.

"How long does it take for your baldness hex to take affect?"

"About twelve hours after ingestion, why?"

I quickly told her about my visit with Junior. Her eyes widened. "Louisa? *Damn.* Katie Sue had guts, I'll give her that."

As I climbed the steps and pushed on the porch door, I noticed a shiny red mobility scooter complete with a grocery basket parked in my driveway. It looked like a cross between a moped and a riding lawnmower. I'd never seen it and wondered where it had come from. Odd.

I waited for my witchy senses to kick in as I went inside, but all was calm in my witchy world.

At least, until I walked into my living room and saw Johnny Braxton laid out on my sofa, his big feet hanging over the arm. A damp cloth rested on his forehead. His eyes were narrowed in consternation, his cheeks were rosy, and all the rest of the skin I could see was covered in inflamed poison ivy.

I was going to need a new sofa.

Immediately.

Marjie sat on the coffee table, one leg bent, her injured leg stretched out. Her cheeks were rosy as well, but her eyes were alight with life. "Take your time," she said. "No hurry. No big deal. I don't mind scaring off the burglar on my own."

I noticed that she was wearing a pair of loose capris and a tee. Her normal clothes. Either she sent someone who was allowed inside her house to fetch them, or she'd stubbornly hopped down the street herself to collect some personal items from her place.

"Hey," Johnny protested, "I helped."

Marjie rolled her eyes. "You helped him get away is what you did."

Johnny scratched his arm. "Nonsense."

"I had the guy cornered and then you—"

"What happened, Miz Marjie?" Dylan asked, interrupting their bickering.

I walked around. Peeked in the kitchen. Roly and Poly were napping atop the fridge. I kept looking for anything amiss—or missing—and saw nothing out of place. Except that my house seemed inordinately clean. That was definitely different. The dust bunnies had been evicted, kicked to the curb. My curtain sheers looked freshly laundered. The wood floors gleamed. A strong lemon scent filled the air, and I spotted the can across the room, atop a bookcase.

I was going to have to ask Aunt Marjie to move in.

"I'd just went into the kitchen to give the kitties a treat," Marjie said, "and when I came back in here, there was a person rooting through the stuff on the coffee table."

My gaze zipped to the piles that were once on the table. Katie Sue's things. The stacks had been toppled.

"Looked to be searching for something specific, and didn't seem to realize I was even here. Probably saw Carly leave and thought the house was empty. Once he found Katie Sue's phone and purse, he turned to go.

That's when I pounced. Good thing I'd been using Carly's pitchfork as a cane, because I caught the bastard by surprise by threatening him with it."

"You keep saying 'he,'" Dylan said. "It was a man? What'd he look like?"

Her lips pursed. "Don't know if it was a man, truth be told. Huh. I suppose it could have been a woman. The guy—the intruder—wore a ski mask along with a black sweatshirt with a hood and black sweatpants and black gloves. I couldn't tell a gender."

With a sinking heart, I realized I'd heard this description before.

"Was he black?" Delia asked. "Or white?"

"Definitely white. I could see the skin around the eyes. Which were blue," she said to Dylan.

He wrote it in a small notebook. That new detail didn't help much. Seemed everyone involved in Katie Sue's case had blue eyes.

"What happened next?" Dylan asked.

"Bugger gripped Katie Sue's purse for dear life and turned to run. I lunged forward and forked him in the ass."

My jaw dropped. "What?"

"Forked him," she repeated, making a jabbing motion as though she were an expert fencer. "Right in the patootie!"

"You're my hero, Miss Marjie," Delia whispered, her voice full of awe.

"He squealed like a stuck pig and fell over," Marjie said, a gleam in her eye. "I had him good and cornered. Until . . ."

"Until what?" Dylan asked.

Marjie twisted to give Johnny a death stare.

"I knocked on the door," Johnny said, glaring right back at her. He scratched his neck.

I winced and went to find some calamine.

"The distraction," Marjie said, "was just what the intruder needed to scramble away. I yelled for Johnny to stop him, but one swipe of the burglar's leg and Johnny was flat on *his* ass. The bastard got away." She let out a weary sigh.

"With Katie Sue's purse?" I asked, bringing the calamine from the powder room. I handed it to Johnny.

"'Fraid so," she said.

"Which way did he go?" Dylan asked.

"Didn't see," Marjie said. "I was too busy tending to this one." She jerked her head to Johnny.

Johnny frowned while spreading pink goo on his arms. "And here I was just trying to help by bringing you that scooter. It's the least I could do since it was my idea to go on that hike."

I almost laughed aloud. Marjie use a scooter? That'd be the day. The woman wouldn't even use crutches unless it came in pitchfork form. And really, after hearing about his "stomach bug" and seeing his case of poison ivy, I think he'd more than paid for his suggestion.

"I don't need no scooter," Marjie said, crossing her arms.

"Well, I'm not taking it back," he said, sputtering as he tried to sit up.

"You will, too!"

"She'll take it," I cut in.

"Stay out of this, Carly Bell," Marjie said sternly.

I raised my voice. "She's keeping it. End of story." I

walked over and grabbed the pitchfork from against the wall. I shoved it in Dylan's direction. "I'm sure there's DNA on that. I want it back, though."

Everyone stared at me. I set my hands on my hips and dared someone to say something.

Dylan opened his mouth, then snapped it closed again, before turning his attention to the coffee table. He poked through Katie Sue's belongings. "You should have told me you had Katie Sue's things here."

I shrugged. "I forgot."

"Doesn't look like much."

I looked at the fallen clothing. "She had packed for only a couple of days."

"What was in the purse?" he asked.

"The usual. A wallet, some makeup. Nothing incriminating at all."

"Bastard broke in for nothing," Marjie said. "But he now has a hiney full of holes, so it shouldn't be too hard to find him. You should get to lookin.'"

"Yeah, Dylan," I said, teasing. "Does Marjie have to do *everything*?"

She hopped over, patted my face, and said, "You're forgiven for the squatter comment earlier." She turned to Dylan. "Start by lookin' at those Calhouns. They're all kinds of shady."

"Better get going then," he said, trying not to smile. "Call if you remember anything else, Miz Marjie."

"You want backup?" Johnny asked, standing up.

If he could see a mirror right now, he'd never ask such a thing.

Marjie jabbed a finger in his chest. "Dylan's right capable. You sit. I'll bring you some sweet tea."

For a second, just a flash, I saw his eyes soften as he gazed at her. Then it was gone. "If the sergeant needs assistance, I aim to help."

Dylan's shoulder radio crackled to life. A male voice came across the line, speaking a code I couldn't decipher. Dylan said to us, "I'll be right back." He stepped into the kitchen.

Marjie glared at Johnny. He sat.

Delia said, "I want Marjie to adopt me."

I fished in my bag for Marjie's potion and handed it to her. "I can help you out as well, Mr. Braxton, with that poison ivy."

"I'm done with your potions. I haven't adjusted to your last one." Lifting an eyebrow at Marjie, he frowned.

I shrugged. "It's your skin."

Dylan suddenly rushed back into the living room and paused long enough to say, "The temporary mail carrier filling in for Earl was just attacked."

"Where?" I asked.

"Next door."

Chapter Twenty-two

Dylan and Johnny ran ahead as Delia and I stayed with Aunt Marjie as she navigated the front steps. She'd set her stubbornness aside for the time being and actually used one of the crutches given to her the night before. One.

"Let me get the other," Delia suggested.

"No," she growled, then to me, added, "and I'm not using that ridiculous scooter, neither."

At the sound of a siren, I peered down the street. An ambulance had rounded the corner. A small crowd had already gathered in front of Mr. Dunwoody's—probably drawn out from Dylan's arrival, and now cemented in place by the EMTs showing up. "Good, because I have plans to give it to someone who will use it."

Her eyebrows shot up. "You givin' my gifts away without asking?"

"Yes," I said. "Now get a move on, or I'm going to stick you in that basket on the scooter and drive you over."

Her lip twitched, but she kept quiet and hobbled next door faster than I thought she'd be able. Delia and I kept near to her in case she wobbled, but she made it just fine.

Using her crutch, she cleared a path through the crowd, loudly yelling, "Comin' through!" and charged through the open gate of Mr. Dunwoody's yard.

All the action seemed to be happening near his colorful wildflower garden. We rounded the flower bed and found Eulalie kneeling on the ground, the head of José Antonio Rodriguez in her lap. She was smoothing his hair and cooing to him that he was going to be just fine. Dylan and Johnny were kneeling next to them, and Dylan was listening as José told them what happened.

The EMTs brushed past us, and set down enormous bags before taking over the care of the patient from Eulalie, who didn't stray far from the fallen postman.

Dylan walked over. "Said he heard something unusual and went to investigate. Someone knocked him on the head from behind and dragged him out of sight. His mailbag is missing."

"An awfully bold attack in the middle of the day," Delia said. "Mr. Dunwoody's yard is wide open to Eulalie's patio, and she's got an inn full of guests who could have seen it happen."

"Not anymore," Marjie said. "Most were reporters or wedding guests who cut their stay short when the wedding was canceled this morning. The inn's all but cleared out."

It was bold. Even though Eulalie's inn now had vacancies, Mr. Dunwoody's yard could be seen from several windows in my house. But then I recalled what

Marjie had supposed earlier—whoever broke in at my place hadn't realized someone was inside.

Which gave me the shivers . . . because someone had been watching the comings and goings on this street quite closely.

"Eulalie was out watering her flowers," Dylan said, "when she heard moaning coming from Mr. Dunwoody's yard. José had been out cold for a while at that point."

Johnny marched over to us, his barrel chest leading the way. "Two mail carriers whacked upside the head in two days? What's going on around here?"

Oh, nothing much, I wanted to say. Just a little extortion plot gone horribly wrong.

"The town is fallin' apart at the seams," Marjie said. "Now help me over to a chair, you big lug. I need to sit down. This blessed crutch is hurting my armpit something fierce."

Concern filled his eyes. Reaching out, he settled a hand at her back and he led her to Mr. Dunwoody's front porch. She glanced back at us and winked. *Ah.* She'd known we couldn't talk openly about Katie Sue's case in front of Johnny or else risk the whole town knowing every detail by supper time.

"Someone's getting desperate," Dylan said as soon as they were out of earshot. "Someone who wants that package Katie Sue mailed off yesterday."

"Can't blame them," I said. "Even though Katie Sue is dead, whatever she was using as ammunition against the Calhoun family is still floating around somewhere."

"I don't get it." Sunlight glinted off Delia's white

blond hair. "If the package was mailed yesterday, it's already in the postal system. What's the point of attacking another mailman today?"

Dylan's eyes narrowed. "Carly, if you mailed a letter to Delia, how long would it take to arrive at her house?"

I lifted a shoulder in a half shrug. "A day? Two at the most. Local letters are processed quickly—" My words fell away as what Dylan was getting at registered. "Katie Sue sent it local."

Delia nodded. "That makes sense now. But not just local. To someone who lives on this road. It's the only reason that mailman would be attacked right here—before he could deliver mail to your house."

She and Dylan both looked at me. I said, "My house? I suppose it's possible."

"Not possible," Dylan challenged. *"Probable."*

"But who could have known it was being mailed to Carly?" Delia asked. "If we know that person, then we know who's behind these attacks."

"I know who," I said. "There's only one person who saw the address on the envelope."

"Who?" Delia asked.

"Louisa Calhoun. The front of the envelope was facing her when we wrestled for it yesterday at the Loon. I don't know what's in that envelope, but whatever it is has Louisa and Warren desperate enough to assault a mail carrier to get it back."

"Warren's already lawyered up," Dylan said. "He's supposed to meet me this afternoon for formal questioning. I'll ask about the envelope then."

"So the family isn't leaving town?" I asked. I'd been

worried they'd slip away and somehow get out of having to answer questions.

"Not anytime soon," he said. "They've agreed to stick around for questioning."

"That's right friendly of them," Delia said suspiciously.

Dylan grinned. "I threatened to charge them with obstructing the investigation if they left, and when Warren laughed at that, I then threatened to reveal to the press just how involved the family was with Katie Sue. Suddenly they decided a few more days in Hitching Post would suit them just fine."

I smiled. "Look at you fighting dirty."

"Care Bear, when you're dealing with pigs, sometimes you've got to roll in the mud."

Didn't I know it.

We all turned and looked toward the Loon. At some point Cassandra and Gabi had joined Warren and Louisa on the front porch. Gabi stood far away from the others, as though having been segregated from the family. To me, the separation was confirmation that she'd outright canceled the wedding, not just postponed. Just as she believed would happen, the fissure between her and the Calhouns had already taken place. Clearly, she had been cast out.

Dylan said, "Let's not forget there are other suspects in Katie Sue's death as well. I still haven't been able to track down the Cobbs."

Which reminded me to tell him about my conversation with Lyla. And her odd statement that her husband had been murdered. He promised to look into it, and as

the EMTs loaded José onto a stretcher, he went to speak
to them.

Eulalie bounded over, her skirts flying out around her.
Her eyes lit with excitement. "Hot diggety, Carly Bell.
Here I was askin' you to find me a man and lo and behold,
one dropped right out of the sky for me to find like a gift
from above. It's fate. *Kismet.*" Dramatically, she pretended to swoon, and then kissed my cheek. "I'm off to
the hospital to keep José company. Doesn't he have the
most romantic name? *José Antonio.*" She sighed.

I couldn't help but smile at her exuberance. "Yeah,
but does he like ballet?"

"Oh, who cares," she said. Then winked and ran off.

"I hope he's single," Delia said.

"Me, too." I wanted it to work out for her, not only
because it let me off the hook of finding her a man, but
because she seemed so happy.

"I wish there were a way we knew for surc if that
package had been in José's bag," Delia said.

I hated thinking that the Calhouns might have gotten
their hands on it. Simply because it may be the only evidence that proved one of them had motive to kill her.

"But maybe it's a good thing if it was intercepted,"
Delia added.

I shaded my eyes against the sun and gave her a puzzled look. "Why's that?"

"Because, Carly, if it wasn't, and it's still out there
waiting to be delivered to you . . . then it places you in
danger, too. And maybe they won't stop at knocking you
upside the head."

I bit my thumbnail. I hadn't thought of it that way, but

it was true. However, I refused to live in fear of what *could* happen. "Katie Sue might have taken a lot of secrets to the grave, and some are out of our control at the moment"—like her phone messages now that her phone had been stolen and that envelope—"but I wonder if there are others we could still discover."

Delia's eyebrow lifted. "What're you getting at?"

"Are you up for a road trip?"

Chapter Twenty-three

A half hour later, Delia, Boo, and I sat in the front of my Jeep, a shiny red scooter in the back. The plan was to drop the scooter at Jamie Lynn's, then shoot down to Birmingham to snoop around Katie Sue's house.

I was beyond grateful to Ainsley for nicking those keys last night. If she hadn't, they would have been stolen right along with Katie Sue's purse this afternoon.

Wind whipped through the open windows, tossing my hair about as I said, "What Dylan doesn't know won't hurt him." We'd been talking about the fact that I hadn't shared my plan with him.

"Are you trying to convince yourself or me?"

"Myself."

"That's what I thought."

I made a face at her. She smiled as she tucked her hair behind her ears. Boo had his head stuck out the window and was happily sniffing all the outdoor scents.

Lyla Perrywinkle Jameson lived in a small farmhouse, about ten minutes from the center of town. Just far enough to have a measure of quiet and enough land for her gardens, but close enough to be part of the community.

I took the scenic route to her place so I could drive past Cletus and Dinah's trailer. I slowed in the middle of the road, grateful no one was behind us. The trailer was set back a ways from the road, and piles of rusty parts that made me long for a tetanus shot sat in a heap near the gravel driveway. The trailer had a blue tarp on its roof, and broken windows had been mended with duct tape. Weeds had overtaken the walkway, a half-dead hedge of rhododendrons had been planted in front of the trailer, the sparse purple blooms on the surviving plants the only bright spot in the whole landscape. There was no sign of the beat-up pickup truck Dinah had been driving lately.

"What're you looking for?" Delia asked.

I shrugged. "I don't exactly know. I keep thinking about what Lyla said, about how Cletus and Dinah didn't need a reason for hurting people, that it's in their DNA. I don't want to believe Dinah would let anything happen to Katie Sue, being her mama and all . . ." Lifting my foot from the brake, the Jeep rolled forward. "But it can't be ruled out."

Silently, Delia nodded, as she stared out at the passing landscape.

Streets narrowed the farther I traveled from the Ring, and the road Lyla lived on was bordered on both sides by acres of woods. I slowly turned into her pockmarked driveway, not wanting the scooter to tip over.

The farmhouse itself had seen better days, with peeling paint and a few missing shutters. But what was lacking in the house's cosmetics was made up for in the land that surrounded the place. Lyla's farm was her pride and joy. She grew just about everything from plants and shrubs to fruits, vegetables, and herbs.

She supplied many of the local restaurants, and on weekends, she sold her crops at the local white elephant sale at Carter Debbs's church, and townsfolk knew they could come knocking on her door if they needed something during the week. She supplemented her income by entering area baking contests, and had made quite a name for herself as a top competitor.

There were some, like Francie Debbs, who didn't appreciate the fierce competition, but I had to admire someone who tried everything to get ahead. Even if I didn't like that person much.

For someone like me, who had been raised on the healing properties of plants, this place was heaven on earth. I envied Lyla for what she could do, because for all my talents, gardening was not one of them. My thumb was as black as could be.

"Doesn't seem like anyone's home," Delia said.

True enough. The front door was closed, and there was no truck parked in the drive.

"No, wait. Look." Delia pointed.

Someone had stepped out the side door, took one look at us and froze as though we'd just shined a spotlight on her. "Isn't that interesting," I said, shoving the Jeep into park.

Delia and I hopped out before the woman could scurry off. After a second, the woman straightened and came toward us, her flip-flops flapping on the stone pathway.

"What're you two doing here?" Dinah Perrywinkle Cobb said, her voice low. "Besides trespassin'?"

Shiny blue eye shadow colored her lids, and thick black liner rimmed her sunken eyes. Her permed blond hair was teased sky high, many of the ends split and broken. Bright red blush had been swiped on hollowed cheeks, and hot pink lipstick stained thin lips. Her teeth were dark and rotting. Skeletal arms poked out of a pink tank top, and Daisy Dukes shorts revealed thin, wrinkly legs. I saw what looked like a syringe in her pocket, noted the needle marks on her arms, and could only shake my head at the choices she'd made in life.

"What're *you* doing here?" I countered. "Trespassin'?"

"Visiting my baby girl Jamie Lynn," she said quickly, her glossy eyes narrowed. She crossed her arms, then uncrossed them. Tapped one foot, then the other. The woman couldn't stand still.

I wondered what she was currently on, what drug. Because it was something. "We're here to see her, too."

"Well, she ain't home. I just checked. That's why I was leaving."

"Looked to me like you were sneaking out," I said.

"Well, I weren't," she countered, tapping her foot in agitation.

Delia slid her locket on its chain. "How'd you get here?"

"Walked."

"It's a bit far," I said. At least two miles from here to her trailer. And in flip-flops, too.

"I got dropped off," she said, changing her story. "I come every Friday afternoon when Lyla's at her fancy gardening club. Jamie Lynn shoulda told me she wouldn't be round today."

"You meet here?" I prodded, wondering how much I could get out of Dinah. "Thought Lyla banned you from her house?"

"She ain't the boss of me. Or of Jamie Lynn, though she likes to think she is."

"I mean, she has good reason—don't you think?" I asked. "To keep you out? After all, you and Cletus killed her husband. That'd make any daughter turn against her mama."

Her eye twitched. "No idea what you're talkin' about."

"No?" I asked. "Well, you should reacquaint yourself, because Travis's case is being reopened in light of Katie Sue's murder and how you and Cletus might be involved with both." I was bluffing the mouth off my face, but hoped to the heavens she fell for it. "The sheriff's office is looking for you right now." That part at least wasn't a lie.

Her gaze darted around, and I could practically see the panic rising beneath the surface. "I didn't have a thing to do with Travis and that phony life insurance policy," she blurted.

Whoa. Phony life insurance? *Follow the money,* Lyla had said. She'd known what she was talking about. "What about Katie Sue? How'd you even know she was in town?"

"Got a note." Her brows furrowed.

"From who?" I pressed. *Come on, come on; keep talking.*

"Don't know. It weren't signed. Told us Katie Sue was back in town, and that she was staying at the Loon."

"Did Cletus ransack Katie Sue's room?"

Her gaze darted around again. She was looking for an

escape route. Whatever she'd taken to get high had dulled her senses enough to talk to us, but it wasn't enough to make her forget that she could get in trouble talking the way she was. "No way. He only wanted to talk to her. Ask about a loan. But he couldn't even get close to the place."

That rang true, considering he'd been hiding in Marjie's yard.

"Why were you watching the chapel last night, and where was Cletus?" I asked.

"When was this?" she asked, scratching her forearm.

"About seven." Her fidgeting was making me antsy. "You were parked at the edge of the parking lot near the Ring."

She scratched her neck. "I don't know," she said. "I think that's about the time Cletus had gone to get us drinks from the coffee shop."

I frowned. It would be easy enough to check with Jessa to see if it was true.

"You didn't see anything going on at Carly's mama's chapel?" Delia asked, narrowing her eyes.

"Like what?" Dinah's gaze jumped around. She was itching to get out of here.

"Like Katie Sue being there?" I said. "Did you see what happened to her? Did Cletus do something to her?"

Her eyes flew open. "I told you. He was getting us drinks. And I was napping, waiting for him to get back. I didn't have nothing to do with what happened to Katie Sue." She spat on the ground. *"Kathryn Perry,"* she mocked in a hoity-toity voice.

"You say *you* didn't have anything to do with the deaths of Travis and Katie Sue," Delia said. "But did Cletus?"

My nerves were on edge, waiting for an answer. This could help crack the whole case.

Again, Dinah's gaze jumped around. "I—"

But before she could say anything else, a truck roared up the driveway, nearly slamming into my Jeep. Cletus hung his sorry head out the window and hollered, "Get in, woman!"

Fear slid into Dinah's eyes as she gave us one last look and took off running for the truck. We watched her go, and listened as Cletus cussed us a blue streak as he reversed out of the drive.

We stood there staring at the dust the truck had kicked up, long after it was out of sight.

Finally, Delia said softly, "Dinah reminds me of my mama."

I thought my aunt Neige, one of the most beautiful women I'd ever laid eyes on, would stroke out at being compared to Dinah. But the sincerity in Delia's voice stopped me from making a joke. "How so?"

"There are just some women out there . . . women who'd do anything for the approval, the love, of a man. Even at the sacrifice of their own children."

Ah. It hadn't been a physical comparison. This might be worse. I studied my cousin, my heart pounding. What had happened to her? I wanted to ask, but I couldn't bring myself to do it. Delia wasn't an open book. She preferred to reveal herself to me a chapter at a time, and I couldn't go asking her to skip pages just so my curiosity could be satisfied. I finally said, "You think Dinah might have had something to do with Katie Sue's death?"

"I think, Carly"—she grabbed her locket—"that if

Cletus wanted it done, Dinah wouldn't think twice about killing her daughter."

We left the scooter on Lyla's front porch, and made the almost two-hour trip to Shady Hollow in an hour and a half.

The ride down had been a somewhat somber one.

This case was taking a toll on me, and apparently dredging up painful memories for Delia. I hoped Dylan was having some luck interviewing the Calhouns.

Fortunately, Katie Sue didn't live in one of the many gated communities in the area, or else we would have had to figure out a way to break in. As it was, we drove down the street, parked in Katie Sue's driveway, and unlocked her front door without incident.

A pile of mail sat on the foyer floor, having been slid through the slot in the door. I gathered it up and flipped through each piece—no sign of a manila envelope. I set the stack on a side table and looked at Delia.

"I don't like this place," she said, holding Boo in the crook of her arm.

I didn't care for it, either. There was a chill in the air that had nothing to do with the air-conditioning. "Let's hurry, then. We're looking for anything related to the Calhouns, especially Warren. Photos, letters, that kind of thing. Anything that would provide evidence for him getting rid of her."

She nodded and headed down the hallway toward the bedrooms. I went straight for the study, which was housed behind two French doors, off the entryway.

I quickly went to her desk and opened drawers, scanned files. Nothing much here. I did find some finan-

cial planning papers and whistled at her net worth—
she'd invested well. But I didn't find a copy of her will.

Two elaborately framed diplomas hung on the wall,
and as I read them, I thought about the girl who so badly
wanted to become a doctor. She'd earned her undergrad
in biology at Clemson, and her medical degree from
Johns Hopkins Medical School.

My heart hurt for her. For all that she had lost, all that
had been taken away from her. My grief quickly turned
to anger at the person who'd thrown her off that bluff.

As my eyes watered, a splinter of truth pierced my
righteousness.

Had Lyla been right? That Katie Sue never knew
when to walk away? After all, she'd resorted to extorting
Warren Calhoun.

Katie Sue had said she was fighting for love, and as I
stood here, I recalled something I'd said to Gabi the day
I'd met her.

*Sometimes wanting something so badly makes you
forget right from wrong. Especially when it comes to matters of the heart.*

Katie hadn't forgotten right from wrong. She knew
exactly what she'd been doing, and had been willing to
take the risk for the man she loved.

As I looked around this empty office, at the chair that
would never be sat in again, at the diplomas that would
never again be put to use . . . I thought about Warren. If
he'd killed her to cover up their affair, I didn't know if
love had been worth the cost.

But maybe to Katie Sue it had been.

I had to admit that Katie Sue hadn't been perfect.

I thought she had been. With her stunning transformation, but again, that had been superficial. Deep down, it turned out that Katie Sue had been as flawed as the rest of us.

I had to remember that. And also keep in mind that no matter the questionable things she'd done, she hadn't deserved the death penalty.

In the living room, light filtered through curtain sheers as I looked around. I poked around bookcases, and when I opened a wooden box, I found a stack of old letters tied with a pink ribbon.

The letters she'd sent to Jamie Lynn—the ones Lyla had sent back. "Return to Sender" was written in bold script on every envelope. Without hesitation, I slipped the letters into my bag. I figured it was long past time Jamie Lynn saw them. I'd make sure they were delivered.

Glancing around, I noted that several pictures were missing from the walls—noticeable by the nails and dust outlines left behind. Curiosity killed me. What had been the subject of the photos? Warren and Katie Sue?

It was obvious the Calhoun goons had already been here. Delia and I were wasting our time in looking for evidence. We weren't going to find anything that linked Katie Sue to the family.

This trip had been a dead end.

Chapter Twenty-four

If setting up three hundred chairs had been a nightmare of a job, packing them up was a little taste of hell. It was ninety-four degrees in the shade, and there wasn't a cloud in the sky.

This witch was melting.

I did have enough sense about me to wear a pair of gloves, though they were now soaked with perspiration and chafing had begun.

Delia and I had made it back to Hitching Post in record time. I'd dropped her off at her shop and had come straight here. Physical activity (and peanut butter) had always helped me work through my troubles, but being here where Katie Sue's body had been found left me more disturbed than when I arrived.

I loaded two more chairs onto the rolling rack. A perimeter of police tape cordoned off the gazebo. It was a bright yellow reminder that there weren't always happily-ever-afters. Mama was beside herself to get that tape removed, the gazebo bleached, and erase any signs that something horrible had happened here. She had four weddings lined up on Sunday, and was worrying that the brides would take one look at that tape and bail.

Short term, it was a valid concern.

Long term, this incident was bound to be forgotten. And if it wasn't completely, it would be written off as a fluke crime. A love affair gone wrong or a family dispute that got out of hand. Explanations that potential couples could nod their heads at and murmur "that's too bad" and happily go on with their own plans. The crime didn't affect them. Their dreams.

As I snapped another chair closed, leaned it on my hip, and reached for another, I recalled something Katie Sue had said the day before.

"Give it a week and no one will even remember I was here."

She'd been talking about after she left town to go home . . . but the truth was, except for a few, like Jamie Lynn and me, she *would* be forgotten soon.

The realization made me so sad, I staggered a bit.

"You might want to sit yourself down on one of those seats before you pass out from heat exhaustion."

I glanced up and found Ainsley striding toward me, her short legs working double time. I put the two chairs on the rack and glanced at what I had left. Twenty at most. "I just want to get it done."

"Your mama's lucky to have you," she said, handing over an iced coffee from Dèjá Brew. My friends and family knew me well.

"I plan to remind her every day for the rest of my life." I took the cup. "Thank you. This is a lifesaver."

Ainsley snapped a chair closed and set it on the

ground. "I went by Potions to see you and was surprised it was locked up."

"Crazy day."

"You should have called me to cover the shop."

"I hate imposing on your day off."

"Carly Bell Hartwell, what are best friends for if not imposing?"

Unexpected tears filled my eyes.

"What's that?" she asked, squinting. "Stop it right now. Stop. It," she said in her sternest mother voice. Then added, "Damn," as her eyes welled too. We could never cry around each other without the other tearing up, too. It was an emotional connection I couldn't quite explain.

"Sorry," I said, inhaling deeply. "There are just some days you really appreciate what you have."

"Some *weeks*," she corrected. She then got in my face and asked, "Is my mascara running?"

"No. Is mine?" I joked, leaning down.

Tipping her head back, she laughed. "It hightailed out of here hours ago by the looks of you. You look plumb tuckered out."

I loved her laugh. It was so infectious that I found myself smiling despite my gloomy mood.

She snapped two more chairs closed and added them to her stack on the ground. "After I saw the shop was closed, I was headed to your place when I ran into your mama, who told me you were here."

I slurped mocha-flavored deliciousness. "What's going on? Did you find something out about Travis Jameson?"

"Damnedest thing about him," she said. "All anyone remembers is that it was an accidental death. A freak accident but an accident."

It had been freak. Travis had been working on the back axle of his truck and had taken off the two back tires and jacked the truck up to work underneath it. Somehow the jack didn't hold, and the back end of the truck had fallen to the ground, crushing him.

I suppose if someone had tampered with the jack . . . it could have been murder. But why wouldn't Lyla have said something before now?

"But that's not why I came," she said, setting another chair in her pile. She then bent down, lifted all six chairs and carried them to the rack and slid them into place.

I stared. "Are you Wonder Woman?"

She said, "Years of practice at the church hall."

I was still in awe. "You need a cape."

"I'll leave the capes to Delia." Her cheeks flushed. "For now."

I didn't think I wanted to know about the flush. I was already traumatized by the kissy noises Carter made.

"Anyhow, I heard you were planning to meet with Jimmy at the Delphinium tonight."

I didn't even question how she knew. Being the preacher's wife was like she had wiretaps all over town. Direct access to all the latest news.

I took another sip and glanced down at myself. "I should probably go home and change first."

She made quick work of three more chairs and barely broke a sweat. "Don't bother. He's not there."

"What? Where is he?" I had the sudden, horrifying image of the Calhouns bumping him off to keep him quiet.

"Shady Hollow. Got himself a job at a fancy country club down there. Making quadruple what he makes here.

And his mama got a job there as well. They left a couple hours ago."

"The Calhouns bought him off." It was better than bumping him off, I had to admit, but it was going to be much harder to get any information out of him now. Not with the Calhouns' deep pockets helping his whole family.

"Sorry," she said.

"Not your fault. Those Calhouns always seem to be one step ahead of us."

"It's probably why they're so dang successful."

Probably, but I'd tell Dylan about Jimmy anyway. Maybe he could get him to talk somehow. But I doubted it. He had little to gain by helping us, and everything to gain by helping the Calhouns.

Ainsley stuck around to help me roll the chairs to the storage shed behind Mama's cottage before she set off for home.

I'd crossed the footbridge and was just headed into the chapel to help Mama figure out what to do with all the flowers when my witchy senses sent a shiver down my spine. I froze, scanning the landscape. Mama's cottage, the shed, the back of the chapel, the woods . . . I didn't see anything, but I was on guard as I picked up my pace.

"Hey!" someone shouted.

I turned and saw Cletus Cobb pop out of the woods like a rabid raccoon. He swaggered toward me, his shorts drooping, his tank dingy. Gooseflesh popped out on my arms as I wondered how long he'd been in there, watching me.

"What do you want?" It was never anything good when he was concerned.

He kept coming toward me, like he was planning to

get as close to my face as Ainsley had been when she asked me to inspect her makeup. I held out my arm. "You can stop right there."

"Why?" he asked, sneering. Greasy hair hung to his shoulders, and spittle gathered in the corners of his mouth. "You scared of me?"

"Should I be?" I asked.

The question seemed to throw him off, and thankfully, he stopped about two feet away. Enough for me to catch a whiff of his horrendous body odor. He had the same glassy eyes as Dinah had earlier, and again I wondered what they were on. Not that it really mattered in the grand scheme of things.

"That depends," he snarled.

"On what?" I was dirty. I was tired. And I was pretty sure I smelled as badly as he did. *Mercy*. My patience was worn thin, and the less time I spent around this cretin the better.

He jabbed a finger toward me. "On you. If'n you keep buttin' into my business, I'm gonna have to do something about it."

"What business is that?" I asked. "The drug business? Because I don't want any part of that. The business where you killed your son-in-law for insurance money? That's being covered by the police who're reopening the case. The business of you stalking Katie Sue? Yeah, I have some questions about that."

Rage infused his face, his coloring going from sickly yellow to scarlet, his lips twisting into a grimace, his eyes narrowing on a target.

Me.

Just as he was about to lunge forward, a torrent of

water blasted him in the head, knocking him sideways from the shock. He gasped and sputtered as Mama raced forward, dragging the hose along with her as she kept it aimed on Cletus. She soaked him head to toe as she shouted, "Get your sorry self off my property, Cletus Cobb, and don't you ever think of coming back!"

He snorted, trying to keep his nose out of the stream as he scrabbled for footing. Finally, he stumbled forward, and Mama blasted him in the ass. He took off sprinting toward the woods, hitching up his pants as he went.

I watched him go as Mama shut off the water. For all his faults, the man was fast as a jackrabbit.

"Shoo-ee!" Mama cried. She turned to me and pulled me into a hug, sweat and all. "Are you all right, baby girl?"

I smiled as she squeezed the life out of me. "I am now."

She finally let me go. *"Pshaw.* You probably could have taken him."

Probably. Maybe. "I'm glad I didn't have to find out."

"Well, you know your mama's always there for you when you need her most."

I knew. For all my mama's craziness and antics, I knew that I could always count on her.

"Lordy, that man fell straight out of the ugly tree—"

"Hitting every branch on the way down," I said, finishing the saying. It was sure enough true. He was ... disgusting.

"That's right." Smiling, she wrapped an arm around my waist as she led me to the front of the chapel. Suddenly, she hooted, laughing. "Did you see his face when the water hit him?"

I wished I could laugh, but it was too soon to find humor in the situation. Maybe tomorrow.

She swiped tears of mirth from her eyes. "Probably hasn't seen the likes of water in some time."

"That's true," I agreed. "He needs a bath but bad."

She glanced up at me, then tipped her head and pointedly said, "He isn't the only."

I laughed. "I love you, Mama."

"Love you, too, baby girl. Now let's get you cleaned up, and you can call that hunky Dylan about this little dustup."

As I followed her into the chapel, I thought Dylan might also want to know about how well Cletus could run. It might be time to get a search warrant for that junky trailer near the river. Because after Cletus's display of running skills, I wouldn't be the least bit surprised if he owned some black jogging gear.

Chapter Twenty-five

Early the next morning, I woke to the scent of fresh coffee. Really strong coffee. Right next to my nose.

I lifted a sleepy eyelid to see Dylan's face peering down at me. "Good morning, Care Bear. Rise and shine!"

I pulled the sheet over my head. "What time is it?"

"Six thirty."

"Who let you in?"

"Marjie."

"I'm disowning her."

"I've got your coffee right here."

I lowered the sheet a bit to peer out at him. Damn him, he was smiling. "It's unnatural to smile so early in the morning."

"Ah, but Care Bear, I remember a time or two putting a morning smile on your face. . . ."

That was a low blow. He was right, of course, but still. "Who made the coffee?"

"Marjie."

I tossed the covers off and sat up. Roly and Poly were

long gone, the traitorous buggers. Dylan handed over the coffee. I breathed in the tendrils of steam and eyed him warily. "What're you doing here?"

He wasn't in uniform, so I hoped that meant he wasn't here on business. I'd had just about enough bad news as I could stomach in a week.

"Putting up sheetrock in the bathroom." He sat on the edge of the bed.

I grabbed my locket. "You're my hero."

"It's time you finally realized that, Care Bear."

Maybe it was. . . .

"Did you have any luck with the search last night?" I asked around a yawn. There had been a full-scale search of the post office in hopes of locating the envelope Katie Sue had mailed.

"No luck," he said. "It's not there."

"Then it had to be intercepted by whoever attacked José in Mr. Dunwoody's yard yesterday."

"It would seem that way. As a precaution, we're sending an armed escort with today's mail carrier. Just in case."

It felt too little, too late.

I stared into my mug, my stomach sinking. If the Calhouns had gotten their hands on that envelope, then there was very little connecting them to Katie Sue's death. No proof of motive at all.

Yesterday, during Dylan's interrogation of Warren, he'd denied knowing of an envelope at all. In fact, the entire interview had been a complete waste of time. Warren, Louisa, Landry, Cassandra, and the two lug nuts all provided alibis for each other during the time

frame of Katie Sue's death—which my aunt Hazel verified. Warren had also flown in a fancy lawyer from
D.C. who ended up threatening the whole department
if they continued to harass the family. The sheriff,
Dylan's boss, had shut things down pretty quick after
that.

Deny, deny, deny.

It infuriated me. If the manila envelope had been intercepted by one of the Calhoun's lug nuts, I was quite
sure that it was destroyed by now. If it hadn't been, I
didn't know where else to look.

It was yet another dead end.

"We'll figure it out, Carly," Dylan said, giving me a
nudge with his elbow.

I looked at him and nodded, unable to voice my
doubts.

He stood up. "Now, not that I'm not enjoying the view
of you in your loose little tank top—because trust me, I
am—but it's time for me to get busy. And time for you to
get your lazy bones out of bed and help me before we
both have to go to work later."

"Just when I was liking you again."

He dropped a kiss on the top of my head and strode
out the door.

I leaned against my headboard and sipped the coffee.
Heaven. When Marjie moved back to her inn, I might
have to start having morning coffee with her. Of course,
it would have to be here since she wouldn't let me in her
house, but that was okay with me. I'd get to keep the
leftovers in the pot.

I let my eyes drift closed and allowed myself to just *be*

for a minute. Birds were singing, and for this very brief moment, all was right in my world.

But then I remembered my run-in with Cletus, and my eyes popped open. When I'd talked to Dylan last night, he said he'd try to get a search warrant processed, but it wasn't going to be easy. The thing was, there wasn't a lot of supporting evidence that Cletus had done anything to Katie Sue. Nothing that tied them together. No overheard threats. No sightings together. No . . . nothing. He was also trying to interview Cletus and Dinah—but so far they'd evaded the police like pros.

Jessa Yadkin, however, had validated Dinah's claim that Cletus had been in Déjà Brew during the time frame that Katie Sue had been murdered. He'd apparently made quite a fuss over the way Jessa fixed his iced coffee. I wasn't ready to rule him out as a suspect. Because we didn't know exactly when Katie Sue had been killed, it was possible he'd been in the coffee shop before or after the deed. It seemed to me he might have made a big ass out of himself so people would remember he'd been in the shop—all witnesses to his "alibi." Of course, we wouldn't know anything for certain until Cletus and Dinah were caught and properly interrogated. Dylan also promised to head down to Birmingham to talk to Jimmy, and I'd had to listen to him lecture me for a solid fifteen minutes last night when I confessed to going to Katie Sue's house.

Lordy, the man could lecture when he built up a head of steam.

I found it interesting that word hadn't broken yet about Katie Sue having been murdered, and wondered if the Calhouns had also paid someone off to keep that out of the news. It wouldn't surprise me. They just got rid of the press—news of a murder would bring the media swarming back.

I wanted to push thoughts of the murder aside, but try as I might, I couldn't. They festered in my brain, and even thinking of the phone call I'd received from Lyla last night didn't help. She'd phoned to say that Jamie Lynn was walking without her crutches and smiling bigger than Lyla had seen in a long, long while. She'd offered to give the scooter back, but I told her to just go ahead and sell it and use the money to buy something nice for Jamie Lynn's birthday.

I finished my cup of coffee and threw back the covers. After grabbing a change of clothes I headed downstairs to take my shower.

Roly and Poly sat on the back of the couch—which, I noticed, had been draped in a sheet. Apparently, Aunt Marjie didn't want Johnny's poison ivy cooties, either. I bent and kissed each of the kitties. Their tails swished happily.

By the time I emerged from the bathroom my stomach was rumbling from the scent of breakfast cooking. I was surprised to see Gabi with Dylan and Marjie. They were all gathered round a kitchen table piled with pancakes, bacon, sausages, and muffins. The two cats prowled around. Even Roly had resorted to begging. She was a sucker for sausage.

"Dylan, I thought you said you woke her up," Marjie joked. "She's sleepwalkin' if I ever saw it."

"Ha. Ha," I said. I poured coffee, added a little milk, and joined them.

"I saw Gabi running this morning and invited her on inside for a bite to eat," Marjie said.

"I couldn't be more thankful. I was starving after my

morning run." Gabi smiled and reached for another helping of pancakes. "One good thing about the wedding being called off is that I can stop worrying about fitting into my dress."

I sipped my coffee and said, "Are you all right?" It had to be a difficult day—she was supposed to be marrying the man of her dreams this evening. Instead her whole world had turned inside out.

"I'm okay." She took a deep breath. "Yesterday, I called off the wedding completely."

"Oh?" I asked.

"I know it's what's best," she said. "It'd just be nice if it didn't hurt so bad."

I glanced at Dylan. After two failed attempts to get married, we knew that pain.

Marjie added two sausage links to Gabi's plate. "Eat all you want."

"Thanks," Gabi said, taking another pancake.

"How'd Landry take the news?" I asked.

"Honestly, I don't know." Gabi looked at me. "He refuses to come out of his bedroom."

I glanced at Dylan—that was odd.

"Bastard," Marjie said, adding a slice of bacon to Gabi's plate.

"I just can't believe how much of my life I wasted," she said. "On him. On *them*, that family. And when I do something for myself for once—choosing not to marry a man who doesn't love me—they treat me like a pariah. Giving me the silent treatment. Going to dinner without me." Her lip trembled. "So much for me being part of the family."

"They suck," Marjie said.

Dylan kept quiet, forking pancakes into his mouth like nobody's business, but I could tell he was listening to every word.

I refilled my coffee mug. "It probably doesn't feel like it right now, but you're better off without them, Gabi. I feel good things for you."

"You do?" Skepticism clouded her eyes.

"I really do."

"Me, too," Marjie said, thumping the table.

Gabi looked at each of us. "But what am I going to do with myself? I don't know how to start over."

I knew she'd just graduated from college. "What's your degree in?"

She laughed, a joyless sound. "Officially? Communications, and I barely scraped by at that."

"Unofficially?" Dylan asked.

"Sororities and pageants."

Marjie barked out a laugh. A *laugh*.

Gabi said, "I know. It's bad. On the pageant stage I came across as this strong independent woman, but behind the scenes the truth was I'd been perfectly groomed by Louisa to be a trophy wife. In all reality, my degree should have been an MRS."

A Mrs. A married woman. An arm piece.

"You don't have to figure it out right now," I said. "You have time."

"That I do," she said solemnly.

After that, we fell into an easy chatter, discussing nothing more serious than the day's forecast (sunny). Gabi seemed in no hurry at all to return to the Loon.

Dylan and I cleared dishes while Gabi and Marjie

chatted about how the aches from their broken bones had pretty much disappeared overnight. I never tired of hearing how my potions helped someone.

I finished cleaning up while Dylan went out to his truck to bring in sheets of fancy moisture-resistant drywall.

"Tell me again why you let that one go, Carly?" Marjie asked.

I eyed her. "Tell me again what game you're playing with Johnny?"

"I'm going to go clean," she snapped, hopping out of the kitchen. Over her shoulder, she said, "Someone around here has to."

Gabi comically tried to dry a mug one-handed and looked at me. "You and Dylan?"

"Long story." I watched him out the window. "Long complicated story."

"Give me the CliffsNotes version. Come on. It's my failed wedding day. Humor me."

I tipped my head side to side, weighing what to say. Finally, I said, "Engaged, his meddling vindictive mama, two failed wedding attempts, a fiery chapel, a bad breakup, broken hearts, separate towns, a tentative reconciliation, and . . . here we are, treading softly. Well, I'm treading. He's clomping."

Her jaw dropped. "Okay, I might need more than the CliffsNotes."

Dylan walked in, carrying the sheetrock. He glanced between the two of us. "What?"

Gabi still looked stunned. "Carly just summed up your two's relationship for me."

"Summed it up, did she?" he drawled. "Did she mention the fire?"

I wiped my hands on the dish towel. "Yes. That's the best part."

His eyes glinted. "Naw, it's not."

"What is?" Gabi asked.

"Yeah, what?" I echoed, curious.

"Well, it sure isn't her cheery disposition in the morning. You should have seen the look she gave me when I woke her up, after I brought her coffee and everything."

I whapped him with the towel.

He laughed, then said softly, "If you must know the best part, it's knowing that if you really *truly* love each other, you can overcome anything life throws your way. Ain't that so, Care Bear?"

Gabi's eyes widened as she looked between the two of us.

Talk about a loaded question. I squeezed the towel. "That is pretty good," I finally said. "But the fire still might trump it."

His gaze met mine, and the tenderness there, the love, nearly did me in. "If so, only because you were arrested because of it. I have your mug shot framed on my nightstand."

He leaned in, gave me a kiss, winked at Gabi, and *clomped* away, taking my heart with him.

Shaking her head, Gabi said, "You know, I don't think I ever really knew what love looked like until just now. That's the kind of love I want."

"I highly recommend you find it without the med-

dling mama-in-law. Or the fire. Or the arrest. But yeah . . .
the rest is pretty good."

"So why aren't you married then?"

Another loaded question. "Broken hearts get put
back together one piece at a time. I still have a few pieces
left to go."

She looked to be contemplating that when the phone
rang. I reached over and grabbed it up. It was the sheriff's station, looking for Dylan.

As I took the cordless phone upstairs, I could only
imagine why Dylan was wanted so early in the morning.
I had my hand over the mouthpiece as I stuck my head
in the bathroom. "Your office."

He dusted his hands off on his shorts and said, "Jackson here." He listened for a second and added, "You're
sure? Okay, let me write it down."

He used a nub of a pencil and wrote on the sheetrock.
It was an address in Nashville, Tennessee, about two
hours north. "Yeah," he said. "I'm on my way." He clicked
off the phone and said to me, "We might have finally gotten a break."

"How?"

"Got a hit on the alert I sent out about Katie Sue's
jewelry. It's sittin' in a pawnshop in Nashville. I've got
to go."

"I don't suppose I can go with—"

"No." He kissed me.

"That doesn't make up for it," I said as he dashed
down the stairs.

"Then I guess I need more practicin'," he hollered
back.

Smiling, I went to the window in my bedroom and

watched him hop in his truck and drive off. My gaze skipped across the street to the Loon.

Opposite me, Louisa was watching the same scene as I was . . . and I had to wonder how long she'd been looking out the window. She glanced up and noticed me. Quickly, she swished the curtain closed.

Huh. I couldn't help but wonder if her nosiness was idle curiosity at the goings-on in the neighborhood . . . or if she was lying in wait for the mail carrier.

Chapter Twenty-six

When I left for work a little after nine thirty, I moseyed down the steps to the mailbox. I opened it
up and pulled out the small pile of mail that had been
stuffed inside only moments before.

No manila envelope.

I turned to the Loon, held up the letters for anyone
who might be taking a gander—like Louisa—and shoved
them in my bag. It was my way of saying, "Look! No
manila envelope! No need to break in while I'm at
work."

I hoped the message was loud and clear, because
Dylan still had my pitchfork as evidence and unless Marjie had secretly brought one of her guns over along with
her clothes yesterday, she was somewhat defenseless.

The cats hadn't looked the least bit willing to come to
work with me, so I decided to leave my bike and walk. I
was starting to wonder if they'd choose Marjie over me
when it was time for her to go.

As I passed the Buzzard, I stopped, stared. Marjie's

front yard had been cleared of weeds. Planters filled with colorful annuals dotted her porch. As I watched, Johnny came around from the backyard, pushing a wheelbarrow. He wore a fishing hat, a short-sleeved shirt, long pants, and tall boots. His skin was still red and rashy.

He spotted me and said, "Looks good, don't it?"

"You *do* have a death wish, don't you?"

Laughing, he said, "What? I'm just doing a little tidying. This spring cleaning is long overdue. Besides, I've already got poison ivy . . . what's this yard going to do to me?"

"It's not the yard you should be afraid of."

"Marjoram doesn't scare me. She's all bark and no bite, that one."

Had this man learned nothing? "I'm not sure which of the two of you is more stubborn." Or crazy.

"A draw, I'd say."

"Does she know you're here?"

He smiled. "It's a surprise."

"I'll send flowers to your funeral," I said, waving good-bye. His laughter followed me down the street. I didn't have the heart to tell him that I hadn't been joking.

I stopped at Dèjá Brew, grabbed my usual, and headed across the Ring to my shop. I quickly went around and turned on lights, adjusted the thermostat, and took quick stock of what needed to be done today. It was a lot. I'd been neglecting the place the last couple of days. There were bills to pay, orders to place, and cleaning to do.

No sooner did I unlock the door than a couple came in to browse around. They held hands, kept their heads bent, and continually smiled at each other.

Just eloped, was my guess. They bought a couple of

my premade items, a few hand soaps, a jar of bath salts. They'd just walked out the door when another person walked in.

Warren Calhoun.

There was no sign of my witchy senses, so I unclenched my hands and wondered what he was doing here.

"I'm not sure we've formally met," he said, picking up a bar of soap and sniffing it.

It was so like what Katie Sue had done, I felt a pang of grief strike me hard. "I don't think formal introductions are necessary, do you?"

"I was told you were feisty," he said as he walked around.

"You probably don't want to know what I've been told about you."

The corner of his lip lifted. "Probably not."

Outside, I noticed two of his lug nuts stood watch. I wondered if one of them had puncture wounds in his patootie, but they were too far away for me to feel their energy.

"It's a lovely little shop you have."

"I think so." I slid my locket along its chain.

"I've done a little research on you, Ms. Hartwell. Reports say you're a witch. That the potions you sell . . . are magical. True?"

"I've done a little research on you, too, Senator. Reports say you're a playboy, that some of your money might not be all that clean, and that if people get too close to exposing who you really are, you have them killed. True?"

He let out a laugh, which surprised the hell out of me.

He said, "I see 'feisty' was an understatement. Let's see. I haven't been a playboy in years, my money is no one's business, and I don't believe in the death penalty ... for anyone."

It was my turn to laugh.

"I'm not sure why it's amusing, Ms. Hartwell, but it's the God's honest truth. Now, I'm not saying I'm a saint. There have been plenty of times I've done something I shouldn't have to protect my family, but you tend to re-assess morality in those situations. Family comes first."

"Said like a true presidential candidate."

Wincing, he said, "Said like a man who's made some mistakes. I'm withdrawing from the presidential election come Monday. I'll fulfill the remaining three years of my term as senator, then I will reevaluate my political aspi-rations."

He'd shocked me again. "Does your withdrawal from the presidential election have to do with Katie Sue's death?"

"My plans have been in place for several weeks now. What has happened to Kathryn is a tragedy," he said, "as she was a bright, lovely, somewhat misguided, young woman, but her death is not the reason for my with-drawal."

"What is?"

"It's a personal matter."

"Personal, like your affair with her?" I prodded. "I bet if that leaked now, then in three years it will long be for-given and forgotten."

Shock flashed across his face, and then he laughed again. "An affair? Did she tell you that?"

His reaction startled me. Well, no. She hadn't. But

her actions had certainly led me to believe it. "Do you deny it?"

"Of course."

What did I think he would say? "I know Katie Sue had dirt on you. The manila envelope? The attacks on the mail carriers? Any of this ring a bell?"

His eyes narrowed. "I've no idea what you're talking about."

Wryly, I said, "Now you're just insulting me."

He quietly strolled to the wall of potion bottles. "Kathryn and I were not having an affair," he stated again.

Frustrated, I let down my guard to read his energy. He wasn't lying about Katie Sue, and it took only a second to realize why he would renounce his candidacy. That reason overshadowed all his other energy.

Stunned, I drew in a deep breath. If Katie Sue hadn't been his mistress ... How had I been so wrong? She'd spoken of love and Warren being a puppet master and getting what she wanted from him ... I was beyond confused.

I took hold of my locket. "How long have you known that you're ill?"

Startled, he pivoted. "Pardon?"

I went about gathering a half dozen ingredients including ginger and white willow bark. "The cancer. How long have you known?"

"A month," he answered. "I haven't told anyone about it. Other than my doctors, you're the only person who knows." Suspicion crossed his features. "How *did* you know?"

"Witch, remember?" I asked, not wanting to explain my empathy abilities. "Are you in treatment yet?"

"No. I wanted to wait until after the wedding." He stuck his hands in his pockets. "I saw the way Gabi's face healed when she used the lotion you gave her. It was nothing short of . . . miraculous. I was hoping you'd have something to help me."

"What have your doctors said?" I asked cautiously.

"They've advised me that the cancer is terminal but they can buy me some time. Six months, maybe a year."

The cancer was, indeed, terminal. I closed my eyes and let out a breath. When I opened them again, I looked at him straight on. "I'm going to give you some advice. You don't have to take it, but I have to give it. Despite any conflict we might have between us regarding Katie Sue, I'm not one to see someone needlessly suffer."

"Go on."

"Announce your resignation from all politics on Monday. Travel. Explore. Tend your garden. Ride your horses. Spend time with the people who matter most."

"What're you saying?"

I bit a nail. "I can make you a potion to help with the pain, but I can't cure terminal ailments. The cancer in your body is everywhere." I held his gaze. "You have two to four months at most. It's up to you how you spend your remaining time, but if I were you, I wouldn't want it to be spent in hospital hooked up to machines."

Shoving a hand into his hair, his voice was hoarse as he asked, "I'll take your opinion under advisement." Looking up, I saw dampness in his eyes. "If I'd sought treatment a month ago . . . ?"

I didn't want to tell him the truth. That a month ago his prognosis might have been so much brighter. This was an aggressive form of cancer—it had done a lot of damage in four weeks.

Then I realized the cosmic irony of it all. He'd put off getting treatment to go to a wedding he'd deviously planned so he could get elected. Now, he'd never see election day.

I figured the truth would only hurt more, so I finally said, "It might have given you a little more time, but your type of cancer is aggressive and invasive ... I doubt your outcome would be any different."

He sat on one of the worktable stools and dragged a hand down his face. "You said you can help with the pain?"

"I'll mix it up now."

"Why would you help me?" he asked, searching my face with ravaged eyes. "Especially in light of Kathryn's hatred of me?"

"I'm a healer," I said simply. "I rarely like to see any-body suffer."

"Rarely?"

"I have my moments."

"Don't we all," he said drolly.

Drumming my fingers on the tabletop, I decided to see how much I could get out of Warren Calhoun. Being ill didn't preclude him from being involved with Katie Sue's death. "Katie Sue told me she was trying to get you to change your mind about something. What was that?" If it hadn't been about him leaving Louisa, I was really at a loss.

"I've no idea what Kathryn wanted from my family," he said.

Another lie. He hadn't quite figured out that I could read his deceptions.

He added, "And I don't have any idea what happened to her. No matter how hard you want to paint me as a villain, I wasn't involved in her death."

I was shocked to feel that he was telling the truth on that matter.

I tried to put together the pieces. He didn't want to tell me what Katie Sue wanted from him, but whatever it was hadn't led him to kill her. Were they two separate matters, after all? Had her killer been a little closer to home?

"Perhaps a closer look at her felonious family is in order," he said as though reading my mind.

Squinting at him, I said, "Did you send a note to them that she was in town?"

"Me? No."

Again, he was being truthful.

I asked, "Do you know who did?"

"No."

A lie. "Was it Louisa?"

"Not at all."

Another lie. So, it *had* been Louisa who'd notified the Cobbs that Katie Sue was in town. What a sweet, sweet woman. Bless her heart.

The thought reminded me of what Katie Sue had said about Gabi—and her wedding. "What did Katie Sue have to do with Gabi?"

His heart rate kicked up. "I don't know what you mean. They barely knew each other."

I was on to something, but I didn't know what. Not yet. "What was in the envelope Katie Sue mailed to me?"

"I don't know."

"Ah, ah." I waved a finger at him. "That's a lie."

His eyes darkened. "I suggest, Ms. Hartwell, that you forget you ever knew about an envelope."

"Is that a threat, Senator?"

"Take it as you will. I, however, am through discussing Kathryn Perry. If that means you won't help me with one of your elixirs, so be it."

Indeed, I was regretting helping him at all, but the damn healer in me didn't want to see him suffer. "I'll be right ba—" I stopped midsentence as another couple came in. I gave them a friendly smile, told them to look around, and said to Warren, "I'm just going to mix this up for you."

He snagged my arm. "Wait—before you do . . ."

"What?"

He dropped his voice. "Do you have anything that cures hair loss?"

Despite my irritation with him, this I had to hear. I leaned in eagerly, wondering if Louisa had gone bald overnight. "You know someone losing their hair?"

"I don't know if it's the stress of the wedding being canceled or what," he said, "but Landry's hair is falling out in clumps."

My mouth dropped. "Landry?"

"At this rate, he's going to be completely bald in a couple of days."

"I, um, think I might have something," I murmured.

As I bustled about, I kept thinking about Landry and his hair. And wondering how in the world he'd been the one who'd gotten hexed.

An hour later, Warren was long gone and I was still trying to figure out the hex situation when John Richard

Baldwin sailed through the door. He was dressed in business casual, and I had to wonder if he was working today or, like his boss, always dressed in his Sunday best.

"Hey, Hilda," he said.

I smiled. "Hi, Uncle John Richard."

"Well, sadly," he said, ducking his head as he walked toward the counter, "I believe you may have to drop the uncle part. Hazel has informed me that her attentions have swayed elsewhere. She cut me loose."

I didn't know whether to think it funny or sad that she actually believed she had a relationship with him.

He said, "Such a shame. Just when I was getting used to the thought of us being family and all."

I eyed him suspiciously. "You didn't whack Earl, did you?"

He laughed. "No, but I'd like to thank whoever did. I had no idea how to dissolve an imaginary relationship."

"That's a new one for me, too, and I've helped plenty of people end relationships."

His smile lit his face. "Can I still call you Hilda?"

"It might be time to switch to Carly."

"Maybe so," he said. "The end of an era. Let's have a moment of silence." He dropped his head again.

He'd clearly spent much too much time with my dramatic family. "What brings you in? You looking for a love potion now that you're a free man?"

"No, thanks. I think I'll bask in my bachelorhood for a while. Caleb sent me over. I've got the goods on Kathryn Perry's will. You didn't hear it from either of us, though. Sharing this kind of info before the will is probated is strictly verboten."

"Look at you throwing around fancy words."

He grinned. "Helps me remember that I actually went to college for seven years."

"And also helps you forget that you're now the best-educated administrative assistant in Alabama?"

"That's right."

"My lips are sealed. What's the scoop?"

He leaned in. "It's not terribly exciting. Everything she has goes to her younger sister, Jamie Lynn. An estate upward of four million dollars. She's invested well."

I knew. I'd seen the financial papers.

In another month, on her twenty-first birthday, Jamie Lynn would have access to a trust worth a million dollars. Now she was set to inherit another four million on top of that.

My word. I couldn't even fathom that kind of money.

"When will Jamie Lynn find out?" I asked.

"Probably in the next week or two. Kathryn's lawyer will contact her directly. Unless she shares the info with you . . ." He zipped his lips.

"Got it."

The door shot open and Gabi came rushing in. Her hair was tucked into a ball cap, she didn't have on a speck of makeup, and there were still vile-looking stitches on her face, but she was still stunning.

"Carly, you'll never guess!" She pulled up short. "Oh, sorry!"

"Gabi Greenleigh, John Richard Baldwin," I introduced.

"Hi," she said to him. "Sorry to interrupt."

"It's okay," I answered, because John Richard had gone suddenly mute. "What's up?"

"I thought about what you said this morning, about

having time to decide what I want to do. And that moment, at your kitchen table, I realized I didn't want to leave."

"I, ah—" I stuttered, wondering what to say without hurting her feelings. "There's no room at my inn."

She laughed. "I didn't mean with you. I meant here in this town. I like it here." A smile lit her face. "I like the people. So, I went into town to find an apartment to rent, but bumped into your mama and next thing I knew I signed a lease to rent the apartment above the chapel."

I'd lived there for years before buying Grammy Fowl's house. "You're sure you want to stay here in Hitching Post?" I asked Gabi. "This town isn't like what you're used to." She had loads of money and could go pretty much anywhere she wanted in the world.

"I think that's why I like it so much," she said. "I just need to find a job now to keep busy, but I can tackle that later. Your mama said I could move in on Monday. Right now she's using the apartment to store all the flowers from my wedding until she can figure out what to do with them." Her eyes glistened.

Maybe a change like this was exactly what she needed.

"I need to get my things from Shady Hollow, so I'm headed back there today to pack up. I've got to run, so much to do, but I wanted to let you know. I can't thank you enough for being a friend to me when I needed one most."

I couldn't help but smile at her sincerity. "You're very welcome, Gabi."

"I'll be back on Monday morning. 'Bye, John Richard." She waved as she zipped toward the door as fast as she'd come in.

He waved back.

After she was gone, he finally found his voice. "She's moving? Here?"

"Yep," I said. "It seems that way."

His eyes went round as MoonPies.

I couldn't help but tease. "How's that bachelorhood looking now?"

"Like the most foolish decision I ever made, and oh, I've made a few." He ran his hand through his hair. "I think I need to get a haircut. See you later, *Carly*."

"Thanks for the info," I yelled as he beelined for the door.

I shook my head, grateful that he hadn't asked for a love potion to use on her, because I wouldn't have given it to him. She needed time to figure out who she was. If love came on its own, that'd be fine, but I wasn't going to push it on her. I would have given him a phony potion, a fake. The old switcheroo.

The old switcheroo.

Mercy! Suddenly, I recalled something Gabi had said about switching her drink for Landry's when she changed her mind about giving him the potion.

She'd given him *her* drink.

It had been the one hexed, not his.

Katie Sue Perrywinkle had wanted Gabi's hair to fall out, and had gone to great lengths to make it happen.

Chapter Twenty-seven

A little while later, I still didn't have an answer to why Katie Sue would be so vindictive toward Gabi. I'd read Gabi's energy the day we'd bumped into Katie Sue behind Marjie's house — there had been nothing but mild confusion at Katie Sue's behavior. No ill will. No hostility.

Whatever it was between them had been one-sided.

It was obvious now, too, that Katie Sue had lied to me about not liking Gabi. The anger she'd felt *had* been directed at Gabi. I'd dismissed it, wanting to believe her, and that was foolish. I needed to learn to trust my instincts more.

I'd called Delia to talk it over with her, but she didn't have any ideas, either. They didn't know each other well at all, had no tiffs with each other, and it left both Delia and me puzzled.

Katie Sue's words rang in my head.

She's just so perfect, isn't she? Perfect upbringing, perfect skin, perfect manners, perfect everything.

Maybe as Ainsley had suggested, Katie Sue *had* been jealous of Gabi's hair all along.

But I kept going back to Katie Sue's last comment that afternoon—the last ones I ever heard her say.

Well, despite her perfection, I actually feel bad for Gabi because she doesn't have any idea that her perfect little world is about to fall apart.

In all that had happened, I'd forgotten those words, but now they rang in my head like a big ol' warning bell.

My palms dampened, and I wiped them on my shorts. Katie Sue certainly couldn't have predicted her own death, which was the catalyst to Gabi's world falling apart, so what had she been referring to?

Gabi's perfect world . . . Her relationship with the Calhouns? The wedding? Landry?

I have plenty of ammunition and a plan to use it to get Warren to see things my way. Love is worth fighting for, Carly, even if I have to fight dirty.

Love—but not for Warren.

Warren's a puppet master, Carly, and he's pulling a whole host of strings.

My mind spun round and round until it stopped on something Gabi had mentioned the first time I met her.

He's only marrying me because his daddy is forcing him to. Some sort of political ploy, an agreement they made years ago.

Oh. My. Word. My heart hammered in against my breastbone as I connected dots. Was it . . . possible?

My head snapped up as Dylan came into the shop. There was a look in his eye, a gleam that had me thinking he'd discovered something big on his trip to Nashville. Something beyond finding Katie Sue's jewelry.

"What, what?" I asked, unable to hide my curiosity as I motioned for him to sit down at the worktable. My theory about Katie Sue's love life could wait a minute or two.

Dylan and I sat face-to-face, our knees touching. *Dang*, but he looked good in his uniform. Not as good as he did in faded jeans and a thin T-shirt, but it was close. Real close.

"You're not going to believe what I'm about to tell you," he said.

I gave him a gentle shove. "I might die of suspense before you spill it. Come on!"

"Katie Sue's jewelry—all of it—is now in the evidence room."

His excitement was contagious. "Tell me everything."

"One of those lucky breaks," he said. "Turns out it wasn't a pawnshop, but an upscale jewelry store that had her things. The owner recognized them as quality pieces, and questioned the seller for the history of the items, guessing correctly that they had been stolen. The seller became squirrelly, and when the owner pushed, the seller said he'd found the jewelry in his truck, just sitting there like Santa dropped it off. When the owner insisted on checking to see if the jewelry was stolen, the seller asked for it back. The owner then suggested they call the police and let them sort it out. The seller ran, leaving the jewelry behind. The shop owned tried contacting the designer of the ring—it was marked—trying to figure who the jewels belonged to, but didn't get in touch with him until early this morning. Wham, bam, boom, my phone rings."

"*My* phone rings."

"Same difference, right, Care Bear?"

"You're killing me here. Who was the seller?"

"Surveillance footage captured his ugly mug perfectly. It was none other than Cletus Cobb."

My exuberance turned to dread. Even though Cletus was a suspect in what had happened to Katie Sue, a part of me hadn't wanted to believe it true.

Family first, Warren had said.

Not always.

"But that's not all," Dylan said.

"What else?"

"I spoke to the designer of the ring."

There was a strange tone to his voice that had me taking notice. "Oh?"

"He gave me the ring's full history. It was commissioned eighteen months ago as an engagement ring. He waxed poetic about the couple, how in love they were, how beautiful a couple they were, blah, blah, blah. It was quite the impression they'd made, and he never could understand why they'd broken up. He himself was heartbroken upon learning the two were no longer together . . . Katie Sue had been engaged to none other than—"

"Landry Calhoun," I said, beating him to the punch.

His mouth fell open. "Again, you've surprised the hell out of me, Care Bear. How did you know that?"

"I just figured it out few minutes ago." I told him about my morning with Warren (including how he hadn't been the one who killed Katie Sue) and how Landry had been hexed. "It all makes sense now. Katie Sue had to be using her ammunition to stop the wedding between Landry and Gabi. She was fighting for love, all right. Her love for Landry."

"You didn't find out what Katie Sue had on Warren, did you?" Dylan asked.

"No. He clammed up and told me to forget I ever saw that envelope."

"Sounds like it was something big," Dylan said, his eyebrow raised.

"I'm not sure we'll ever know."

"Well, there's an arrest warrant out for Cletus and Dinah—she was driving the truck. If nothing else, they're facing federal charges because they crossed state lines with the stolen jewelry. I'm hoping that'll scare them enough to spill what they know about Katie Sue's death."

What they *knew*. What they had probably *done* was more like it.

I kept shaking my head. "I feel sick." This wasn't how families were supposed to be. Families were supposed to be about love and happiness and forgiveness. My heart was broken for Katie Sue . . . and for Jamie Lynn, whose dreams of a big happy family weren't ever going to come true.

He pulled me off the stool and into his arms. "I'm sorry, Care Bear."

I buried my face in his neck and breathed in the scent of him. It soothed, it comforted, but it couldn't shut off my thoughts.

"If not for that stupid wedding," I said, "Katie Sue wouldn't have come back to town in the first place, and wouldn't have even been put in the path of Cletus and Dinah. Cletus probably caught sight of Katie Sue's jewelry and hatched his evil plan."

"Probably," Dylan admitted.

I lifted my face to him. "Louisa Calhoun holds some

guilt in this as well. She wrote the note to Dinah and Cletus, telling them Katie Sue was back."

"Why would she do that?"

"Revenge is my guess, for Katie Sue threatening to interfere with the wedding."

"While we wait to hear news on Cletus and Dinah, I think we should pay a visit to the Calhouns before they leave town. Get this full story. Even though it looks like none of them had anything to do with Katie Sue's murder, they're still guilty as sin for those attacks on Earl and José."

"We?" He *wanted* my help?

"Let's double-team them," he explained. "I'll ask the questions; you read their energy."

I smiled. "I really do like it when you fight dirty."

"That's because I learned it from you."

"Hush. When do you want to go?"

"Now?"

"Let me lock up."

"We met a couple of years ago. I'd just left law school and Kathryn was finishing up medical school—her rotation was on Cass's floor. It was just after her accident."

I looked at Cassandra, who was intently studying the grain in the wood flooring. I recalled what Gabi said about why Cassandra didn't want Landry marrying her: That she wanted him to marry for love. Had she meant Katie Sue?

"Landry," Warren said, a warning in his voice.

He stood next to the fireplace, one hand in his pocket, the other gripping the mantel. He wasn't pleased by our conversation with his son. Neither was Louisa, who sat in the library nook. If looks could kill, Dylan and I would be in coffins right about now.

Sitting next to her mother, Cassandra continued to keep her gaze averted, as though she couldn't bear the words Landry spoke.

Sitting across from Dylan and me, Landry said, "Enough, Daddy. *Enough.* I'm tired of the lies."

He'd finally grown a backbone, it seemed. Too little, too late.

Dylan had already informed them that arrest warrants were out for Dinah and Cletus, and that they were the prime suspects in Katie Sue's death. It had been a tactical ploy on his part to tell them, hoping it would lower their guard. They were likely to be more forthcoming if they knew they weren't viewed as murder suspects any longer.

The inn was empty save for the lot of us—an order carried out by Warren. Hazel, Earl, and the lug nuts were out in the garden. No doubt their curiosity was killing them.

After a few minutes of speaking with Landry, it was clear why he'd been locked in his room and refused to see Gabi: Grief had stolen the soul straight out of the man.

Dark circles colored ashen skin beneath red swollen eyes that kept looking over our shoulders, as if waiting for someone to walk through the door. His face was set in a tight grimace, his shoulders hunched, his body weak from not eating.

His devastation pulsed through me, and I clamped on to my locket and willed the emotions to stop. But even then, I could still feel the pain thrumming beneath the surface of my skin. The ache. The desperation. The yearning to be with her. The overwhelming longing to be dead, too.

Did his parents have any idea how suicidal he was? I imagined not, or they'd show some measure of sympathy for the man.

Instead, they seemed more worried about the secrets he might reveal. *Family first,* my ass. That phrase was just a justification to keep a reputation intact. It had nothing to do with actual love for a family member.

A cowboy hat was pulled low on Landry's forehead, probably to cover up his rapid balding. He clasped his hands tightly, squeezing, squeezing so hard my knuckles ached.

"Why the secrecy about the relationship?" Dylan asked.

Landry looked toward his father.

There was moisture shimmering in Warren's eyes. Maybe the man had a lick of decency after all.

"As soon as it became clear that the two were serious, my team ran a background check. Kathryn's colorful history was . . . an obstacle," Warren said. "We advised Landry to sever ties with her. For the family's sake. Landry knew there were other plans in place for his future. Plans he'd agreed to when he left law school," he added pointedly.

"Is that when he agreed to marry the woman of your choice in exchange for getting him off the hook from that cheating scandal?" I asked, figuring that was exactly what happened. Had his marriage-of-convenience to Gabi already been set in motion at that point?

"Yes," Landry answered. "The plan was to start making music and in a few years settle down with someone suitable who'd help bring in younger votes. After a few years of marriage and a kid or two, and once I was *re-spectable* again, I'd then run for governor. Only, except for the music, I didn't want any of that. It was a future that had been planned for me by my parents, without much of my input at all."

Warren flushed a dark shade of red, his anger infusing his skin with color.

Louisa went to get a drink from the wet bar.

I fisted my hands so tightly my nails bit into my skin. I wondered whether Landry would have opted for the jail time back in law school if he could have peeked into the future to see how his "agreement" with his father ended up.

"When I realized how serious it was getting between Kathryn and me, I tried to break it off," Landry said, shaking his head. "Numerous times. I knew I had a duty to fulfill, and I keep my word. And Kathryn understood. But try as we might, we couldn't quit each other. I proposed. She said yes. We kept it secret and tried to figure a way to spin her background for public sympathy, a girl from the wrong side of the tracks who made something of herself by becoming a doctor. That kind of thing."

"But?" I asked. They had broken up after all.

"The presidential election happened," Landry said. "My choice in wife was deemed not good enough, and my debt to my father was called due. As a man who honors his word, I had to end things with Kathryn for good."

Tears pooled in Cassandra's eyes as she watched her brother. She was working her pearls like no one's business and looking like she'd rather be stuck in my mama's pond than here.

"For God's sake," Louisa snapped, her hand tight

around her drink. "Doctor or not, the press would have torn that girl to shreds, and our family reputation right along with it. This family has lofty plans. A president." She glanced at Warren. Then her gaze slid to Cassandra. "Another senator." She stared at her son. "And a governor, once you were settled with a family."

Landry glared at his mother, and I could feel his disdain for her. *Ah,* I suddenly realized. Warren hadn't been the only puppet master.

I looked toward Warren. It was obvious by the way Louisa was speaking that he still hadn't told her of his diagnosis. There would be no White House for him. And by the way Landry was behaving, I suspected a Calhoun governorship was out as well. He'd had enough of this family. I glanced at Cassandra—she was the last hope for this family to remain in politics. With Cassandra's popularity, I figured Louisa would redirect her daughter's future to include the White House before Warren was cold in the ground.

"Those were your plans, Mama. Not mine," Landry seethed. "Not Kathryn's."

I couldn't hold my tongue. I said to Louisa, "Don't you think what Katie Sue had been through with her family would have made her more relatable to the public? Everyone has skeletons. Everyone's been touched by addiction. She stopped the cycle."

Louisa's icy gaze turned on me. "You have no idea the level of scrutiny we're under. You saw the media circus here this past weekend, and that was for a happy occasion. If the press knew of Kathryn's past, they would not have let it go. Ever. Imagine a wedding. A baby. Every event, the press would seek comment from her family.

They'd be back in her life again, whether she liked it or not. They would get bolder, braver, looking for money. Bringing her down with them."

I hated that she was right. It still wasn't fair. Wasn't decent.

"And in light of what happened to Kathryn," she continued, "I think it's safe to say I was right."

"You might not have been," I snapped, "if you hadn't told her family she was back in town."

Landry's head whipped around to look at his mother. "That was you?"

She ignored him. "As it is now, no one knows how close our family was to Kathryn, and for the sake of the upcoming elections, I'd like to keep it that way. Once we leave here, we leave Kathryn Perry behind. Gabi will come to her senses, and everything will be right back on track."

Landry jumped up. "Don't you understand?" His gravelly voice broke as he added, "There is no leaving her behind. She's a part of me. Of who I am. It'll never be the same. *I'll* never be the same! I'll never marry Gabi, so just let it go."

"You made a deal, Landry," his mother said tightly.

"Screw the deal!" he shouted.

"Don't speak to your mama that way, son," Warren said, his voice strong and sure.

Right. Because proper Southern boys didn't raise their voices to their mamas. Even when his life had been destroyed.

Louisa's lips pressed into a thin, grim line.

Landry paced like a man trying to outrun his grief.

I said, "The night Katie Sue was killed, were you sup-

posed to meet with her after dinner?" I asked, guessing
he was who Katie Sue had met with instead of Jamie
Lynn. "Is that why you rushed off as soon as the meal
was done?"

Nodding, Landry said, "I was late."

"Did you meet up?" Dylan asked.

"For a couple of minutes, but then Lyla showed up,
and I took off. I came back here. It was the last time I
saw Kathryn."

I squeezed my locket, because the energy in the room
was starting to close in on me. The weight of Landry's
emotional pain was overwhelming in itself, but I could
also feel Warren's pains as his body was being eaten
away from the inside out. I could feel Louisa's rage. Cassandra's grief—she'd kept quiet through all this, but it
was clear she sided with her brother. Louisa's heart was
pumping a mile a minute, a heel blister was bothering
Cassandra, someone's thigh hurt something fierce, Warren's chest was tight, and Landry, poor Landry, was bone
weary, every muscle in his body aching.

"What about the extortion?" Dylan's unwavering gaze
was on Louisa.

"What extortion?" Warren asked, his voice dropping.

Louisa's energy immediately flipped from anger to
distress. Whatever Katie Sue had on the family, it was
big. There hadn't been a bluff.

Dylan didn't let up. "What was in Katie Sue's envelope that y'all want back so badly that you'd have two
mail carriers attacked?"

No one answered, but all their energies were filled
with anxiety. Each and every one of them knew what had

been in that envelope, yet none were willing to say what it had been.

This family was too much for me to deal with. *Mercy.*

Energy swirled. Anxiety. Anger. Grief. Pain. Desperation. Muscle aches. Deceit. It swirled and swirled around me until I could feel the color drain from my face.

I fought a wave of dizziness as Dylan said, "Landry, you want to answer that?"

Landry swallowed hard. "I told her not to do it. To let things be . . . but she was stubborn and wouldn't listen."

"That's enough, Sergeant Jackson," Warren said, stepping forward. "Anything else you want to ask us will be done with our counsel present."

Dylan stood. "Landry?"

Landry looked at his mother. Their eyes locked. A battle was being waged.

Fear pulsed through the room. Fear and hurt. A wave of queasiness hit me hard, and I sucked in a deep breath.

The phone rang, and I immediately jumped up to grab it. The tornado of energy swirling around me broke apart, and I took a deep breath to help regain my equilibrium. "The Crazy Loon, this is Carly, how may I help you?"

"Carly Bell, it's Marjie. Lyla Jameson just called round looking for you. Jamie Lynn collapsed at home this afternoon. She's in a coma on life support, and the doctors don't think she'll last the night."

No! No, no, no. My heart cried.

"Which hospital?" I asked, my voice hoarse. She rattled off the name of one of Huntsville's finest. I thanked her and hung up.

"What's happened?" Dylan asked.

"It's Jamie Lynn."

"Kathryn's sister?" Landry asked. "What's wrong?"

"She's dying."

"Go," Dylan said. "I'll meet you there later."

I ran for the door, never looking back at the Calhouns.

I hoped to never see any of them ever again.

∼๏ Chapter Twenty-eight ๏∼

I raced down the hospital hallway toward Jamie Lynn's room. The corridor tried to be cheerful, with brightly colored paint on some walls, lovely murals on others, and artwork created by pediatric patients, but the only word to describe the ambiance was dreary.

"Thanks again for coming with me," I said. "It was good timing you showing up at my house just as I was leaving."

Delia raced alongside me. "Right. Good timing."

There was something in her tone . . . I stopped and touched her arm. "Not good timing?"

Fluorescent light made her blue eyes seem even bluer. "There might have been a dream involved."

"What kind of dream?"

She shrugged. "A dream telling me that I should be at your house at that moment. I can't explain them."

"Nothing else?"

"Not last night."

"Well, whatever the reason, I'm glad you're here."

We'd made one stop at Potions before heading over, and I hoped we weren't too late.

The quiet of the hallway was suddenly shattered by a woman shouting, "You son of a bitch!"

We kicked into a run, rounded a corner, and saw Lyla Jameson pummeling Cletus Cobb. Dinah was trying her best to pull her daughter off him.

It had been Lyla screaming, and she continued to do so as she wailed on her stepdaddy. "You sick, twisted, evil man!" she yelled as she punched. "You've gone too far! Too far!"

Delia and I reached the melee at the same time as two security officers. They quickly pulled the pair apart. And even though she was being restrained, Lyla still tried to kick Cletus. Tears streamed from her eyes.

"Settle down," one of the guards boomed.

"Crazy bitch!" Cletus spat. A bruise was already forming around his eye.

Lyla stopped kicking and turned her tear-streaked face to her mama. "How could you?"

Dinah looked to Cletus and wrung her hands.

"Ain't nothin' to do with your mama," he said. "It was Jamie Lynn's decision. Got it right here in writin'."

It was then I noticed papers clutched in his filthy hand.

"Liar!" Lyla shouted. "Mama! Do *something*," she cried. "Don't let him kill her!"

Dinah just stared at the floor.

"What's going on?" I asked. "Lyla?"

Her head dropped and she sobbed.

Tears filled my eyes. "Someone please tell me what's going on?"

Delia walked over to Cletus and snatched the papers straight out of his hand. The guards didn't so much as blink. I had the feeling they'd seen similar situations played out before.

"Hey!" Cletus shouted.

The guard holding him tightened his grip. "Settle. Down."

Cletus sneered. "Jamie Lynn signed them papers clear as day!"

Delia scanned the documents and said, "One's a power of attorney giving Dinah rights to make decisions for Jamie Lynn. The other's Jamie Lynn's living will." She let out a sharp breath. "It says she wouldn't want to be kept alive by artificial means."

"He wants to pull the plug," Lyla cried. "Don't let him! Please don't let him."

I glanced over Lyla's shoulder, through the narrow window of a closed door and into the room just beyond. Jamie Lynn lay unmoving, the machines around her bed the only things keeping her alive.

"It's what Jamie Lynn wanted," Dinah said, shrugging.

She was lying through her rotted teeth.

"No! No, it wasn't!" Lyla countered. "I don't know what you did to trick her into signing those papers, but I'd bet my life you have a will at home with her giving you everything when she died! You knew you couldn't take out life insurance on her because of her sickness, so you went straight for an inheritance. You *bastard*!" She kicked again.

I could have sworn the guard let her land a blow before pulling her back.

Neither Cletus nor Dinah denied the accusation and my heart sank. They'd taken advantage of Jamie Lynn's illness in the worst possible way. And not only that, but by killing Katie Sue, they upped their inheritance by four million dollars.

It was such a sick, twisted plan that I couldn't even believe how evil their souls had to be.

To Delia, I whispered, "Call Dylan. He's at the Loon."

She handed me the papers and strode off. I'd told her all about my afternoon on the ride over, so she knew Dylan had been looking for this pair.

Quite the crowd had gathered, and when a doctor came running up, his long white coat flying out behind him like one of Delia's capes, the nurses slowly dispersed.

"This isn't the place," the doctor said. "Get them out of here."

"I ain't done nothing!" Cletus shouted, wiggling. "She's the one who attacked me! I want her arrested for assault! I'm pressin' charges!"

"Then take her away," the doctor said in a low tone to the guards. *"Now."*

"Come on, Miss," the guard said, tugging on Lyla.

"Wait," I said, jumping in front of him. "Can't she stay? Her sister's dying."

A hovering nurse said, "The police are on their way."

The guard said to me, "Take it up with them when they get here."

Lyla reached for me. Tears soaked her face. "Don't let them pull the plug. Save her, Carly. Save her!"

Her sobs carried down the hallway as the guard led

her off. The other guard, who held Cletus, let him go with a little shove before he followed his colleague.

Cletus adjusted his tank top. "Now, what's got to be done? We don't like to see our baby Jamie Lynn suffering none."

Such rage built inside me that it took all I had not to jump on him as Lyla had done. "Nothing is to be done," I seethed. "Not by you at least."

"I got the papers," he said.

"Actually, I have the papers," I said, holding them up. "And I intend to call a lawyer and get the courts involved. You're not pulling the plug. Not now. Not ever. And if she eventually dies from whatever it is ailing her, you won't be collecting any inheritance of hers, either."

Saliva gathered at the corner of his mouth. "You don't got no say-so."

"Maybe not me, but the law does. I'm pretty sure that neither of you can make Jamie Lynn's decisions from federal prison. There's video footage of you trying to pawn Katie Sue's jewelry. There's a warrant out for your arrest right now, and you're wanted for questioning in Katie Sue's murder."

"Katie Sue?" Dinah said. "Oh no. We ain't have nothing to do with that."

Cletus jabbed a finger at me. "Don't go blamin' us for that. We didn't lay a finger on that girl."

His gaze jumped to something over my shoulder, and he reached out and grabbed Dinah's hand. In a split second, he took off, knocking over a cart of medical supplies on the way. I glanced back just as Dylan zipped past me, giving chase.

Delia came running back. Catching sight of Dylan she said, "That explains why he wasn't at the Loon when I called."

The doctor looked at me, his eyes wide. "Are you really getting a court injunction?"

"Yes."

Shaking his head, he let out a weary sigh. He said, "Don't know how much time you have."

"Can I see her?" I needed to see her.

"You family?"

I grabbed Delia's arm. "We're her sisters."

He eyed me dubiously but said, "Only a few minutes. She's scheduled for a brain scan."

A brain scan. To determine if she were brain dead. One of the steps needed before pulling the plug.

I nodded, and holding hands, Delia and I went into Jamie Lynn's room. I closed the door behind us, and quickly slipped a vial out of my purse.

"What're you doing?" Delia asked.

"Something I've never done before, and lord have mercy, I pray it works." I held up the vial. "Straight Leilara. Grandma Adelaide once told me she believed that a large dosage of the tears could bring someone back from the dead. That's never been proven, of course, but I'm hoping that a large dose brings someone back from being *mostly* dead."

"But . . . isn't there a limited supply of the tears?"

I held up the bottle. "This tiny container is a half-year's worth."

She gasped. "Won't you run out?"

"It's a risk I have to take." My heart pounded. "I can't let her die like this. She'd been doing so well after her potion yesterday . . . I don't know what went wrong. I have to figure it out."

Delia nodded. "Hurry up then."

I quickly went to the bed and looked down at Jamie Lynn. She already looked dead.

"What's wrong?" Delia asked. She was standing in front of the door's window so no one could peek in.

"The best route of ingestion is the mouth, but it's all taped up because of the ventilator."

"Her IV?"

"I don't have a syringe."

"Her eyes," Delia said.

Yes! Her eyes. They were taped closed, but that was easy enough to remove. I used the vial's dropper to suck up the tears. Holding up an eyelid, I poised the dropper over Jamie Lynn's vacant pupil. One drop. Two. I switched eyes and repeated the process. Sweat dampened my palms. This was more Leilara than ever used on a person before. Two more drops. Four. Eight. Ten. Twelve.

"Come on, Jamie Lynn," I urged, pausing to look for any changes.

"Anything?" Delia asked.

"Not yet."

Two more drops, three, four. Suddenly, I jumped when Jamie Lynn's machines started beeping like crazy. Delia ran over to the bed as Jamie Lynn blinked her eyes, trying to focus on me.

"You did it!" Delia whispered, her voice full of awe.

I held up the vial. "With some to spare, too."

Jamie Lynn groaned, trying to speak, as nurses rushed into the room. I surreptitiously slipped the vial back into my purse as Delia and I were pushed into a corner. We looked on as doctor after doctor came rushing in. The word miracle floated on the air.

Delia squeezed my hand and looked at me. "Leila Bell would be proud."

I let out a relieved sigh. Jamie Lynn was alive.

We just had to keep her that way.

⊸ Chapter Twenty-nine ⊸

"Where are you off to this early?" Aunt Marjie asked the next morning. She leaned against the kitchen counter, which had been scrubbed immaculately clean. The whole house smelled lemony-fresh from the dust polish she'd used. "Leaving before you had your coffee and everything. Must be in a hurry."

I was. "I'm off to bail Lyla Jameson out of jail."

The Huntsville police had arrested her last night, and nothing Dylan could say or do could sway them. It wasn't likely the charges would stick considering that Cletus and Dinah were on the run. They'd gotten away, slipping into the dark night like the two slippery snakes that they were. The police, however, did let Dylan speak with Lyla, and he'd told her all about the night's events. When he left her, she was sobbing tears of gratitude.

It had been a long night for everyone, and was undoubtedly going to be a long day. The manhunt for Cletus and Dinah was still under way. I'd already spent a half hour on the phone this morning giving Ainsley ev-

ery last detail of what had happened. And last night, I
had an idea how to help my mama get rid of all those
flowers, so after I bailed Lyla out of jail, Delia and I were
going to load up our cars and take the flowers to the
hospital to give them out to the patients. They would add
just a little bit of cheer to chase off the dreariness. After
that, I wanted to visit with Jamie Lynn and try to figure
out how Cletus got those signatures, and see if I could
read her energy again to see if the Leilara had cured
whatever had been ailing her in the first place.

"You're a good girl, Carly Bell."

I slipped my purse over my head and across my body.
"Don't let it get around."

She laughed. Who was this woman?

"I've been thinking," she said.

"About?"

"It might be high time for me to move on back home.
My leg don't hurt at all anymore, and stairs aren't a problem."

My heart sank. "You sure? You're more than welcome
to stay as long as you want." I swallowed hard. "The cats
have really loved having you here."

"The cats, you say?"

Both sat at her feet, swishing their tails.

I bit a nail and nodded.

Marjie pursed her lips. "Maybe one more day. That's
it, though. I've got a man to whip into shape and a life to
be getting back to . . . and so do you."

I smiled, glad she wouldn't be leaving today. "The man
or the life?"

"The man you have is already whipped. Head over
heels for you. It's the life with him you need to work out."

I knew. "Your yard is looking mighty nice," I said, teasing her, changing the subject. I didn't really want to talk about a future with Dylan. I didn't even want to think about it. Or hope for it.

She smiled again—*mercy!*—and said, "It's coming along."

Realization dawned. "Aunt Marjie . . ."

"What?" she asked, crossing her arms.

"Are you using Johnny Braxton to fix up your house?"

"I ain't using nobody. If he has the desire to do it as a gift to me, who am I to complain?"

"And you wouldn't have planted those seeds in his head, would you have?"

Her eyes softened. "I learned it here."

Puzzled, I said, "Learned what?"

"Watching Dylan around this place. Hanging sheetrock here. Laying tiles there. Doing whatever he can to get the job done."

"I don't understand what you're getting at."

"Carly Bell," she said softly, "the job he's doing is not fixing this *house*."

Not the house? "Now I really don't understand."

Sunlight streamed through the windows. "Every day that man's here, he's fixing a piece of you. Patching together your broken heart as surely as he patches a hole in the wall. Open your eyes, girl. Open your heart. You'll see it's working just fine again."

"I—I mean . . ."

"What?" she prodded.

Holy hell, was she right?

The phone rang once, twice. I was too stunned to answer. Marjie plucked it out of its dock. After saying hello, she covered the mouthpiece. "Speak of the devil," she whispered to me.

My chest felt tight, and I was suddenly anxious. I was scared and hopeful at the same time.

"Uh-huh," Marjie said. "I'll tell her. Yup. 'Bye."

"What was that?" I asked.

"Said he's still tracking Cletus and Dinah, but wanted to let you know the post office was broken into last night."

"Broken into?" It hit me why. "My word. Katie Sue's envelope?"

She nodded. "Video caught the suspect, but he was covered head to toe—so no ID—but the culprit left the post office empty-handed."

"So the envelope is still out there somewhere."

Marjie nodded.

"Great." I'd hoped to never see the Calhouns again, but if they were still on the hunt for that envelope, no way were they leaving town just yet. Dylan had told me how after I left the Loon last night that Landry had clammed up. He'd sided with his family instead of standing up for the woman he'd loved. The coward.

I glanced at the clock. "I need to go. I don't want Lyla sitting in that cell a minute longer than necessary." I'd tried bailing her out last night, but had been told to come back first thing in the morning.

I gave the cats some loving, then headed for the door. I had so much on my mind. Beyond Katie Sue's murder, and that missing package, I had to decide what to do with Dylan.

Every day that man's here, he's fixing a piece of you. Patching together your broken heart as surely as he patches a hole in the wall.

Hand on the doorknob, I turned back to face my aunt.

"What?" she asked. "You forget somethin'?"

"You learned it here?" I said, repeating what she said just minutes ago.

"What're you talking about?"

"You said you learned it here. The fixing, the patching."

Was that what was truly going on with her and Johnny? Was she letting him fix *her* heart one insult at a time?

"You've gone daft," she said. "I don't know what you're talking about."

Oh, but I did. I smiled.

Slowly, a return smile crept across her face. "Now git on with you."

As I walked out to my Jeep, I couldn't help but wonder at the way fate worked sometimes.

Turned out Johnny Braxton hadn't needed a love potion after all.

But the question remained if Marjie did.

"I can't thank you enough," Lyla said when I dropped her off at her house. "I'll pay you back the bail money, every cent."

"No rush," I said. "I know you're eager to get back to Jamie Lynn, but I have a few questions I hope you don't mind answering."

"I am eager, but at this point, I'd do just about anything you wanted. Come inside."

I parked and followed her into a large airy kitchen. Light spilled through the windows, highlighting old wooden floors and distressed cabinets. It was a cozy space, inviting, which made it all the more strange that my witchy senses had just kicked in.

"Tea?"

"Do you have coffee?" I asked, missing the cup I hadn't had this morning. I sat at a worn wooden table.

"Sorry." She smiled. "We're a tea-drinking family."

"Is it caffeinated?"

"Definitely."

"Fill 'er up." Could Cletus and Dinah be nearby? That might trigger my warning system. I listened for any unusual sounds and heard nothing.

"What do you want to know?" She worked quickly, efficiently as she set a tea kettle on to boil, grabbed mugs from the rack on the counter, and pulled tea bags from a turquoise canister on the countertop.

"Why do you think Cletus killed Travis?"

"I don't think." She opened a cabinet and removed a small sugar dish and a crock of honey, took two tiny spoons from a drawer, and set it all on the table. "I *know*. Travis had been working some with Cletus back in those days. Odds and ends. Construction. That kind of thing. Then one day we get this notice in the mail from an insurance company about Travis needin' to come in for a physical to complete his life insurance policy. Only, he hadn't signed up for any policy. We thought it was junk mail and tossed it. The next week, he and Cletus were working on Travis's truck." Her bottom lip pushed out as her jaw clenched. "Next thing I know, Travis is dead."

"I'm sorry," I said.

"Me, too. More than you know. I loved that man somethin' fierce. Still do." She unwrapped the tea bags and put them in the mugs. "Anyway, 'bout a week later, my mama's asking if Travis had a physical before he died. It was then that I put it together. She and Cletus had tried to take a policy out on Travis and were too high to realize it wouldn't be processed without him taking a physical and having his signature."

"Did you go to the police?"

"I did. They said they didn't have enough evidence that a crime was committed. But I knew. And they knew I knew."

"Did you tell Jamie Lynn?"

She shook her head. "It would have hurt her too much to know her mama was a murderer. But I did forbid contact with them, using their addiction as an excuse. But if Cletus had her signature on those papers, she's been seeing them somehow."

"Here, every Friday while you're at the garden meeting." I told her how Delia and I bumped into her mama. And also how Jamie Lynn believed her mama deserved a second chance.

"I should have told her more about them. Maybe this wouldn't have happened."

"You were trying to protect her." It made sense now why Lyla had always kept a tight rein on her little sister.

"Fat lot of good that did me."

The tea kettle whistled and she poured steaming water into the mugs and carried them over to the table. Wearily, she sat next to me. If she'd had a wink of sleep the night before, I'd be surprised.

"I have these," I said, reaching into my purse and pulling out the stack of letters I'd taken from Katie Sue's house.

Her mouth dropped open. "My Lord! I thought these were lost and gone forever. I'm so glad you have them. Jamie Lynn will most definitely want them now."

"What do you mean?"

"She stubbornly refused to read them when she was younger. She'd write 'return to sender' on them and stick them back in the mailbox."

I stirred a little honey into my tea, swirling the liquid round and round. "Jamie Lynn sent them back? Not you?"

"Not me. I wanted Jamie Lynn to have a relationship with Katie Sue. It was Katie Sue and her stubbornness that segregated herself from us."

"I'm confused. I thought you refused to let Katie Sue see Jamie Lynn unless Katie Sue gave you money."

She spooned sugar into her tea. "Not true. I never asked for money."

I almost choked on my tea. "Then I have this story all wrong."

"Most people do. Because I didn't make my side public. I didn't want to put Jamie Lynn through that. I've never said a bad word about Katie Sue in front of my sister, and I never will."

"What's true?"

"It's true I sued for custody and won. Everything else is . . . muddled. I never wanted Jamie Lynn's money. It was hers. She earned it, just like Katie Sue had earned hers. All I wanted was to give Jamie Lynn a home with a surrogate mother and father to replace the crappy ones she'd been born to. I wanted her to know love and comfort . . . and safety. I'd grown up in the years after I moved out and realized what a brat I'd been about not helping with my granddaddy. But I was twenty-five, Travis and I had just bought this place, my gardens were taking off, and we were making decent livings. I was in a good place. I was happy. I thought it was time Katie Sue had a chance at happiness, too."

"All the court battles . . ."

"Katie Sue wouldn't let it go. She never could just walk away. She wanted Jamie Lynn and that was that. She couldn't see the bigger picture if it hit her in the face."

I sipped. "What bigger picture?"

"That I was also trying to help Katie Sue."

A chill went through me, another warning, and I wrapped my hands around the mug for warmth. I listened again, but there was no hint that we weren't alone in the house. "How so?"

Tears filled Lyla's eyes and she backhanded them away. "She had the whole world in front of her. She was so smart. So motivated. She was always telling me how she was going to go to her fancy college, get her fancy degree. Could she really do that with a ten-year-old girl to look after? I wanted her to live her dream."

"Did you tell her that?"

"Of course. She wouldn't listen. She was convinced I only wanted the money, that I couldn't have anyone's best interests at heart other than my own. She said I was just like my mama."

"Ouch." Dinah Perrywinkle Cobb had certainly made her mark on this family.

"Yeah. She laid down an ultimatum. Either I let Jamie Lynn live with her, or Katie Sue would never see any of us ever again." Lyla slid her mug side to side between her hands. "I thought she was bluffing."

"She wasn't."

"No."

"Then the letters starting coming, and Jamie Lynn was

so hurt by Katie Sue's leaving that she sent them straight back. Eventually, they stopped coming, and we never saw hide or hair of Katie Sue again until this week."

"When you tracked me down in Dèjá Brew and told me to keep Katie Sue away from Jamie Lynn . . . You were protecting her again, weren't you?"

Biting her lip, she nodded. "It about killed Jamie Lynn the first time Katie Sue left, and she'd been healthy as horse. I didn't want Katie Sue doing it to her again. She's been so frail . . . Maybe I was wrong about it, but I couldn't take the risk. Jamie Lynn is everything to me." She picked up the stack. "I'll bring them with me to the hospital."

It was time for me to go. I pushed away from the table. "I have a stop to make first, but then I'll see you over there." Another shiver went down my spine. "And be careful, okay? Cletus and Dinah are still out there somewhere."

"I will." She walked me to the door. "Thanks for everything, Carly. I have to admit I might have been wrong about you."

I stepped on the porch and looked back at her. "I might have been wrong about you, too. So we're even."

As I drove off, headed toward my mama's I couldn't help but feel sorry for all the Perrywinkle girls and the scars left behind by their childhoods. It was too late for Katie Sue to heal those wounds, but I prayed there was time enough for Jamie Lynn and Lyla.

~⊛~ Chapter Thirty ~⊛~

"This is going to take a few trips," Delia said not ten minutes later as we were loading up our cars with flower arrangements. My mama and daddy were busy getting the chapel ready for the four weddings today, but occasionally would pop out with an armful of flowers. I had the feeling it was going to be an all-day process.

"More than a few, I'd say." Good thing it was only a little past eight. I shoved an arrangement of beautiful pink-tipped white hydrangeas in the back of my Jeep and when I straightened up, my head spun. I leaned against the open door.

"You okay?" Delia asked.

"A little woozy." I shook my head a bit trying to clear my vision.

"What've you eaten today?"

"A cup of tea."

She smiled. "We'll stop for some food on the way to the hospital. You shouldn't skip breakfast."

"Yes, Mom," I teased. I'd agreed to go, but I wasn't hungry. In fact, my stomach roiled angrily.

Delia said, "Your mama would be lecturing you worse than me." She turned to go back into the chapel for another load.

I tried to pick up another of the hydrangea arrangements from the curb, but my legs wouldn't move. My hands started to tremble and my heart thudded erratically. I was suddenly having trouble breathing. I gasped for breath. Panic sluiced through me.

Black spots swam in front of my eyes. "Del—" I tried calling for Delia, but her name had wedged in my throat. I slumped to the ground, gasping, writhing in pain.

Delia was by my side in a flash. Sheer terror clouded her eyes. I had the feeling she just read my energy and knew exactly how bad off I was.

I tried to speak, but there were no words. My airway was closing.

"Help!" I heard her shriek. "Someone help!"

Delia disappeared, leaving me alone as my lungs shut down. I couldn't even cry out in pain, even though my whole body felt as though it was being put through a grinder. All I could do was gasp for breath as I tried to fight off the darkness clouding my vision. I stared helplessly at the hydrangeas, so beautiful for such an ugly moment. But they, too, had an ugly side, I remembered. They were highly toxic.

As soon as the thought wandered in my head, I realized what was happening to me. I squeezed my eyes closed, already knowing what my ultimate fate would be.

I'd been poisoned. Just like Jamie Lynn.

Delia yelled, "Don't you dare die on me!"

I opened my eyes, and I could feel the tears leaking from their corners, but I was powerless to tell her what was happening.

She knelt next to me, busily doing something . . . I couldn't quite see. Items were flying left and right. "Yes!" she shouted, apparently finding what she was looking for. She stuck her face right in mine and said, "You're going to be fine. Just hang on!"

I wanted to believe her, I did. But the pain was too much, and my chest felt ready to explode.

Her determined face was the last thing I saw before I slipped into the darkness.

"Your dreams suck," I said two hours later. I was propped up in my bed, the ceiling fan circling lazily above my head. Roly and Poly hadn't left my side since my daddy carried me up here.

"What'd they do now?" Delia asked, making the mattress dip as she shifted to face me.

"Well, they certainly didn't warn you that I was going to be poisoned this morning, did they?"

"Can't blame them for that—I never went to sleep last night. I was so wound up about what went down at the hospital that I didn't go to bed. How about we talk about you ignoring your witchy senses?"

I rolled my eyes and rubbed Poly's chubby belly. "I didn't *ignore* them. I acknowledged them. I just didn't know why I was getting them."

"How about they were trying to tell you not to eat the poisoned honey?"

"Yeah, I missed that part." A quick call to Jamie Lynn at the hospital verified that her mama had given her the honey. The police went and confiscated the crock, and we'd have the results soon as to what was in it.

It was the perfect plan by Cletus and Dinah. To slowly poison Jamie Lynn until she eventually succumbed to her mystery illness. Lyla had been safe from the poison only because she was allergic to honey. Had Dinah even remembered that? Or had it been part of the master plan to hide the poison in plain sight?

The current speculation was that the honey held a low dose of poison, meant to take a toll over time, until Dinah and Cletus got wind that Jamie Lynn was feeling better. It was my guess that when Delia and I saw Dinah coming out of Lyla's house the other day that she'd added more poison to the honey to push Jamie Lynn's health over the edge. I'd seen a syringe in Dinah's pocket and assumed it had been for drugs, but now I suspected it had held poison meant to kill her daughter.

Fortunately, it hadn't. Jamie Lynn had made a full and complete recovery and was being released today. The Leilara had completely cured her. There would be no lingering symptoms.

But she wouldn't be truly safe until the Cobbs were found. There was hope that would occur really soon. Dylan practically had to be pried from my side when a call had come in from someone who'd spotted the truck belonging to Cletus and Dinah. He promised he'd be back as soon as possible. I didn't bother to tell him that there was no rush, that I was perfectly fine and in fact felt better than ever. I'd seen the look in his eye when he rushed to Mama's chapel and saw me still lying on the ground. He could come back. And he could stay as long as he wanted.

Delia fluffed a pillow behind her back. "And, now we know why my dream told me to accompany you to the hospital last night, don't we?"

"I suppose," I said grudgingly as I watched Roly knead my stomach. I rubbed her head.

It had been the Leilara that saved me. Delia remembered I had put the vial with the leftover tears in my purse the night before. She'd laughed as she told me how she'd tipped my head back and dumped what was left of the vial into my mouth, and then squished my jaw shut so no liquid would seep out.

I came to only seconds later, amazingly none the worse for wear. Even the paramedics had agreed I didn't need to be taken to the hospital, but I could have sworn I heard my daddy ask them if they had any tranquilizers for my mama. She claimed I took ten years off her life. Then she amended it to fifteen. By tomorrow, it would be twenty.

If Delia hadn't gone with me to the hospital, hadn't seen me use the Leilara and slip it back into my bag . . . I would be dead.

Voices floated up the stairs. I had a really full house down there. My parents. The Odd Ducks. Ainsley and Carter. Caleb. I could hear my mama rehashing what had happened, her voice rising and falling dramatically. They'd all been up to see me, and it had been too much for my senses, so I pleaded that I needed to rest. I volunteered Delia to watch over me, because no one trusted that I wasn't going to just up and quit breathing. They'd insisted I needed someone with me at all times until they truly believed I wasn't about to die.

"So," Delia said, stretching out her long legs. "I think

we can both agree my dreams trump your witchy senses any day."

"Maybe so." I glanced at her.

"What?"

"You know that was your chance to get rid of me forever, right? With my death the Leilara secrets would be passed on to you."

"Oh," she said, linking arms with me and resting her head against mine, "damn. I didn't have time to think things through."

"You're wicked."

She laughed. "How could I have let you die? I'm just starting to really like you."

Smiling, I said, "I really like you, too."

"Well, that's good. Now, how about you promise not to get poisoned anymore?"

"I promise. Thanks for saving me."

"You're welcome." After a moment, she added, "How long are you going to humor your parents by staying in bed?"

"I'll give it another hour."

"I bet you won't last twenty more minutes."

She might be right about that. I was already itching to get up. To do something. To *live*. The only thing keeping me up here was all the energy swirling around downstairs.

There were heavy footsteps on the stairs, and Delia and I both craned our necks to see who it was.

"Knock, knock," Dylan said, tapping on the door. "Oh, good, you're still alive."

"How long?" I asked. "How long until people forget I almost died today?"

"Never, that's when." Dylan came over to the side of the bed, kicked off his shoes, took off his gun and set it on the nightstand. "Scoot."

Delia, the cats, and I scooted over. Dylan climbed in next to me, and suddenly my queen-size bed felt like a twin.

He dropped his head back on the headboard and said, "I just have a few minutes, but wanted to give you an update."

"Did you find Cletus and Dinah?" Delia asked.

My whole left side was pressed against his body, and he took hold of my hand and held it tight.

"Found them down at an old hunting shack along the river. They're both in custody, blaming each other for everything that happened. You've never seen two people turn on each other so fast. They're both looking at life sentences and possibly death penalties."

Good riddance.

"That's not all. Jamie Lynn's will and a syringe were found in their truck. The syringe is being sent for testing to see if it did in fact have poison in it."

"Case closed?" I asked.

"Case closed," he said.

He stayed with us a while longer until finally leaving to deal with a "mess of paperwork" as he put it, but agreed to come by for supper.

Delia slid off the bed and said, "I should go, too. I need to check on my shop and Boo."

"You'll come for supper, too?"

She swung her locket on its chain and smiled. "I'll bring dessert."

"Something chocolaty?"

"Is there another kind of dessert?"

"It's like we're related or something," I quipped.

"Yeah," she said, heading for the door. Then she stopped and said, "I was thinking earlier that there was a time when I never dreamed you'd be part of my life. And now I can't imagine life without you in it. That's so strange, isn't it?"

Emotion swelled in my throat, stung my nose. "Definitely strange. And completely wonderful."

She smiled, then sailed through the doorway, her cape flying out behind her.

Chapter Thirty-one

I'd lasted in bed only fifteen minutes before almost losing my mind with boredom. I cleaned my room for another hour before finally going downstairs.

Fortunately, by that time the house had mostly cleared out. Only the Odd Ducks remained behind, and they sat quacking on the sheet-covered sofa as I came down the steps.

"I think *I* need to almost die," Eulalie said. "You look wonderful! Fresh and rested."

Smiling, I said, "I think that has to do more with the Leilara than almost dying."

Eulalie leaned toward me. "Got any extra?"

"Not a drop to spare," I said, flopping into an armchair.

"You sure, Carly Bell?" Hazel asked. "Because Eulalie here just learned some distressing news, and needs a little pick-me-up."

"Oh?" I asked. "What kind of news?" I hadn't heard anything, but I was a little out of the loop today.

"José Antonio is married with four kids." She stuck out a tongue, raspberried, and folded her arms with a huff.

"It's so rude of him," Hazel declared. "He could have said something sooner."

"Like on the way to hospital?" I teased.

"Exactly!" Eulalie cried. "He didn't let on while I had him propped in my lap and my fingers in his hair, now did he? I swanee, he had the thickest hair. . . ."

Marjie sat silently, a content look on her face. I was truly going to miss her.

"So the hunt is back on for you, Carly Bell," Eulalie stated. "I'm counting on you to find me a man. Make him a good one, will you? That cutie pie John Richard is back on the market, isn't he?"

Hazel surged forward. "I thought he was a child!"

Eulalie said, "I could be a cougar. *Rwwwar!*"

Shuddering, I quickly put an end to that idea. "He says he's going to be content in bachelorhood for a while."

Hazel clucked. "I've gone and damaged the poor boy. I am a hard woman to get over. It might take him months. Years, even."

"Maybe a decade," Marjie egged on.

"This is what I'm sayin'," Hazel said solemnly.

"Oh, please," Eulalie said. She stood. "Carly, we're headed out for some lunch. Would you care to join us?"

"Any other day and I'd say yes, but I think I'm just going to putter around here for a while and then head over to take care of Mr. Dunwoody's yard." I'd forgotten to do it yesterday, and I was afraid I might have doomed his plants. One hot summer day was enough to scorch them brown.

Eulalie kissed my cheek and said, "I'm mighty glad you didn't die this morning."

"Thanks, Aunt Eulalie."

She waved and walked out the door. Marjie rolled her eyes and followed, barely hobbling at all.

Hazel kissed my cheek, too. "Run over to the Loon if you need anything. Dotsie's tending the desk, and she'll take good care of you."

"Thanks, Aunt Hazel."

As she headed for the door, she said, "We're collecting casseroles to take over to Jamie Lynn and Lyla. We'd like to fill up their freezer so they don't have to worry about cookin' none in the next week or so."

If the call had gone out for casseroles, the sisters wouldn't need to cook for a month, at least. Hitching Post rallied around their own.

"I'll make a sausage and egg casserole," I said. "Give them something to heat up at breakfast."

"Perfect." She blew me a kiss and walked out.

I went to find my favorite comfort food—peanut butter—and grabbed a spoon to eat the peanut butter straight out of the jar.

Poly slunk into the room, once again proving his ability to sniff out peanut butter from great distances. I grabbed another spoon and dabbed it in the jar. I bent and put it on the floor for him, giving his ears a scratch as well.

Out the window, I glanced into Mr. Dunwoody's yard and could practically hear the flowers begging for water. Slipping on my flip-flops, I headed over. He was due home tomorrow, and I hoped I could revive the poor little buds before he returned.

For the next hour, I dragged the hose around the yard, giving everything a good soaking—even myself.

Although I wasn't much of a "yard" person, I actually enjoyed the time outside. I supposed almost dying tended to put that kind of thing in perspective.

I was trying really hard not to think about how close a call it had been this morning. Of that moment of panic . . .

Shaking my head to clear the thoughts, I wound the hose onto its hook and noticed I had a blister starting near my toe. Chafing from wet feet and the little plastic thingy rubbing in between my toes. And I'd gone and given my potion cream to Gabi.

"Shouldn't you be resting?"

I looked up. Ainsley was giving me her best "mama" look. "I'm all rested out." I limped over to her.

"What's wrong with your foot?"

"Blister."

"You're just not meant to work outside, are you?"

"Apparently not." I smiled. "What're you doing here? You just left an hour ago."

"Brought you a peach cobbler," she said, holding up a dish.

I eyed her warily. "Not made from those rotten peaches in your yard, are they?"

Her eyes twinkled. "You'll have to wait and see."

"Why are you really here?"

Her lips pursed. "Just wanted to make sure."

"What?"

"That you're really okay." Her eyes welled.

"Stop!" I said, already feeling mine filling.

She gave me a little bump with her arm. "Fine. Now

that I've seen you, I'll just put this in your kitchen and go. Don't be staying outside too long. You'll melt for sure."

She speed walked toward my front porch.

"Ainsley?"

She faced me. "Hmm?"

"Thanks."

She beamed and disappeared into the house.

I took some time to deadhead flowers, refill birdfeeders, and sweep the porch. It was hot, and I thought Ainsley might be right. I was melting. It was time to go in.

I gimped toward my front door and veered off to the mailbox before remembering it was Sunday, but then I suddenly realized that not only had I neglected to take care of Mr. Dunwoody's plants yesterday, I'd also forgotten to get the mail from his box the past two days.

I trudged back toward his house, annoyed with the blister. I wanted to laugh at myself—after the pain I'd been in just that morning the blister should seem like nothing. A blip. But it was a bothersome little blip for sure. I kicked off my flip-flops and hotfooted it down the sidewalk, *ooh*ing and *ouch*ing as my feet touched the hot cement.

I jumped onto a patch of grass and stood there and laughed. I probably looked like an absolute crazy person, but I didn't much care. And as I stood there, welcoming the laughter—my chest constricted at how much I had almost lost.

No, no. I wouldn't go there. Couldn't. It was over. Done with. I glanced down at my feet, at the blades of grass clinging to my skin and eyed that silly throbbing blister, its painful bubble seeming to be there to remind

me that life wasn't perfect. It wasn't guaranteed. And
that feeling pain was sometimes better than not feeling
anything at all. Like when you were dead. Or paralyzed,
like Cassandra Calhoun.

My head snapped up. Wait a sec.

I eyed the Loon. I'd been sitting in there yesterday
and *felt* Cassandra being annoyed by her own blister. A
blister on her heel.

A blister she shouldn't have been able to feel at all.

My jaw dropped as I realized something that I missed.
When I read paraplegics, my own limbs felt heavy. Dead
weight. I hadn't felt that from Cassandra.

It suddenly hit me *why*.

An immense sadness swept over me, and I want to
shout "no" at the top of my lungs. Cassandra was the genuine Calhoun. The one that helped hungry children and
fought for all the injustices of everyday people. She was
the Calhoun who could make a difference in this world,
make it a better place.

But she'd been keeping an enormous secret.

She wasn't paralyzed.

That. That was the dirt Katie Sue had on the Calhoun
family, I was suddenly so sure of it.

As I hotfooted it to Mr. Dunwoody's mailbox, I recalled what Landry had said about how he'd met Katie
Sue at the hospital after Cassandra's accident.

I tried to recall all the information I knew of the accident, and all I kept coming back to was how Cassandra's
accident had salvaged Warren's reelection campaign after it tanked with Landry's scandal.

She had saved his election. The accident had surely
been real, but how exaggerated had her injuries been?

And how many people, beside Katie Sue, knew that Cassandra was faking her paralysis?

I'd bet my witchy senses that each and every Calhoun knew—it was why they'd been so protective of that envelope. They'd been trying to protect Cassie.

I had to call Dylan. Pulling open Mr. Dunwoody's box while doing a two-step on the hot ground, I grabbed the pile of mail inside. I turned and sprinted back to my house, and was halfway there when I realized one of the large envelopes in the stack had a coffee stain on its edge.

I stopped and pulled it loose. My breath caught.

Sure enough, Katie Sue had sent the package to me, but she'd addressed it wrong, putting down Mr. Dunwoody's address instead of mine. It was a mistake Earl would have caught right off, but José Antonio would have had no idea.

I ran up the steps and headed straight into the kitchen. I'd just grabbed the phone when my witchy senses sent a tingle up my spine.

It couldn't be a coincidence to me finding that package.

This time, I listened to those senses. I quickly dialed 911, put the phone in the junk drawer, and closed it tight. After I stuck the coffee-stained envelope deep into the trash can, I went to grab my pitchfork, but I'd forgotten Dylan still had it as evidence. I heard the planks on the front porch creak, so I did the only thing a sane witch could do—I went out the back door. I stuck close to the house, keeping my head low. I carefully peeked in the living room window and saw Cassandra Calhoun limping around my living room.

Limping, because I was fairly sure that thigh pain I'd felt yesterday at the Loon had also come from her — and the forking Aunt Marjie had given her. Not quite in the patootie as she thought, but the upper thigh.

I hoped it was infected. Positively festering.

Like I told Warren, I had my moments.

She wore a pink bandanna to cover her hair and black spandex running clothes that sent my mind reeling. The black clothes. Running shoes . . .

Dinah and Cletus's claims of innocence in Katie Sue's death rang through my head. Had they been telling the truth for once in their lives?

Had it been Cassandra who dragged Katie Sue through those woods and threw her off the cliff? I recalled how she'd bragged about her upper arm strength, and I felt queasy. Why? Why had she done this? Even if Katie Sue was threatening to reveal that Cassandra wasn't paralyzed, why not just claim she'd been miraculously cured?

Before making a dash for it, I peeked into the window one last time and saw Cassandra suddenly spin around. She aimed a gun at the front door.

The door Marjie had just hopped through.

"No, no," I whispered. My heart thudded against my rib cage as fear sliced through me.

"Where is she?" Cassandra demanded.

"Where's your wheelchair?"

"Where's Carly?" Cassandra repeated, steadying the gun on the center of Marjie's chest.

"No idea," she said.

"She was just here."

Marjie shrugged. "I wasn't."

"Call for her," Cassandra said.

"No."

"Call. For. Her," Cassandra said, taking a step toward her, her hand shaking as she pointed the gun.

"No."

"I will shoot you."

"I don't give a hoot."

Cassandra shot. Marjie jerked backward as the bullet grazed her arm. "Call her!"

I went running. I couldn't let her shoot Marjie again, and I knew Marjie was stubborn enough to keep quiet.

I dashed up the front steps. "I'm here!"

Blood oozed from Marjie's arm, but she looked more pissed than hurt. Thank the Lord.

"Where's the envelope?" Cassandra asked, tears streaming down her face.

"What're you going to do, Cassandra? Kill us both?"

She sucked in a breath in an attempt to control the tears. "If I have to," she said.

"Well, what's two more at this point?" I asked, edging toward her. "It *was* you who killed Katie Sue, wasn't it?"

Backhanding tears from her face, she hiccuped. "I loved Kathryn like a sister." Pain crumpled her features. "How could she do that to me? It wasn't my fault my parents wouldn't let her marry Landry."

I tried not to look at Marjie. I wanted to keep Cassie's attention on me.

"I don't know," I said softly, trying to be sympathetic. It wasn't easy with a gun pointed at me. "When did you find out that she was threatening to reveal your secret?" How long had she planned to kill the woman her brother loved?

Wiping more tears, she said, "I heard my parents arguing about it after the rehearsal at your mama's chapel. I couldn't believe what I was hearing—until then I had no idea that Kathryn had threatened them. My daddy wanted to give in to Kathryn's demands, but Mama wouldn't budge. She kept saying Kathryn would never go through with it, but I knew Kathryn. She was—"

"Stubborn?" I supplied.

Cassandra nodded. "I disguised myself and went to find her after that terrible dinner. I wanted to hear her side. I found her in the gazebo." More tears spilled over. "She wouldn't tell me where the envelope was. Said she was standing up to my family, and though she hated to hurt me, it had to be done. I was so angry. I slapped her. She fell and hit her head on the corner of one of the benches." She winced. "Blood went everywhere. I panicked—I couldn't let anyone see what had happened. I dragged her into the woods." In a quick burst, she said, "I took off her jewelry to make it look like a robbery and . . ." She gave her head a shake.

"Tossed her off the cliff?" I supplied, hating that I felt any sympathy for her. In a heated moment, she'd lost control. And lost everything she'd worked so hard to accomplish for herself—even though her popularity had grown from a lie, there was no denying all the good she'd done through her charitable work.

However, it was a far sight less than what Katie Sue had lost.

And now . . . the cover-up continued as Cassandra dug a bigger hole for herself. It was a wicked web she'd woven.

She nodded. "I didn't know what else to do to . . . hide . . . Kathryn." Watery eyes searched my face, and she drew in another deep breath. "And then I had that jewelry, but as I made my way back to the inn, I saw Kathryn's mama sitting in her truck—she was parked at the curb passed out behind the wheel—and her step-daddy was paying me no mind as he walked back to the truck with two drinks from the coffee shop. Kathryn had told me all about her upbringing and how horrible her mama and stepdaddy had treated her. It didn't take me but a second to decide to toss the jewelry into the back-seat and keep on walking."

"You wanted them to be arrested for the murder."

Without a lick of remorse, she said, "Yes. I hated them on Kathryn's behalf. They never were charged for the abuse they heaped on her. Maybe now they'd be pun-ished for that."

Her twisted reasoning made me queasy. The Cobbs might have abused Katie Sue, but they hadn't *killed* her—as Cassandra had. "Do your parents know what you did?" I asked.

Her face registered her horror at the thought. "Heav-ens, no. Oh God. I don't even want to think about that. I need that envelope. Please get it," she asked so nicely it was hard to imagine that she had killed someone.

"I'm sorry. I just ran it down the street and dropped it in the mailbox," I lied. "It'll be a couple more days be-fore it gets here again."

She narrowed red-rimmed eyes. "You're lying."

"Why would I?"

Having no answer, she said, "I need that envelope. I've worked too hard to let it fall into the wrong hands. The election is in my sights. . . ."

"You earned that Senate seat," I agreed, glancing

around for some sort of weapon. "All your charity work. The tireless fund-raising. And let's not forget your accident. Was that planned, Cassie? That you take a literal fall to save your father's reelection?"

"It was worth it," she said, her tears finally slowing. "I was promised his Senate seat in exchange. Think of all the good I can do as a Senator," she said. "If I hadn't had that accident, no one would even know my name. I'm not outgoing enough for public office. My disability is what made me famous."

She would have been a wonderful Senator. That was the shame of it all.

Her eyes had turned a bit wild. "Get the package, Carly. I'll give you ten seconds before I shoot the old lady again."

"Old?" Marjie barked.

This really wasn't the time.

"Ten."

"Cassie, the police are going to figure out you killed Katie Sue. Your DNA is on the pitchfork. There's no getting away with this. You went too far."

"Nine."

"How'd she know?" I asked, trying to keep her talking. "How'd Katie Sue know you weren't paralyzed?"

Blinking, she said, "We hung out a lot. She noticed how toned my legs were. She promised to keep the secret as long as I helped her sway my parents in her favor. We became good friends." She snuffled. "I didn't want to hurt her. I really didn't. Please believe me. I just had to ... protect myself."

"Put the gun down, Cassandra," a voice from the kitchen said.

My heart lurched as Dylan came into the room, his handgun pointed at her.

Cassandra spun around and swung the gun between Dylan and me. "I'll shoot," Cassandra threatened, now using both hands to control the gun because she was shaking so hard.

I met his gaze and immediately went into panic mode. I'd just gotten him back. If she shot him . . .

"You don't want to do that," Dylan said. "You're not so into this that you can't get out again."

Cassandra was distracted by his words. That was good. Now all I needed was a weapon of some sort. I glanced at Marjie. She motioned toward the side table.

I followed the motion. A can of furniture polish rested atop a stack of books. I took a baby step sideways. Then another. I reached out and was able to wrap my hand around the can. I quickly stuck it behind my back and took a baby step forward, toward Cassie.

"This can't be fixed," she said. "I'm ruined. I've embarrassed my family. I . . ." She raised the gun to her temple.

"Cassie," I shouted. "Here's the envelope!"

She turned to me. I sprayed for all I was worth, a lemony scent filling the air. Cassandra let out a scream. Dylan lunged for the gun, and wrested it out of her hand. She dropped to the floor, crumpled and sobbing. Sirens screamed as cruisers pulled up in front of the house.

I dropped down next to Marjie. "Are you okay?" I asked, eying her wound.

"Takes a lot more than a flesh wound to take this old bird down."

"Old?"

She gave me a look. "You have excellent aim with furniture polish. I wouldn't have known it by the dust in your house. . . ."

I laughed to keep the tears away. Dylan glanced over as he cuffed Cassie. I was sure the relief I saw in his eyes was mirrored in my own.

"I've been thinking as I've been sitting here," Marjie said.

"About what?"

"I might need a place to stay while recuperating with this here arm wound."

Smiling, I said, "I think I know just the place."

"Does it have a vacancy?"

"For you? Always."

"Child, you know I love you, right?"

I kissed her cheek. "I won't let it get around."

~~ Chapter Thirty-two ~~

Two weeks later, I woke up and found myself pinned to the bed by floppy felines. Poly was stretched across my legs, and Roly was on my chest, her head lovingly bumping my chin.

My father was working at Potions today, so I had planned a rare morning of sleeping in, but here it was a little after six and I was wide awake.

After the past two weeks of chaos, I was trying to enjoy the peace. The quiet. But the silence seemed to amplify the thoughts in my head. The ones I didn't like to think about.

In the two weeks that had passed, Cassie had been arraigned on murder charges—she pleaded not guilty by reason of insanity. A few days later, Warren had announced his resignation from politics, and the media assumed it had been because of Cassie's arrest. There had been no mention of his illness at all. Both he and Louisa had been to every court date Cassie had, standing by their daughter.

Landry had gone into seclusion, but his latest song, "Can't Quit You," had soared to number one on the country charts and was holding steady.

Katie Sue's infamous envelope had contained a disk documenting Cassandra's medical history and the cover-up undertaken to hide the fact that she hadn't been paralyzed.

My heart still ached for Katie Sue when I thought about all she'd gone through to fight for the man she loved. It was a lesson I'd taken to heart.

"Up, up," I said to the kitties, trying to push them aside. "The coffee's not going to make itself, especially now that Marjie's back at her house."

They lazily yawned and stretched, and I tossed back the thin sheet. I tugged the shade to get it to roll upward, and I looked out at the quiet street below. Dawn was breaking on the horizon, and the road looked like a photo on a postcard.

Mr. Dunwoody's flowers were thriving.

Marjie's front porch was being rebuilt.

Aunt Hazel's bras hung from a clothesline.

Aunt Eulalie was in her yard doing tai chi.

A normal day in the neighborhood.

Across town, I imagined Jamie Lynn and Lyla waking up, too, to start work in the garden. They hadn't attended a single court date of Dinah's.

They'd gotten word last week about Katie Sue's will, and it had only taken a day for Jamie Lynn to announce that she was starting a foundation that would help people with disabilities to buy the mobility equipment they needed. She didn't want anyone to need a wheelchair and not be able to afford one.

I saw her out last week on a date with Junior McGee and she never looked happier.

Which made *me* happier than I could ever express.

The honey and syringe had been filled with highly toxic hemlock. It was a miracle Jamie Lynn had lasted as long as she did, being poisoned every morning. But now . . . she had her whole life ahead of her . . . and a lot of time to come to terms with Katie Sue's death and what her mama had done to her.

She wasn't the only one grieving. Gabi was, too. For Landry. As much as she knew he hadn't been the man for her, she'd loved him. It was going to take some time for her heart to heal. In the meantime, she was working part-time at my mama's chapel and had already won the hearts of many of the townsfolk.

Little Orphan Gabi was an orphan no more. The people around here had unofficially adopted her, stitching her square onto the edge of the crazy quilt that was this town. She was now here to stay. Hitching Post had a way of holding on to its own.

I flipped on a light in the bathroom, brushed my teeth, ran a comb through my hair, and glanced at the newly tiled shower. It was a thing of beauty, but still needed grout before I could use it. Dylan had been here every chance he got, working every spare moment. Patching my walls.

Patching my heart.

I switched on the light in the kitchen and smiled, knowing Dylan would be over later this morning, back to work, and he'd stay for supper. I was fixin' his favorite roast chicken. He'd stayed late last night to finish the tile and had planned on sleeping in as well.

The cats ran to their dishes, meowing pathetically. I fed them, washed my hands, and filled the coffeemaker. I opened the cabinet for a mug and froze.

My eyes filled with tears.

I reached in and pulled out a Professor Hinkle mug that had been glued back together, its cracks sealed tightly.

A note hung from the handle. It read, "See? A little glue and it's good as new. What do you say, Care Bear?"

I recalled what Dylan had said to me not that long ago.

But that doesn't mean we can't glue back together what was broken. Rebuild on what was a solid foundation.

My heart raced as I picked up the phone and dialed a familiar number. A sleepy-sounding Dylan answered on the second ring.

"Is something wrong?" he asked.

"Nothing's wrong," I said. No, for once, it all felt right. "I was just wondering if you wanted to come over."

"I thought we said ten? Did I get the time wrong?"

"No," I said, hugging the mug to my chest. "I just thought you might want to come over sooner."

"Like when?"

"Like now."

"Now?" He suddenly sounded wide awake.

"That's what I was thinking."

"Carly . . . I mean . . . What . . ."

I smiled at his stammering. "Dylan," I cut in.

"Yeah?"

"In light of recent events, don't use the lights and siren, but I'm okay if you break the speed limit. Seven minutes?"

"I'll be there in five, Care Bear. I'm already on my way."

Read on for a sneak peek at the next novel
in Heather Blake's Wishcraft Mystery series,

Some Like It Witchy

Coming in May 2015 from Obsidian.

Something wicked this way came.

It blew into the Enchanted Village as surely as the
warm breeze that rustled oak leaves barely unfurled from
tight buds.

Villagers had been coaxed out of their homes by an
early mid-May heat wave to bask in the warmth after a
long, arduous winter. Flowers bloomed, morning dew
glistened on vibrant green grass, and sunshine beamed
down.

It should have been bliss, but as I stepped off the front
porch and scanned the village square, I couldn't shake an
uneasiness that had the baby-fine hair at the back of my
neck standing on end.

My companion, Curecrafter Cherise Goodwin, paused
in her descent of the steps to look at me, concern etched
in her eyes. "Something wrong, Darcy?"

Wind suddenly gusted, carrying bad juju along with

the sweet scent of lilac from colorful bushes that dotted the landscape.

There was evil in the air, whirling around along with the magic that made this village so very special.

Long strands of dark hair flew across my face. "'Something wicked this way comes,'" I said, properly quoting Shakespeare's *Macbeth*. Looking around, I tried to see something, *anything*, that would explain the feeling.

The Enchanted Village, a themed touristy neighborhood of Salem, Massachusetts, was truly magical, filled with Crafters, witches who'd lived on this land for hundreds of years. As a fairly new Wishcrafter—a witch who could grant wishes—I believed it to be the most extraordinary place in the whole world. I'd moved here almost a year ago from Ohio, and now I couldn't imagine living anywhere else.

Being enchanted, however, didn't mean this village was immune to wickedness. There'd been several murders here over the past year. Cases I'd helped solve. I'd become accustomed to trusting my instincts, and right now I couldn't shake a strong sense of foreboding.

In her fifties, Cherise knew this village inside and out, and as a Crafter she knew not to dismiss seemingly random feelings outright. She had the decency to wait a few seconds.

"Nonsense!" She came down the steps and linked arms with me. "It's a glorious day. A more flawless one I couldn't have conjured even with the best weather spell out there. Breathe deeply, Darcy. Raise your face to the sun. Take it all in. It's the perfect day to buy a house, don't you think?"

Cherise had hired me through my aunt's personal

concierge service, As You Wish, to help her house hunt within the village. Years ago, she'd moved out of the neighborhood, closer to the Salem coastline, and she was now at the point in her life where she wanted to come home, so to speak.

Two doors down, she slowed to a stop in front of her dream house, and leaned on a wrought iron fence that enclosed a weed-infested yard.

The old Tavistock place.

The large bungalow had been minimally maintained over the years—only enough to appease village ordinances.

Cherise's hand curled possessively around a bulbous finial as though she already owned it. "It needs some work, I admit. But I think it's a good investment. Don't you?"

The two-story Craftsmanesque bungalow had three gables, one centered on the second floor, and two smaller ones that flanked it on the lower level. The front porch sagged, and a rotting pergola to the right of the house had collapsed under the weight of out-of-control vines. A few of the stones on the front-porch columns had long ago crumbled, and the blue clapboard facade of the home was in desperate need of new paint and repair.

I wrinkled my nose. "Don't you think the cottage on Maypole Lane is a better choice? The location isn't as good, true, but it's cheaper and you would have minimal renovations."

The sun made Cherise's eyes sparkle. "Darcy, you're not trying to talk me out of this house so you can have it for yourself, are you?"

I had to confess to a pang of envy. There was something about this house that had drawn me in the moment I laid eyes on it. It was a visceral connection—one I couldn't quite describe. I'd love to own it, put my stamp on it, and bring it back to its original glory. "You know I do love it, but it's just not . . . for me."

Though I wished it were. I really did, which was all kinds of silly. My life was . . . settled.

I couldn't really imagine moving out of As You Wish, leaving behind all the things that were starting to feel like home. Then there was Nick Sawyer to think about. Our relationship had never been better, and because we'd been dating for almost a year, it was becoming clear that it might be time to take the next step—and he already had a lovely house a couple of blocks away.

But this house . . . I sighed. It felt like it was supposed to be mine.

"And hardly a realistic possibility," I added, trying to talk myself out of the impossible. Though I had a decent inheritance from my father, it wasn't near the amount of money I'd need for a house like this. "I don't have your kind of resources, Miss Moneybags."

She laughed again and squeezed my arm. "If I get it, I promise to take good care of it."

If I couldn't have it, then Cherise was a great choice. She would honor the character, the history. But it was a big if. The other buyers didn't seem to be backing down.

"Let's go have another look, shall we?" Cherise finally let go of that poor finial, and I followed her to the front door. She knocked, then tried the knob.

"Locked," she said, glancing at her watch. "It's unusual for Raina to be late. She's always early."

"I'm sure she'll be here soon. It's a busy time of year for her." The spring housing market had exploded. Magickal Realty, owned by Raina and her husband, Kent, had dozens of listings in and around the village. "And don't forget that TV guy is following her around, asking every question under the sun."

"True enough," she said, grinning. "What a hoot it would be to have a show filmed here, no?"

Maybe. It also presented some issues. Certain things around here couldn't be easily explained. Like how Wish crafters showed up on video as bright starbursts. The show needed a special permit to shoot, and it was coming up for a vote through the village council soon. Right now, the decision was split.

We sat on the sagging top step to wait. I glanced next door to Terry's and saw a curtain swish. He'd been watching us. I had to wonder what he thought about possibly living between two ex-wives.

If I were him, I'd consider selling the place.

"Oh, here comes Calliope," Cherise said, standing up and dusting off her knee-length shorts.

Calliope Harcourt had her head down, reading something on her phone, as she hurried along the sidewalk. After she made an abrupt right turn to come onto the walk, she gasped when she finally lifted her head and realized she wasn't alone. She dropped a binder she was carrying and laughed as she picked it up. "I should pay more attention. Hello!"

In her early twenties, Calliope was a recent college graduate, and intelligence shone in her blue eyes. She was a tiny thing—barely five feet tall with an oval face, rectangular glasses, and shiny auburn hair pulled back in a loose bun. Wearing dress pants, a short-sleeved floral-print top, and ballet flats, she looked every bit a bookworm.

"You seemed engrossed," Cherise said, smiling.

"An e-mail just came in from Kent to draw up a contract when I'm through here. He and Raina are running me ragged. Plus, dealing with that TV crew . . ." She smiled, not seeming to be bothered in the least. She glanced around. "Raina asked me to meet her here with papers for you to sign, Ms. Goodwin. Is she inside?"

"She's not here, dear," Cherise said. "We've been waiting for her to have our walk-through."

"That's strange." Confusion filled her eyes, and her eyebrows dipped. "I know she had a morning meeting with that TV producer. Maybe it ran late." She shrugged. "Let's go in. At least you can look around while we wait for her to get here."

Calliope tucked her binder under her arm and bent to tackle the lockbox on the door. A second later, she had the key in her hand and was slipping it into the door.

My envy level spiked a little as I walked through the door, still wishing this place was mine. Sunlight streamed through the windows, and dust particles danced in the beams. The house had been emptied of furniture, and all that remained were the bare bones of the place.

Although those bare bones were in need of a little TLC, they were . . . extraordinary. The scarred wooden floor, the original hand-carved mantel and fireplace surround. The built-in bookcases. An archway led through to the dining room, which had French doors opening to a spacious backyard.

"The ceiling needs a lot of work," Cherise said, eyeing it critically.

It did. Water stains looked like rusted clouds. "You'll need to find out where that water came from. My guess is the roof."

"Undoubtedly. Did you see the rotting shingles?" She fanned herself with her hand. "Central air-conditioning would be nice, too," she said, adding to the list.

It would. Saunalike, the house was hot and humid, and I longed to open the windows to let in some fresh air. Unfortunately, all the sashes had been painted shut. The single-paned windows were just one more thing that needed updating.

Cherise headed into the kitchen and looked around. "It's beyond repair."

Old, cracked wooden cabinets hung from loose hinges. The white tiled counter was stained, a lot of the tiles chipped. The linoleum flooring seemed to have been waxed with a layer of grease, which made footing slippery.

Cherise lifted a pale eyebrow. "What would you do in here?"

"Maple cabinets, bronze hardware, a light-colored granite countertop," I said, lying through my teeth. I didn't want Cherise to know what I'd do—it would be too painful to see it be built in someone else's house. I'd enlarge the window above the kitchen sink—which I'd replace with a deep farmhouse-style one. White cabinets, brushed nickel hardware, and a Carrara-marble countertop.

"I was thinking that, too. It would be lovely."

As she headed for the staircase, Calliope glanced around. "It sure has potential, doesn't it?"

"It does," I said softly, trying to hide my longing as I admired the craftsmanship of the bannister. "Any more offers come in?"

"A few," Calliope said, trailing behind me as I climbed the steps. "The deadline is still tonight, however. Best and final."

"Any hint of how high the bidding has gone?" I asked.

She laughed. "You know I can't say."

Pesky rules.

Upstairs, Cherise wandered around the master bedroom, chatting with Calliope about the changes she'd like to make, which included busting out a wall to add a balcony or a deck.

"Oh, and I'd love to knock this down"—Cherise motioned to the wall dividing the master from the second bedroom—"and create an expansive walk-in closet." She strode across the room to the adjoining bath. "Then I'd take out the existing walk-in closet and enlarge the bathroom."

I walked over to the closet to see how much space it would add to the bath. Pulling open the door, I happily inhaled the scent of the cedar boards that lined the space. As I scooted inside just far enough to grab the chain dangling from the light, I stepped in something wet and figured the roof had leaked in here, too. But as the light flashed on, I looked down to find I'd stepped in a large puddle of . . .

I shrieked.

. . . blood.

A little farther into the space, Raina's body lay curled in a fetal position, her eyes wide and vacant, her head bleeding profusely.

Stumbling backward, I nearly knocked down Cherise and Calliope as they raced over to see what was going on.

Calliope immediately slapped a hand over her mouth. "I think I'm going to be sick." She ran for the bathroom.

Cherise moved in for a closer look, bending down to reach across the pool of blood on the floor and take hold of Raina's wrist. Looking for a pulse.

Light glinted off a golden chain resting in Raina's open hand, and I could see a flash of color from a gemstone amulet.

The hairs rose on the back of my neck again, and I took a closer look at the closet. Some of the cedar paneling had been pried loose, but clear as day, the letter *A* was written in blood on one of the wooden boards.

Something wicked . . .

"Do you feel a pulse?" I whispered, not sure I could speak any louder if I tried.

Cherise shook her head and sadness filled her eyes. "We're too late. Raina's dead."

Also available from

Heather Blake

A POTION TO DIE FOR
A Magic Potion Mystery

Carly Bell Hartwell, owner of a magic potion shop
specializing in love potions, is in high demand. The
residents of Hitching Post, Alabama, are frantic to stock
up on Carly's love potions after a local soothsayer predicts
that a local couple will soon be divorced. Carly is happy
for new business but her popularity is put on pause when
she finds a dead body on the floor of her shop, clutching
one of her potion bottles in his hand.

The murder investigation becomes a witch hunt and all
fingers are pointing to Carly as the prime suspect. With
her business in trouble, Carly has to brew up some serious
sleuthing skills to reveal the true killer's identity before the
whole town believes that her potions are truly to die for...

**"Blake has taken the paranormal mystery
to a whole new fun, yet intriguing, level."**
—Once Upon a Romance

Available wherever books are sold or at
penguin.com

facebook.com/TheCrimeSceneBooks

P.O. 0003440804

OM013